S.R. Burks

FATAL DECEPTION

The Complete Two-Part Series
Special Edition

A NOCTURNA PRESS BOOK

Dedication

I would like to dedicate this book to four extraordinary women who have been a huge part of my life, and who helped defined who I am today. First, to my grandmother, who was like a second mother to me, especially when my own mother had passed. You were always there, even through your own illness. She gave to me the second person I dedicate this book to, my mother. Thanks, Mom, for making me a strong woman who was able to raise two beautiful children to adulthood, my two daughters, to whom I also make this dedication. Having you two in my life gave me strength to pull through my battle with cancer and win. You gave me a reason to get up in the morning and to face what life had to offer. And don't we have the greatest adventures?

My love, always and forever.

The Light that Shines

Though the tempest is raging and the gales are roaring, all is not lost. For there is a peace within that calms the waters and stills the air. When all hope seems fleeting and despair encompasses you, be not afraid; for a refuge is within your grasp. It shines like a bright light beckoning unto you. This light glows within our hearts helping us to overcome adversity, giving us strength to endure, and inspiring us for a better day. But above all else, it can tie all of us together, our family and friends.

FATAL DECEPTION: PART I

Prologue

A lonely traveler made his way down a dark road, heading home. The moon was absent on this night, the bright shining stars attempted to beacon the way. The outline of the mountain tops, against the sky and the lights from the city meant his journey was coming to an end.

It had been a grueling business trip that his boss had arranged. He'd been told his expertise was required to close a deal. He'd been reluctant to go, but it was perfectly clear that it wasn't a request. And after two days of negotiations and three days of travel, he was completely exhausted.

At last, the man reached the winding road leading up to his street. He was glad to be home, and to his new bride of just one month. The honeymoon wasn't yet over, which was the primary reason he'd hated to go on that trip. He wanted nothing more than to greet her with a lingering kiss; take a long, soothing bath; make passionate love; and to fall asleep with her in his arms. Now that would make it all worthwhile.

He pulled the car into the driveway, gathered his things, and entered his home. He threw his keys and coat next to the door in the foyer and dropped his briefcase on the floor. He stood there for a few moments, searching for his wife's whereabouts, calling to her a few times. He started up the stairs, when he received no response.

She had been standing before the mirror, her favorite pastime, admiring herself. She heard him drive up, and initially thought it might be another car coming through. But when the reflection of the headlights, passed over the windows and danced across the room, she knew he had come home.

She ran from the room and dashed down the stairs, into the sitting room, stopping briefly to check on the champagne she had on ice, and found it was chilled just right. She wanted his homecoming to be a very special one.

She was dressed in white sheer-lace lingerie; very much aware this would get his attention. She smiled in anticipation and moved over to the camel-back sofa, placing herself seductively on it and awaited his entrance. She heard him calling her, but wanted to play a little game; she wanted him to search for her.

Indeed, he was like a blood hound picking up a scent. When he caught the fragrance of her perfume, he followed its trail. He staggered momentarily in the doorway, his eyes falling on the scene before him. There, laid a beautiful, enticing creature. He could barely catch his breath.

When they'd first met, he'd felt she could never love him. He was nearing sixty years old, and although he was fit as a man in his forties, she was only twenty-seven. She was tall and blonde with beautiful crystal blue eyes. Yet, to his surprise, she did fall in love with him. In the few months they'd known each other, she'd shown him that and more.

She smiled when she met his gaze and was pleased at her effect on him. She sat up and poured them each a glass of the sparkling beverage she had chilled. Holding one up to him, she beckoned him to come and sit next to her. He happily obliged.

Their eyes became fixed on each other's. He took several sips of the champagne, and a tingling sensation flowed through his body, not from the drink alone, but also from her loving gaze. Her eyes were speaking to him, and he was physically responding. He let out a soft sigh, finally in a place of serenity. He was just beginning to relax when, without any warning, she jumped to her feet.

"Come!" she said. She took his glass away, took him by the hand, and led him to the staircase.

Her eyes never faltered from his as she guided him up the stairs and into the bedroom. She began to disrobe him. He was enjoying the attention he was receiving and it took nearly everything in him to contain himself. Once he was completely free of his clothes, she looked over his body, admiring his fit physique. She noticed his package and knew what was on his mind.

"Not just yet," she said. She shook her head laughing as she turned and walked away. "Follow me," she commanded as she moved into the master bath.

He followed but wondered what she was planning. At once he saw that she had drawn him a bath. He tested the water and quickly slipped in.

Submerging himself, the soothing warmth caressed his aching muscles. "Nice… this is just what I needed," he said. "Thank you, Baby." He deeply appreciated her thoughtfulness. He sunk further down into the water to unwind.

She watched quietly from the foot of the tub as he closed his eyes. She was leaning against a wall where a radio was perfectly placed on a tiny shelf. She turned it on. Soft easy music coursed through the air, calming him even more.

His eyes opened and he basked in her lustful appearance. "Come join me," he said, extending his hand.

She looked into his amorous eyes as regret formed in hers. "I wish I could," she replied. "But I can't."

"Oh, come on," he pleaded playfully.

Her back stiffened and her eyes suddenly changed into cold hard orbs. "No!" she repeated. "I must bid you farewell."

He was confused, and not sure of what she had just said. "What?" he asked, replaying her reply in his mind and hoping he'd misunderstood.

An answer he would get–but not one he was expecting. She fixed her eyes on his, drawing his attention away from her hand, which she had slid behind the radio. She quickly turned away as his eyes caught the falling device.

A blood-curdling scream erupted from him and was quieted to a vibrating hum when the radio impacted the water. Emanating from behind her were the sounds of sizzling, and his body splashing about in the water. Then there was silence. An eerie stillness consumed the room as the electricity within him had been spent.

She didn't look back, simply walked to the bed and sat down. After a few moments of composing herself, she picked up the phone, punched three numbers, and waited patiently until a voice on the other end responded.

"What's your emergency?" It came through loud and clear.

"Help!" The young wife screamed into the phone.

"Ma'am, calm down so I can help you," said the voice.

"My husband! I think he's dead!" she cried hysterically.

"You say your husband is dead, Ma'am?" the voice asked.

"Yes, yes, yes! Oh, please help me!" she pressed on.

"Someone is on their way now, Ma'am. Tell me what happened."

"He was taking a bath... and listening to music... as he always does. I—I—don't know if he tried to get up and change the channel, or what he was doing. That's all I know." She fell into a deep thought.

The voice pulled her out. "Ma'am?"

Then she continued. "I heard a splash and saw the lights flicker. I ran as quickly as I could to the bathroom." She grew quiet, once again.

"Okay, I understand. Go on, Ma'am." The voice was very sympathetic.

"I just turned away," she said. "It was just, too... too horrible to see. Please come. Please help me..." Her last words trailed into a whisper as she laid the phone down.

The voice from the other end repeatedly called out to her. She just sat and stared, eyes glazed over. In the distance, the sirens could be heard approaching.

Chapter 1

Ben McBain was a well-known agent for numerous high profile celebrities including actors, musicians and sports figures. If they had money or something to sell, he was their agent.

Many said he had "Midas' touch"; that everything he touched turned to gold. His clientele were all millionaires, due to his hard work and know-how. His philosophy: 'keep them happy, and they keep you rich'. It worked every time. And it also made him the most sought out agent around.

Usually he would be out and about, doing what he does best, making money. But on this particular day he decided to work in his office.

He was sitting behind his desk going over some paperwork when the intercom buzzed. Without looking up from his task, he pressed downward on the button.

"Yes! What is it?" he snapped, remembering he had told his secretary he didn't want to be disturbed except in extreme emergency.

"Sir, you have a visitor," she humbly replied. He paused for a moment staring at the paper but not really seeing it. What part of 'extreme emergency' didn't she understand?

"Miss Taylor, don't I pay you well?" he blasted. He sensed a hesitation on the other end.

"Yes, Mr. McBain, you do!" Her voice was shaky.

"When I said I didn't want to be disturbed—that's exactly what I meant. I do not want to be disturbed! Get their name and make an appointment." He relieved the button, ending the conversation.

Suddenly, there was a commotion at his door which caused his head to shoot upward. The door had swung open, and his secretary was struggling to keep someone from entering.

"Sir—" Miss Taylor started to address him with fear in her eyes.

"What the—" His eyes became fixed on the tall, dark-haired beauty who had barged into his office uninvited. Then he paused as recognition took place. "Deidra? Is that you?"

She smiled happily when he recognized her. He quickly made his way to her and they tightly embraced. "How have you been?"

"I've been just fine, Ben." she replied.

Ben looked over to his secretary who seemed wary. He nodded his head and reassured her everything was all right.

"It's okay, Miss Taylor, you can go. In fact, take a break!" He said with a smile.

Miss Taylor gave him a bewildered look. She wondered what had come over him. She let out a long sigh and left them to their reunion.

"So, to what do I owe this pleasure?" he asked returning to his seat.

She quickly began. "The magazine I work for will be doing a spread on retired sports superstars next spring. They want pictures along with an article on what their lifestyles have been since leaving sports. I'm personally taking care of all photos and interviewing—with the help of a very small crew of course." She shifted in her seat as she relayed this to him.

"Go on," he urged, reaching over to a small box atop of his desk, removing a cigar, and placing it in his mouth. He had given up smoking. But now and then when pressed with business, he liked to chew on one. It helped him think things through.

"Well," she continued. "They have athletes from every venue. But they wanted to include wrestlers, since professional wrestling is very popular."

He stared at her with blank eyes, preferring not to tip his hand. She squirmed in her seat, knowing what a hard nose he could be.

"I told them I knew you, and that two retired wrestlers who were once the greatest in the industry, were clients of yours. And that are you could probably get them on board." She finished, and waited for him to respond.

He sat quietly, twirling the cigar in his mouth, eyes straight ahead, and pondered the idea.

"Have you been on the internet lately?" she interjected. People are still talking about these two and are quite curious as to how they are doing."

He sat back thinking of the two brothers in question, Marc and Cain Caldwell. Their characters had been more than dominant in the promotion; there would never be another two like them.

She rose from her seat, and began to move about. She really wanted to drive home the pitch, and she knew that money was the key to get McBain's consideration.

"Listen, Ben, if you could get them, could you imagine the magazine sales alone? It would make you a lot of money," she pressed.

His eyes lit up at her last words. He stood to his feet, still deep in his thoughts. He raked over the idea in his mind and paced the room. It would be tricky, he thought, but there must be some way to get them to agree. He turned to look at her, then out the window. "Give me some time, Deidra. I need to think. I'll get back to you as soon as I get their consent," he said.

She ran over to him, and wrapped her arms about his neck. He pulled away from her. "But there is one thing you should know if I get them to do this: stay clear of their family and of questions pertaining to them. They spent years concealing them from the madness, and we don't want to start now," he warned her.

She nodded her head in understanding. "Thank you! You are the best godfather a girl could have," said Deidra. She kissed him on the cheek and left the office—mission accomplished.

Ben continued to peer out the window. His mind drifted to his old friend, Deidra's father. He heard he was very ill. They hadn't spoken in some time, and he felt it was a good time to catch up with him.

Chapter 2

A woman reached the top of a small hill and paused.
She placed her hands on her knees for balance,
exhausted from her daily jog. She peered down below
while trying to recapture her fleeting breath, and sway
her racing heart from leaping from her chest. She
drew in the morning air, filled her lungs with the fresh
oxygen and rejuvenated her body.

She had moved into her new home several days
before, and come to this spot each morning, secretly
surveying the neighboring ranch below, and noting
everything she could about the people who lived
there.

It was ironic how things had come about. She'd had her eyes on these two properties for years, waiting for them to become available.

She knew that both properties had at one time been a complete ranch, and it was her desire to obtain both. So when she was notified one part was up for sale, she pounced on it. But she was very disheartened to learn the other wasn't for sale, and probably never would be.

In the distance, a rumbling sound brought her out of her thoughts. Her eyes shot to the direction of the sound and observed two motorcycles speeding down the road side by side. They were neck and neck. One was noticeably larger than the other. The dust was rising like a heavy cloud behind them.

On the porch of the house they were approaching, stood a huge man leaning on one of the posts. He watched as the two closed the distance to the house.

Suddenly, and without warning, the smaller bike let out a burst of speed and left the larger one in its dust. It then came to rest in front of the man on the porch. He looked down smiling and nodded his head as the larger bike joined them. "Well, Bro, she beat you!" he proudly shouted, as the other large man turned the key and shut off the engine.

The smaller biker pulled off her helmet to reveal thick red hair, and piercing green eyes. Her skin was darker than that of her father, who was of Irish descent. It was a terrific blend of cool cream and the warm tone that came from her mother's African-American heritage. She watched the men in amusement.

"Yep," said the second biker, a tall, muscular man. He who wore a black and white bandana; his hair, past his shoulders, was pulled back into a braid. He dismounted, and pulled the dark glasses from his face mirroring the same piercing green eyes as the young woman's. They met with hers proudly. "She beat me." He took off his gloves and gave her a quick pat on the head.

"Oh, Dad! Must you do that?" she protested, snatching her head from under his hand.

"What?" he asked, looking confused, as she sneered and ran into the house. She was tall and a beautiful, and but for her eyes and hair she inherited from her father, she was the picture image of her mother.

"You have a good kid there," his brother reminded him. He looked at him then to the doorway where she had just disappeared.

"Yeah, that she is. Her mother would've been proud of how she turned out." He turned from his brother, and looked over the ranch he'd bought for the love of his life.

"It's been seventeen years now, Marc; nearly eighteen," said Cain. "Alondra will be off to college soon. You've got to start thinking about what you're going do with your time. 'Specially since you won't be able to use her as an excuse for not dating. She'll be out there seeking a life for herself. You're gonna have to live yours." Cain stared at his brother, studied him, and waited for a response.

But Marc said nothing. He looked at Cain, then back out at the open ranch. He could hear his brother's footsteps fading into the house, but he didn't turn around. He remained still. It had been a long time since the death of his beautiful wife, Clarice. She had blown into his life and out just as quickly, leaving him with a broken heart, and a newborn to attend to. Caring for Alondra may have been what helped him get through his grief.

He bent down to pick up a dry piece of grass, and fumbled with it between his fingers. He went deep into thought of what life would be like after she left for college. They had been inseparable since her birth. It would take some serious readjusting for sure. He tossed the grass in the air, and watched it struggle to the ground.

"Marc, phone call!" a feminine voice called out, interrupting his train of thought.

He turned to the house, and to the door where a kindhearted, brunette stood. It was Cain's wife, Blair. Cain and Blair had moved in after Clarice died. Marc felt that having Blair around gave Alondra the feminine support she needed.

"Okay, thanks, Blair!" he yelled, and started toward the house. No one was aware they were being watched.

The Caldwell's new neighbor had seen everything from her vantage point. She'd been searching for these people for years, for they had a mutual acquaintance. She'd vowed to seek them out. She would find them if it was the last thing she ever did. It was ironic that trying to buy the property gave her the information she needed. It was there all the time, right under her nose. She turned away, and jogged down the road back home with one thought in mind. She would make her introduction soon.

Chapter 3

Marc entered the house to take the phone call Blair
had announced. Alondra was rushing down the stairs,
and jumped from the last step onto the floor. Her
hair was wrapped in a towel, evidence that she had
just taken a shower and shampooed her hair.

"Girl, you know better than to come down here
with your hair wet," Blair chided. "Why do we spend
money on a hair-dryer if you're not going to use it?"

"I want it to air dry!" Alondra replied tartly, and
pranced into the kitchen for a snack.

Marc smiled at the exchange very grateful for the
love Blair had given his daughter. She filled in very
well. He turned his attention to the phone. "Hello,"
he answered.

It was Ben McBain. "The other day an offer came across my desk," said Ben. "A well-known magazine is doing articles on retired sports figures. It's all about their lives after retirement."

Marc was silent.

Ben took the cue. "Well, being your agent, and always looking out for you, I thought it was a good idea for them to include professional wrestlers," he lied.

"And?" Marc shifted from one foot to the other.

"I informed them that you and Cain were the top characters in your promotion, and that are you're still quite popular on the net. I also told them it would boost their sales," he said proudly, lying still about his role in the plans.

Marc would have to give it some thought. "Let me talk this over with the family, and I'll get back with you," he replied and abruptly hung up the phone.

Cain was standing in the living room doorway listening. "What's going on, Brother?" he asked.

Marc swirled around, half-startled. He'd just been pondering how to convince Cain to do the shoot. He exhaled sharply. "Some magazine is doing a story on retired athletes," said Marc. He then walked past his brother and entered the living room.

Cain turned to follow, and took a seat in a chair. "What does that have to do with us?" he asked.

Suddenly, Blair joined them and took a seat on her husband's lap. "What's going on?" she asked.

"Marc was just about to explain," said Cain. "It's something about a magazine article."

Marc knew it would take some convincing to get Blair on board as well. She was just as much part of this as they were, and it was her home as well. He wasn't sure if she'd go for it. "McBain says they want to do an article about our lives since we left wrestling," he explained.

"Hey, that's cool!" Alondra exclaimed as she came bounding in and sat near her dad.

"Alondra," he sighed. "You know we've tried to keep you away from that world. And we've been very successful. No one but our close friends and colleagues even knew about you or Blair." He looked at Blair when he said this.

Blair looked in his eyes. She always knew how important it was to him to keep them safe.

"And if we agree to this, then the secret will be out there," Cain interjected.

Blair leaned back into him for security. All the years of being married to him, no one knew whether he was married or not, whether he had kids or not. They knew absolutely nothing about her, or of Alondra, who now stared at the ground, not fully understanding.

"Alondra," her father said calmly. "There are a lot of crazy fans out there mixed in with some of the greatest. You just don't know which is which until it's too late." He pulled her to him to clarify the intensity of the situation. She had never been to any of his shows in all the time he was active. He never wanted to take that chance. Neither did Cain.

"And with the magazine people being here—unless we send you two away—they will see and know exactly who you are," Marc concluded.

Cain looked at his brother, and wondered if this was a good idea. Did they really want to make such a drastic sacrifice?

"Do we have to decide today?" Blair questioned aloud.

"No, we can all think about it," said Marc. "And if everyone gets on board, then I'll give Ben a call." He looked at everyone, and got nodded heads in agreement.

After thinking everything through for a few days, they all agreed they were comfortable going ahead with the article. Marc gave Ben a call, and it wasn't long after that Deidra made arrangements to visit the ranch.

"Marc, they're all ready to go," Ben informed him by phone one morning.

"When?" asked Marc.

"Three days?" Blair screamed, after hearing the news. "I can't get this house in order in three days," she rambled.

Cain looked over to Marc and they both smiled. He walked up behind his wife, and wrapped his arms around her.

"Relax baby," he breathed in her ear.

She did just that. Peaceful in his warm embrace, she exhaled.

"This house is already clean, but I know you, and I know you want to see your reflection in the wood... so I already hired a cleaning agency," Cain cleverly admitted. "They'll be here first thing in the morning and they'll do whatever you want." He kissed her sweetly on the neck. "So calm down, before you rupture something," he said teasingly.

She smirked and then smiled as he walked away. She would try her best.

Chapter 4

Two days had passed since everyone was told when the photo and interview crew would arrive. It was very early in the morning and Blair was busy in the kitchen preparing breakfast as usual when she thought she heard a knock at the front door. After glancing at the time, she was sure it couldn't have been someone knocking. A few minutes passed when the knock was repeated. She wiped her hands on her apron and cursed under her breath, wondering who could be calling so early in the morning. She unlocked the door, opened it and peered through the screen door. "Yes? May I help you?" she looked at the four unfamiliar persons standing on her porch.

"Hello," said a dark-haired woman. Her bright blue eyes were striking even through the screen. "Is either Mr. Caldwell in?" she asked.

Blair stood for a moment, and then realized who they were. "Wait! Are you from the magazine?" she snarled. They weren't supposed to be there until the next day.

"Yes!" said the woman very cheerily.

"Oh no, you have got to be kidding?" Blair shouted. Blair turned her head to the side staring at the wall trying to retain her composure. Already, she wasn't too keen with having just three days to prepare for the invasion, but to come a day earlier than expected was absolutely unacceptable. "You weren't supposed to come until tomorrow!" She turned back to glare at them.

"No, it was scheduled for today," the female visitor insisted. "I gave Ben McBain the information."

Blair shook her head. She wouldn't listen to any explanations. "No, we are scheduled to begin tomorrow. My family is still asleep. If we were expecting you today, we would all be up and ready for you." Blair was standing firm, and would not be moved.

And as relentless as she was, the slightly younger woman was just as determined. They had traveled a long ways, she and her crew, to have to turn back now was out of the question. "Well, I'm sorry for the inconvenience," she said smartly, "but we made arrangements for today. And who are you—the housekeeper?"

Maybe it was the way Blair's expression contorted her face. Maybe it was the way her eyes turned from wide browns to black slits. Or maybe it was the way the door slowly opened, and she silently moved through it to come and stand just inches from the taller woman, but the men slowly moved backward off the porch, and allowed the one who had asked the insulting question to deal with its aftermath.

Blair then opened up very colorfully, and, not wanting to be outdone, the visiting woman was giving it right back.

Marc was settled comfortably into a deep, restful sleep. His large, powerful body was lazily sprawled over his bed as he lay on his stomach oblivious to the outside world. But even though he tried to remain in this blissful slumber, some obnoxious thing was trying to distract him. It was the sound of distant voices. They became increasingly louder and inevitably he was thrust from repose into blatant consciousness.

His eyes shot open. He flipped his enormous body over, causing the bed to creak in protest for the assault, and snatched the clock from its perch on the nightstand as he glared at the time. "Six o'clock!" he boomed.

The voices continued to rise from downstairs. They were women's voices, and were quite boisterous. He jumped out of bed, grabbed his jeans, and swung open the door. He slammed it against the wall as a warning. He was now officially awake. His feet hit each and every step with a loud stomp as he made his way down the stairs seeking out who and what was this going on so early in the morning.

That's when he saw her, a beautiful, tall raven-haired woman arguing with a familiar, and very feisty, Italian, brunette. Marc's foot hit the floor with such a vibrating thump that the stranger turned her attention away from Blair and her crystal blue eyes penetrated the green pools staring at her.

"What's going on out here?" Marc roared. His voice rumbled and overpowered the situation, bringing their quarrel to a halt.

The younger woman moved past Blair, and slowly toward Marc. She explained what she had been trying to get across to Blair.

"I'm so sorry, Sir!" she said, her lashes fluttering. "As I was trying to make your wife understand—"

She was then sharply cut off by Blair. "Wrong again, honey! I'm not his wife—or the housekeeper!"

By this time the entire house was awake and Alondra and a sleepy-eyed Cain joined the group. Cain tried to calm his wife and Alondra went to her father's side hooking her arm in his.

The woman's eyes settled on the exotic-looking, pretty, young, red-head. "I'm so embarrassed. This is your wife..."

Blair simply laughed. The woman looked around not sure what it was she had said that was so funny. She could also see that the young lady she was referring to was not amused.

"I'm not his wife, I'm his daughter," said Alondra. She glared strangely at the woman then turned, and walked away to the kitchen.

The woman rubbed the back of her neck, and allowed a long breath to escape. "Now that I have thoroughly made a complete fool out of myself–" she started.

"No, you haven't," said Marc. "I'm not married, so let's clear that up before another female enters the room. She died years ago at childbirth. You should know that since you're gonna be spending some time with us."

"Well," Blair said smugly. "I'm going to finish making breakfast, and let you two deal with this." She returned her gaze to their guest. "Have you and your men eaten yet?"

"No, Ma'am, not yet," said the woman. She then forced a kindly grin. "And you can call me Deidra."

Blair stared for a second, that name now burned in her mind forever. Then she replied, "My name is Blair. I'm married to Cain." She then turned and walked away.

"Deidra, huh?" Marc repeated.

She looked up at him and smiled.

"You can call me Marc. You're a little early, as she was trying to tell you. Was there a mix up?" he asked as he glanced at the equipment outside the door and to Cain who was in the yard talking with the camera crew.

"I'm not sure," said Deidra. "I told Ben we'd like to start today and he said it was all set."

"Knowing Ben, as I do, he probably did this on purpose. Well… where would you like to start?" Marc asked, watching the men setting things up.

"I don't know," said Deidra. "Maybe with your wife?" she suggested.

Marc's head snapped around causing her to step backward. She saw the rage in his eyes.

"Let's get something straight," he said. "My wife and daughter are not to be spoken of—is that clear? I've kept my daughter safe from the public eye for some time now, along with the fact that I'm a widower. It is nobody's concern. This is about Cain and me–not even Blair." He was very emphatic.

"Yes, of course. I didn't know," she lied; knowingly full-well what Ben had told her. "I'm very sorry."

Marc rubbed his eyes and let out some air. "No, I'm sorry," he said. "I shouldn't have bitten your head off. You had no idea." Marc looked at her really well for the first time. It was then that he realized how clear her eyes were, like an angel.

"Okay, but if I should ever over step my bounds, please feel free to correct me," said Deidra. "I want this to go smoothly; and more importantly… I want you to feel as comfortable as possible," she said sweetly, staring purposefully into his eyes.

He smiled and nodded.

Chapter 5

"I don't like her." Alondra said, walking back into the kitchen. She'd heard and seen the exchange between her father, and Deidra.

"You don't even know her, now stop and help me get this food on the table," said Blair. "We've got a long few days ahead."

Alondra did as she was told, and carried a platter to the dining room table. She paused momentarily to see that Deidra was alone, likely because her father and uncle had gone to change. She was fumbling around with something.

Feeling someone staring at her, Deidra looked up into the stern eyes of Alondra. She didn't back down. If she was going to be here a while, the little girl would have to know something–that she doesn't scare so easily.

Alondra caught her drift. Just as quickly as they had locked eyes, they released them. Alondra turned away from her, and walked back into the kitchen to finish setting the table. Deidra smiled wickedly, feeling she had won this round, but knew there were a few more ahead. This job wouldn't be as easy as the others. She hadn't known about the daughter or about the brother's wife. But then, it wouldn't matter, she thought. She went to the porch to talk briefly with Marc and Cain who had reemerged from the house.

When everyone was full to the brim from Blair's terrific breakfast, they thanked her and rose from the table. Two of the crewmen began taking plates from the table to assist her in cleaning up. They felt that was the least they could do for such a hearty meal. But she wouldn't have it, and politely shooed them away.

During the meal, Alondra kept peering over her fork at Deidra. There was something definitely not right about that woman, and she was going to find out what it was. Especially, since she seemed to have caught her father's eye. Deidra was very aware that Alondra was watching her. Feeling uneasy, she tried to push it out of her mind. Marc seemed to have much to say to her and she couldn't let Alondra distract her. She breathed easily after the meal, knowing her work day could begin. And she felt more at ease knowing Blair and Alondra wouldn't be involved in the interview process. "Wow, I don't feel like doing a thing after that wonderful meal," she said, walking out the front door with Marc at her side.

"Yeah, Blair is a damned good cook. And she always cooks big meals, even though Cain and I are the only big eaters," said Marc. He walked to the end of the porch, propped his foot up on the bottom rail, and leaned over the top. He loved to do this after his meals, even more so at night. Looking over the ranch in the peace and quiet always seemed to give him a little time with Clarice.

"I can see that Alondra doesn't eat much," Deidra added. "She just picks at her food."

Marc turned his head in her direction, puzzled. "No, Alondra eats okay—just doesn't seem to gain weight," he replied.

"Well, maybe it was having unexpected company for breakfast," she surmised.

Marc stood up and turned completely to her.

"I guess I was too busy talking to notice she didn't eat much," he stated.

She looked at him then turned away slowly.

Marc watched her carefully.

"I don't know, Marc," said Deidra. "But I did a study on eating disorders a while back. I'm not saying she has one, but you may want to watch her closely. You did say she eats, but doesn't gain weight."

Marc's eyebrows furrowed, and he decided to change the topic. "What would you like to do first—photos, or story?" he asked in a serious tone. "And remember what I told you before; my daughter, wife, and sister-in-law are not to be discussed." His warm green eyes had become somewhat cold.

"Understood," Deidra insisted. "We can start with photos. I would like to get some shots of you around your beautiful ranch," she conceded and moved on.

Just then, Alondra ran out to the porch. "Dad, Aunt Blair and I are going to town. Can we take the Yukon?"

"Yeah, the keys are on the table," he replied.

Alondra shook her head. "I couldn't find them," she said.

"All right, I'll go look for them. Back in a minute, Deidra," said Marc.

When he left to go inside, Alondra moved to his spot and unknowingly stood just the way he had been standing.

Deidra noticed this. She truly is Daddy's girl, she thought.

Alondra stared coolly into Deidra's eyes.

"You miss your mom very much, don't you?" Deidra asked abruptly.

Alondra was flustered. "What do you know about my mother? Oh, wait—I see! My dad told you, huh? Well, he may be fooled by you, but I'm not. So never ever talk to me about my mother!" Alondra screamed, brushed past her, and nearly knocked her to the ground.

Deidra braced herself against the wall of the house, at that same time Marc and Blair were headed their way. They watched as Alondra stormed toward the garage.

Both pairs of eyes went to Deidra, but Blair rushed to catch up with Alondra. She would have to give that girl a good talking to about disrespecting company.

"Once again, I am so sorry," Deidra pleaded to Marc. "I was trying to strike up a conversation. I guess I should have taken your advice," she said. She looked up at him knowing what was going to happen.

"What did you say to her?" he said. His eyes were fixed on the garage where he could hear Blair fussing at Alondra, and watched as Cain left the men setting up, and went into the garage to defuse things.

"I was trying to get her to like me by sympathizing with her," said Deidra. She began to walk around in circles wringing her hand. Her plans could be in jeopardy if she couldn't talk her way out of this.

"How?" he turned from the garage as the SUV exited with the two women inside. Alondra was turned completely to the window not looking at anything in particular, and it appeared that Blair's mouth was going a mile a minute. Cain followed the vehicle out of the garage and watched as it went down the road.

"I tried to make her understand that I knew how much she missed her mother," Deidra continued. "She seemed so sad staring out like you do."

Her eyes turned a soft crystal blue as she let him know how much she knew he missed his wife. Marc wanted to scold this woman for the last time, but their eyes linked for a moment, and in that time it seemed as if it was just the two of them, and no one else in the world existed. Somehow, he'd forgotten the previous few moments.

Suddenly, his brother approached. "I'll tell you, Marc, Alondra really has Blair's goat, but she sure loves that girl," he said with a smile. "Maybe we should have kids of our own. She's really gonna miss Alondra when she goes away to school." He hadn't noticed the exchange between the two before him.

Marc broke his gaze and turned to his brother. "You should've started on that a long time ago," Marc kidded.

Cain chuckled and looked to Deidra. "Say, Josh wants to know when you'll be ready to take pictures."

Deidra was still staring at Marc. "I'll go and let them know," she replied lowly. "I think in front of your ranch house would be a nice start." She moved past Marc, brushing him gently, but intentionally.

He felt a tingling in places he hadn't felt in a very long time.

"Nice," Cain said as he nudged his brother.

Marc didn't respond. His eyes were set on her as she sauntered over to the other men.

Later, Deidra directed the photo sessions. She knew exactly how she wanted to present the two brothers, comfortably at home on the ranch. She chose places which seemed especially marvelous, many of which exposed the lush green acres and splendid views.

She also took interest in Marc's motorcycles, and he noticed. Deidra hoped Marc would ask her for a spin. She felt much more at ease now that Alondra wasn't around glaring at her every movement. She would freely touch Marc from time to time, and took it upon herself to position him for the photographs. Their eyes caught each other's more than a few times. Cain noticed there was something between the two, and all he could do was hope the best for his brother.

Chapter 6

It had been a busy day for the two women of the house. Blair had only meant to spend a couple of hours away, but since Alondra was so upset, she thought it best to keep her out until the magazine crew had surely gone. They went to a movie and then to a spa, which it seemed to relax them both. It had been a very pleasant day.

Growing up, Alondra was a tomboy. And Blair wanted her to know that that was perfectly fine as long as she never forget to pamper herself. She often treated Alondra to spas for manicures and massages; she wanted to preserve the feminine side of her. This was part of the reason Marc appreciated having Blair in his daughter's life. She was doing something he wouldn't have been able to do.

"So now how do you feel?" Blair asked, as they walked to the truck. Alondra had a smile on her face. She enjoyed these outings with her aunt who knew exactly what to do when she was upset.

"You know I feel good," she replied happily.

Blair nodded in agreement as she unlocked the door and got in. She began to ramble through her purse then and found a piece of paper. "Boy, we have a lot of groceries to get. I think I'll drop the list off at Sal's market and have them deliver this time around. Why don't we grab a bite to eat?" she asked.

Alondra suggested a new café she'd seen and they drove away. Neither noticed the vehicle that had been following them since they arrived in town, and was now behind them.

It had been a long day, and evening began to approach. Deidra wanted to leave before nightfall, so she told the crew to pack up and call it a day. Cain secretly called Blair to let her know.

While the camera crew packed up, Deidra slipped away to get one final look at those motorcycles.

Marc noticed and began to follow. "Do you ride?" he asked.

Deidra was startled as she hadn't seen or heard him come in. She was usually very aware of her surroundings. "A little," she replied. "I'm not the expert that you are, I'm sure," she said.

"Maybe we can go for a spin when this is all over," he said. He rubbed his hand over one of his bikes staring down at it.

She smiled from what he had just implied. "Is that an offer for a date?" she asked. She wanted to be clear on what he was saying.

Marc's eyes slowly moved up to meet hers, and stared deeply into them. "Maybe," he said with a grin before turning to leave the garage.

Deidra stood for a few seconds, and watched him leave. She began to hug herself, laughing. Her plan was going beautifully; better than she could have hoped.

Blair was eating with Alondra when she got the call that they could come home. She told Cain that he and Marc should fend for themselves for dinner before hanging up.

"What did Uncle Cain want?" Alondra asked while her aunt slid the phone back into her purse.

"The magazine folks are packing it in, that's all," said Blair.

"Excuse me..." said a voice from the table behind them.

Alondra and Blair turned in response.

"Yes?" said Blair, staring at a woman with dark, auburn hair and light brown eyes who rose from her table and came over to them.

"Hello, my name is Geraldine, but people call me Geri." She extended her hand to Blair who took it hesitantly. She was still unsure why this woman was making her introductions.

"What can I do for you?" Blair asked.

"I'm your new neighbor," said Geri. "I moved in several days ago. I saw you come out of the road leading up to your ranch. I went for a hike the first day to get to know my place and saw the young lady racing bikes with a man I presume to be her father. You're pretty good, girl!" Alondra smiled charily.

"Oh, it's a pleasure to meet you. I'm Blair, and this is my niece Alondra. I heard someone had brought the Anderson's place. I'm sorry I haven't got around to welcoming you. So much is going on at our place, especially today. Why don't you join us?" Blair asked.

"Don't mind if I do," said Geri. She reached over to grab her food, drink, and belongings and Alondra went over to help.

Blair was surprised to see Alondra take to this woman so easily, as she was usually on the defensive.

Chapter 7

"Well, guess what'?" Cain hung up the phone as Marc entered the house.

"What?" asked Marc.

"The girls are sitting in a restaurant at this very moment, and you know what that means," said Cain.

"Oh no," Marc replied. He shook his head and started toward the kitchen. There was no use putting off the inevitable. Cain followed.

Marc opened the refrigerator while Cain came up behind him. They stared into it blankly seeing so many different containers filled with food making it hard to figure out what was what. The two were too busy trying to plan what they were going to eat, to notice they had company.

"Gentlemen," said Deidra, garnering their attention.

They looked up simultaneously.

"I was coming in to let you know that we're heading out, but I see that you two are in need of a helping hand, so I'll send my men on, and then I'll solve your problem." She took complete control of the situation.

Marc and Cain watched her disappear through the kitchen door then turned to stare at each other. Each knew what the other was thinking.

"I don't know, Marc," Cain finally said.

"Yeah, I know what you mean; Blair and her kitchen..." said Marc.

By that time, Deidra had come back in and pushed them out of the kitchen.

They were just hoping Blair didn't get back in time to see another woman moving around in her domain. Maybe they could make it seem like they'd invited her to stay. They just sat back, and hoped whatever she was going to do would be quick.

It didn't take her long to whip something up. The smell emanating from the kitchen made their stomachs jump for joy. They soon forgot the dilemma. She put together some leftovers with fresh sides and prepared the table. The men watched her move around the place like she belonged there.

She set the food on the table, and called them to eat. Everything looked and smelled good. They all sat down and began their meal. They laughed and talked about everything from the business to motorcycles. They were just finishing up when Blair and Alondra walked in. And they weren't alone.

Blair thought the smell coming from the kitchen was pretty good and wondered what the guys had cooked. She went to the dining room. When she walked in, three pairs of eyes darted over to her.

She looked suspiciously at the table, and how it was set, knowing the guys hadn't done it, and then her eyes came to rest on Deidra. She suddenly realized Deidra was there alone, without her crew.

Cain jumped out of his seat, and took Blair's shoulders guiding her into the kitchen to divert a storm. Their voices were subtle at first. Then they grew louder. Marc readjusted himself in his seat. Deidra's eyes fell on her half-eaten food, not wanting to look at Marc just yet. She knew he was uncomfortable.

Just then, they heard a noise at the entrance of the dining area. Their eyes came to rest on Alondra standing with someone else. Marc stared at his daughter, who glared at Deidra and rushed off to the kitchen.

Geri felt a little out of place. Marc's eyes squinted out of curiosity. He wondered who this newcomer was and rose from his seat to greet her.

"Hello, I'm Marc," he said. He extended his hand and she rested her hand in his.

"I'm Geraldine," she said. "But you can call me Geri I met your sister-in-law and daughter in town. I'm your new neighbor. It's seems like a bad time to come visiting." She let out a light chuckle.

Marc nodded and smiled. He couldn't put his finger on it yet, but there was something very familiar about her. And she was incredibly beautiful without trying. Her skin was smooth and sienna; her makeup was very subtle; her eyes were endearing and gentle. She'd quickly taken his breath away.

Upon realizing this, Deidra cut between the two and introduced herself.

"And I'm Deidra," she said and offered her hand. Geri took it, and thought she felt Deidra put a little pressure into the squeeze.

"It's nice to meet you both," said Geri. She drew her hand back and put it in her pocket.

Suddenly, the noise from the kitchen stopped, and Marc, Geri, and Deidra watched the door swing open as Blair stormed out and rushed upstairs with Alondra close behind.

Cain reentered the room. He wanted to apologize to Deidra, but stopped in his tracks. His eyes were fixed on their guest. "Hello," he said. His voice was a little shaky.

Marc's eyes rose to look at his brother. He sensed something was the matter.

"Hello, Sir. I'm Geri," said the new neighbor to Cain. "I moved into the Anderson's place."

Cain was frozen in time for several moments. He couldn't take his eyes off of her and was suddenly speechless. Alondra came down the stairs and noticed this.

"Uncle Cain… I think you need to check on Aunt Blair," she said. She then cast an evil eye toward Deidra.

"Yeah…" he breathed. "I don't know what's gotten into her lately. She's been acting really strange," he said, breaking his gaze. He turned away, but unnoticed to the others, he watched Geri as he ascended the stairs. Something had puzzled him.

Everyone else stood around uncomfortably.

"I guess it would be a good time for me to leave," said Geri.

"I suppose I should too," said Deidra. "After I clean up of course..." she added.

"No, you've done enough, thank you," Alondra spat.

Marc quickly stepped over to his daughter. "Wait just one minute young lady—you apologize for being so rude!"

Alondra stood defiantly, but knew not to push her father too far. She pouted, and looked down at the floor.

"It's okay, Marc," said Deidra politely. "We're all a little edgy today."

"I don't need you to help me out!" Alondra snapped again, shooting her a heated glare.

"Alondra Caldwell!" Marc boomed. The explosion of his voice causing the Geri and Deidra to jump, but Alondra had been down this road many times, and looked to the far wall.

She forced a 'sorry' from her pursed lips, then walked out to the porch.

By now, Cain and Blair were coming back down to join them.

"I owe you an apology for my own actions," said Blair. "I don't usually act that way. If I can be frank, it could be P.M.S.," she said with a little laugh, hoping to lighten the mood. Then suddenly something occurred to her and she went deep into thought.

"It's okay, Blair, I understand," said Deidra with a smile. "Well, it's been a long day, and I have to be back here in the morning. I'd better go. May I use your phone to call a taxi?" she asked Marc, her lashes subtly fluttering.

He looked at her strangely. "What are you talking about? I wouldn't dare let you call a taxi. I'll take you to town," Marc reminded.

She smiled innocently. "Thank you very much," she said, her eyes fixed hungrily on his, unbeknownst to him.

Alondra stepped back inside. "Well," she said. "When you take her... you can also take Geri to her place. Her car broke down at the restaurant where we met her."

"What happened to your car?" asked Marc with concern.

"I don't know," said Geri. "It just wouldn't start. I had it towed to the garage. Hopefully, they'll be able to tell me something tomorrow."

"Well, if they don't let you know by the afternoon, give me a call. I'll get them cracking," Marc boasted.

"Thanks," she replied sincerely. She smiled a beautiful smile that tugged immediately at Marc's heart.

There was something about her. He had an aching feeling that he knew her from somewhere and began to stare just as Cain had.

Deidra piped in, purposely breaking the connection. "Shall we go?" she chimed.

Marc turned from Geri and acknowledged Deidra. "Sure," he replied.

He started toward the door and Alondra and Geri followed. Cain watched as they disappeared. He watched from the doorway and noticed how Alondra had interacted with Geri.

"Alondra has really taken to the new neighbor," he said aloud.

But Blair's mind was going over something far from what was going on. "What?" she breathed, slowly coming out of her own little world. She'd come to realize something.

"I said Alondra has taken to the new neighbor pretty quickly. Is something on your mind?" asked Cain.

"I think I'm going to call Dr. Simmons tomorrow, and make an appointment," she replied.

Cain became concerned, and went to her side. "What is it, Baby?" he asked, caressing her shoulders.

She looked up and saw the concern in his warm hazel eyes. "Don't worry, Cain. It's probably nothing serious. Probably just hormones," she admitted.

But her words didn't ease his feelings. "I'll go with you," he insisted.

She wanted to protest, but knew it would be in vain. And she loved him for it.

He pulled her close and held her tight. Inside he felt there was more to what she'd been feeling than hormones alone.

Chapter 8

Marc was silent as he drove down the county road that would first lead to Geri's house and then to town. Deidra sat beside him and Alondra and Geri sat together in the back seat where they conversed quietly. Deidra said nothing while she stared at the road ahead.

When Marc neared the entrance to Geri's place, Alondra got an idea. She scooted forward in her seat, and placed her hand on her father's shoulder. "Dad, wait! Since you're going into town anyway, why don't we check on Geri's car? The garage should be still open."

He stopped the car momentarily and thought about it. "That sounds like a good idea. You don't mind, do you Geri?" he asked.

"No, not at all," she replied. "But I don't want to put you out." She was grateful for the help. She knew how male mechanics sometimes try to take advantage of women if no man is around.

Deidra slightly tensed in her seat, then turned her head, and stared out of the side window shielding her disappointment.

"You're not putting anybody out. It's my pleasure," said Marc.

He continued down the road and Alondra and Geri began to chatter amongst themselves.

They first arrived at Deidra's hotel. She thought about asking to tag along, but felt it better not to. She would have to bide her time. She would be with him tomorrow... and for sure there wouldn't be an Alondra or a Geri to stand in her way. She bid them goodbye, and watched them drive away.

She stood there for a few moments after they had long disappeared from sight. Then she slowly went into the hotel lobby. She was in a trance-like state as she walked to the elevator. The doors had barely opened before she squeezed past them. When the elevator finally came to a stop on her floor, she stormed out of it and rushed down the hallway to her room. Upon entering, she closed the door and threw her bag across the room. She stood for a few moments with clenched fists, angered at the events of the day. It hadn't gone as planned. Geri's arrival was an unexpected, and unpleasant, surprise.

She went to the bed, snatched a pillow from it, pressed it into her face and let out a blood-curdling scream. Temporarily relieved of her emotions, she tossed the pillow back to the bed and went into the bathroom. She doused her face with cold water, lethargically raised her head, and gazed at the reflection in the mirror for a very long time. "There is nothing to worry about," she said to the person staring back at her. "Just a little obstacle that will be dealt with if necessary." She turned away and ran herself a hot bath.

"Okay, Jack, what's wrong with the lady's car?" asked Marc as he walked around checking the car out. It was an old Pinto wagon.

"Marc, this car has had its last run. She should look into getting a new one," said Jack.

Geri was distraught. She'd had this car from the time it came off the floor. It was her first new car. She pleaded with the mechanic, "Can't you do something to get it running again?"

Marc's eyes returned to her. There was something about how she looked, and the way she talked, her mannerism just seemed so damned familiar, and yet he knew he didn't know her.

"I'm sorry, Lady. I can, but not in clear conscience. You'll only wind up stranded on some road somewhere, and that's not what I'm all about." He looked from her to Marc who stood listening with his arms crossed over his chest. She looked at Marc, her light brown eyes a little wet with emotion.

"This was the very first car I bought for myself, right off the floor," she said. She went over to her car and rubbed the hood.

Marc walked over to her, and caught her arm gently.

"I'm sorry, Geri," he said. "I know this is hard, but he's right. It'll certainly break down again, and who knows where or when? It's too risky." He tried to reason with her.

She knew he was right. She looked over to Jack and nodded her head. It was time to let the car go.

"All right," she blurted. "Junk it!" She turned and left the garage crying and Alondra followed.

Marc shook Jack's hand and thanked him for being honest. He left the garage to join the ladies.

The ride out of town was a somber one. Geri sat in the front this time, next to Marc and didn't say a word. Alondra sat behind her father not pressing Geri to talk.

This time when Marc neared Geri's drive, there was no protest. He took the winding dirt road into a clearing, revealing the one-story ranch-style house. Geri opened the door, and jumped out before Marc could unbuckle his seat belt. He followed her to the porch steps and she turned around.

"Thank you so much for your help," said Geri. "I want you to know how much I appreciate it, and I feel a little foolish for acting the way I did back there. I can only imagine what are you think of me, first impressions and all." She let out a small chuckle, and looked down at her fidgeting fingers.

"Don't worry about it," said Marc. "I know how it feels to have to give up something important to you. And your first car is always the hardest to let go.

I know that too." He smiled at her. His eyes softened when she gazed in them.

The moonlight played just right on her eyes. They seemed even brighter, and for that moment his heart seemed to go back to another place and another time, long ago.

"I'd better letter you go," she said. "I don't want to keep you. I understand you have a very long day ahead. Thank you again for everything." She purposely interrupted their moment. It was hard to do, but she was feeling something, and she couldn't allow herself to get attached; not right now.

"Yeah, I guess that slipped my mind," he said. "But if you need a ride any place until you find another car, don't hesitate to call me. You know what?" An idea popped into his head. "We should be wrapped up with this by Saturday. Why don't I take you to a nice car place I know?"

She was taken aback, and didn't quite know what to say. "I don't know…" she said. "I don't want to make a nuisance of myself." Geri started to back up towards her front door.

"I'm not gonna take no for answer," said Marc. "Even if I have to cancel these shoots. Then there will be a big problem with the magazine folks… And you don't want to see that now, do you?" he stood leaning on the railing with one foot propped on the lower step. His eyes staring up at her like a school boy looking at his crush.

"All right," she said with a smile. "Since you put it that way. I certainly don't want to see you get into hot water with the magazine. Especially since you have gone out of your way to be neighborly." She had eased her way back to the edge of the porch and wrapped her arm around the post. Her eyes became fixed on his.

"Good," said Marc. "Then it's a date." His voice was low and deep, but soft. Not wanting to leave her but knowing he had to, he gave her a smile and turned and walked away.

He glanced up at the moon, and for the first time in years his heart felt full. Something it hadn't been in a very long time; not since Clarice.

Geri watched him walk away. He stopped and gave her one last lingering gaze before entering the vehicle, then he drove away.

Alondra, who'd jumped into the front seat, and had watched the two interact, and was very happy about what she saw. Maybe, just maybe, Geri was someone worthy of her father's love.

"You like her don't you?" she asked s they drove away.

Marc cleared his throat coming back to reality. "Yeah, why wouldn't I like her?" he asked. "She's a nice lady."

She stared at him with a grin. His eyes darted back and forth between her smiling face and the road ahead. "Look, don't go getting any crazy ideas or making more of this than it is," he warned.

"I won't," said Alondra. "I'm not going to do a thing, I promise!" She sat back in her seat, and looked out the side window, smiling. Yes, her father definitely liked Geri.

Chapter 9

Geri had watched Marc's car disappear around the bend, and stood for a while, looking at the moon. She hadn't counted on this thing with him. He was a very good-looking man; he was tall, broad, and handsome. And there was something about the way he looked at her that made her heart skip a beat. "I can't believe this," she whispered aloud. "Did what happened with him, really happen?" She couldn't ignore what she was feeling. He made her feel wonderful. She sat back in a chair and wrapped her arms around her and smiled.

She basked the moon light. It was a beautiful night in more ways than one. It had been a long time since she had feelings like this; not since her husband

Stan. Suddenly, her tranquil moment was interrupted by another thought. Stan... he'd been nearly twenty years her senior and had died a horrible death–a radio had supposedly fallen into the tub while he bathed. The details were suspicious.

She left the porch, and went into the house to prepare some things. Her first contact had gone better than expected.

Marc stared through the window of his darkened room. The moon seemed more enchanting tonight for some reason. He remembered a night like this many years ago; the night he met his wife Clarice.

He had gone to a fair with Cain and Blair, and wasn't paying much attention to where he was going. He and Clarice bumped into each other. Her brown eyes were mesmerizing, her perfect smile and soothing laughter captivated him. He paused as the memories replayed in his mind.

But just as he thought about Clarice, Geri's face filled his mind; her smile and laughter, the way the moonlight gleamed in her eyes. "No! This isn't happening," he told himself. "I just met the woman today, and already I'm falling for her. What in the hell is wrong with you man?"

He turned from the window and sat on his bed. He took the picture from the nightstand. It had been there for what seemed like forever. It was of Clarice. "I fell in love with you right then and there," he said softly. He gently put the picture back in its place and guilt overtook him. He mustn't betray the only woman who had ever truly captured his heart; the one and only woman for him. He lay back on the bed, his eyes closed, and succumbed to the darkness.

Chapter 10

The next morning seemed to come quickly to Blair. She was up early preparing breakfast for her family, knowing the magazine crew would arrive soon. And no quicker than she had put on the coffee, the front doorbell rang. "They don't waste any time," she groaned. She let the men in and they commented on how good everything smelled.

Marc was just descending the stairs when Deidra walked through the front door. She busy looking at a camera, and didn't notice him staring at her. She fumbled around with it for a while longer, looking through it to see if it was working right by panning around the room, and came upon Marc standing on the bottom step. She jumped back with a start.

"Marc!" she yelled with her hand covering her heart and trying to catch her breath at the same time. He smiled and stepped down on the floor still looking at her.

"You really get into your work don't you?" he said.

She set the camera back in its bag. "Yes, it's all I have right now," she said. She looked at him and then quickly away.

He stared for a moment. "I can't believe a beautiful woman like doesn't have a special someone somewhere," said Marc.

Deidra headed for the living room. "You'd be surprised." She said passing him.

He followed her, wanting to pursue this further, as she had caught his interest now. "Then tell me about it," he said, taking a seat.

"Look Marc, I'm flattered to think you have some interest in my private life, but I'm not here to talk about me. I'm here about you and your brother," she snapped without blinking an eye.

Marc stood to his feet, and ran his hand over his head. "Well, I guess you straightened me out. It'll be straight to business then. I've instructed you on what will and won't be mentioned in this interview so you have every right to set your own boundaries, and I will not cross them again." He left and went to the dining room, leaving her standing in silence.

Deidra stood to her feet clenching her fists. What had she done? She wanted to scream hard and loud, but knew it wouldn't be wise to reveal her temper. She would have think of a way to smooth things over. She just needed to breathe and calm down. She inhaled, allowing the oxygen to flow through her body, then slowly released it.

Alondra was coming down the stairs, and saw her father was clearly upset as he left the living room. She was curious as to the cause. She came to the door peering into the room, and to her surprise, there was Deidra. She was about to go check on her father when she noticed Deidra had a weird expression forming on her face. She continued to observe from the hallway, and saw her doing the breathing exercises. Not one to know when to hold her peace and when not, she entered the room. "I use to take a psychology class," said Alondra. "The breathing method was often used to calm a person with anger issues."

Deidra flipped around and glared at Alondra silently.

"I see you know something about that," said Alondra. "I think everyone should. You never know when it will come in handy." Alondra finished and left the room.

Deidra stared after her until she was no longer in her sight, her heart rate increasing as she began to breathe through her nose. Obstacles! Why must there always be obstacles? She yelled to herself.

Chapter 11

After breakfast Alondra joined her aunt in the kitchen. "Something is wrong with that woman," she said to Blair.

"Are you at that again?" Blair asked. "Do we have to leave today to keep the peace?" Blair stopped what she was doing, and turned to her niece.

Alondra sat down, and began to fidget with something on the table. "No!" She said, knowing where this was going. And after the way her aunt has been acting lately, she didn't want to ruffle her feathers.

"Good! Because I have a lot of things to get done around here. Yesterday set me back, and besides, I have to go into town tomorrow so I won't be able to get them done then." She seemed to drift off somewhere.

"Aunt Blair, are you all right?" she stood up and went to her.

Blair smiled and touched the side of her face with the palm of her hand. "I'm fine, Baby." She reassured her then thought of something that might keep Alondra distracted so she could get some chores done. "You know what? I was thinking... Geri is over at her place all alone. Maybe you could go visit her, and help her get settled in." Blair nodded with a big smile on her face.

Alondra turned away allowing this suggestion satiate in her mind. "Yeah! That's a great idea. I like her." Blair continued to be amazed at how quickly Alondra took to Geri.

"Can I ride my bike?" she asked as she started out the kitchen door.

"Ask your dad, hon." Blair advised.

"Okay, I will," said Alondra. "But don't think I don't I know you're trying to get rid of me," she said with a chuckle before getting on her way.

"That girl is too smart for her own good," Blair said quietly, shaking her head.

Deidra was with her crewmen giving them instructions. Cain was in the garage, busy with something and Marc was standing on the porch observing everything. His head turned when Alondra came out onto the porch.

Deidra glanced over when she saw Alondra come out of the house. She didn't like that girl. She too thought she was too smart for her own good. That's when she decided to go for broke, and walked towards them.

"Dad, I'm going over to visit with Geri. Can I ride my bike? I'll go straight over and come straight back when I'm done," she promised.

"Does she know you're dropping in on her uninvited?" Marc asked. He then noticed Deidra coming their way.

"Aunt Blair suggested it. I could help her unpack, you know, be neighborly," she said, smiling innocently.

He walked to the other end of the porch and thought about it. He wasn't sure if he wanted her to be riding alone. "Why don't I take you? Then, when you're finished you can call, and I'll pick you up," he said. He also wouldn't mind seeing Geri again after they hit it off last night.

"You're leaving?" asked Deidra, coming in on the last of the conversation. Marc's eyes automatically went to her.

Alondra didn't acknowledge her at all.

"Just for a minute," said Marc. "I'll be right back." He then went inside for his keys.

Unknown to Alondra, Deidra had a death stare on her, but she suddenly turned around and saw it.

Deidra tried to soften her eyes, but Alondra caught it in time, and felt a chill run up her spine. She knew there was something wrong with this woman. She'd witnessed too many strange things. She was definitely going to keep an eye on her.

"Okay, let's go, Alondra," said Marc. "Deidra, I won't be long."

Marc and Alondra went to the garage where Cain was finishing up with his work and looked up to see his brother and niece climbing into the SUV.

"Where are you two going?" he asked.

"I'm going to help Geri get unpacked. Aunt Blair suggested it. She felt it was best if I was out of the way." She wittingly informed her uncle.

"Okay! But why are you going, Marc? She can driver herself," said Cain, looking at his brother curiously.

"I'm just going to make sure it's okay with Geri," Marc explained.

But Cain wasn't buying his story. He grinned slyly and Marc gave brushed it off. Cain laughed and went to the house as they drove away. But he caught a glimpse of something fly from behind the garage. It was a bucket. He wondered how it happened, and then saw Deidra come from that direction. He shook his head, puzzled.

Cain was still scratching his head when he went upstairs to find Blair who was sewing something as he came in. She looked up to see his expression.

"What's wrong, Honey?" she stopped what she was doing and watched as he went to the window.

Cain saw Deidra at her Jeep saying something to her crew. Then she climbed in and left.

He turned to Blair as if wanting to say something, but didn't know quite how to say it. "First," he began. "Why is Marc taking Alondra over to Geri's instead of letting her to ride her bike or take one of the cars?" he sat down near her staring at what was in her hands.

"Marc took her to Geri's?" Blair asked. She was surprised. "That's strange. I told her to ask him if she could ride her bike. I didn't think he would take her over there like a child. He has to realize she's nearly grown up."

"I think it's more than just treating Alondra like a child. It's Geri." Cain interjected.

Blair froze for a moment. "Geri? What do you mean, Geri?" she asked.

He gave her familiar look.

"Oh!" Blair's mouth swung opened, and her eyebrows rose. "He's been so lonely for so long, and now two women have him going." Blair laughed.

Cain stood and went back to the window wondering where Deidra had gone.

"One I'm not so sure about," he said under his breath.

Blair's eyes squinted seeing something was still troubling him. "Cain, tell me, what is it?" She came to join him at the window.

"Deidra," he replied. "A little bit ago, a bucket came flying from the back of the garage and I wondered how it happened. When I came to the house and looked back, I saw Deidra come from back there. It's very bizarre."

"Really?" asked Blair. "Where is she anyway?" She slid her arm around her husband warmly and both stared out at the yard below.

"I don't know," he said.

Chapter 12

Geri was just getting back from her morning jog, and entered the house through the kitchen. She closed the back door behind her, but in her haste, didn't secure it. She continued to the bathroom, removed her jogging clothes and jumped in the shower. As she relaxed under the hot water, she thought of Marc. She'd been thinking of him all night and all morning. But soon her thoughts drifted to another person; someone who was very odd.

Earlier, she'd been up on the hill watching the magazine crew from afar and got a glimpse of Deidra. That woman was a pain for sure. She remembered the pressure Deidra applied in the handshake they shared, and how she seemed to be very territorial with Marc.

She even caught Deidra tensing up a few times. Geri got the feeling that Deidra had a temper you didn't want to cross. She shook Deidra from her mind and her stirring thoughts immediately went back to Marc Caldwell.

"Let me go see if it's okay first." Marc said to Alondra when they parked in front of Geri's house.

Alondra stayed in the car while he knocked on the door. He waited for a time then knocked again. He knew she couldn't be gone because she had no car. Receiving no answer, he decided to look around back to see if she was there. As he came around the house, he saw that the door was open and proceeded to call to her through the screen door only receiving silence.

Marc suddenly became alarmed. He entered the house, looking around and calling her name without any response. He made it to the living room and noticed she still had some things unpacked, but everything else appears normal. But suddenly he heard a noise and looked down the hall. His heart stopped at first glance, not because Geri had emerged wrapped in nothing but a towel, but because she looked like someone else, someone more familiar. He blinked to clear his eyes, not believing what he saw.

"Oh!" screamed Geri. Startled, she ran into her bedroom.

Marc just stood still, feeling very awkward. Then Geri returned in her robe.

"I'm so sorry," said Marc. "I knocked a few times, then came around to the back and saw your door was open. When you didn't answer my calls, I got worried. Marc tried to explain to her why he was standing in her living room uninvited, and still reeling from what he thought he saw.

"Is there something I can help you with?" asked Geri, somewhat shyly. She was flushed and didn't look up at him. She was too embarrassed.

"Alondra took a liking to you, and she doesn't do that with many folks. She wanted to come over and help you unpack. I told her I had to ask you first…"

As he continued his explanation she looked up at him for the first time. Her demeanor had quickly changed. He noticed and didn't know what to make of it.

"Oh yes!" she replied. "I would like that. Where is she?"

Geri went to the door and Marc noted how excited she'd become at the mention of his daughter.

"Alondra, come in!" she called anxiously from the doorway.

Alondra climbed out of the car and went inside. "Hi, Geri," she said. "My Aunt Blair thought it would be neighborly to come help you since we hadn't come by before… and I thought it would be fun. Is it okay?"

"Of course it is," said Geri.

She looked over Alondra with such adoration. Marc slowly neared, observing Geri doting over his daughter, and thought it was harmless, but seemed a little strange, since they'd only just met. Then his eyes shot up to something in the distance that neither of the ladies noticed. He stared for several moments. What he'd seen had disappeared from sight.

Deidra sped down the road toward the highway having seen enough. She hit the steering wheel repeatedly with her clenched fist. Her face was contorted; her eyes were paling as her anger was becoming uncontrollable. "I thought he was only taking that little brat of his over there to drop her off! So why was she sitting in the car while he was inside alone with that woman? Then she comes out in her

94

bathrobe! What were they doing?" she was yelling at the top of her lungs, tears welling in her eyes.

She couldn't go back to ranch. She took out her cell phone and called Josh. She said she wasn't feeling well and to pack it up for the day. She threw her phone onto the seat and blazed down the dusty road to the highway. She would have to regroup and deal with things tomorrow.

Cain and Blair had come downstairs to see what was going on. They knew Deidra had left, and hadn't come back. They saw Josh coming towards the house while the others were packing the equipment up.

"What's going on, Cain?" Blair asked, concerned that something had happen to Deidra. Cain moved onto the porch to meet Josh.

"Is anything wrong, Josh? Is Deidra okay?" asked Cain.

"I don't know, Mr. Caldwell," said Josh. "Something is weird. She left but didn't tell us where she was going. The she just called saying she wasn't feeling well and to pack up for the day. We do have a deadline to meet. And I'm so sorry, Sir, for the inconvenience."

"Don't worry about, Josh," said Cain.

"I hope she's all right," said Blair.

Josh just shrugged his shoulders and went to join the others.

Cain just stood in silence.

"We should call Marc and let him know Alondra can come back home," said Blair. "Well, wait. I remember something. This morning, Alondra started in about how something is 'wrong with that woman'. She was talking about Deidra again. I just thought she was doing it because she didn't like her. But it's an odd coincidence." Blair began to walk into the house, pausing at the door then turned to see Cain was still standing unmoved.

"Maybe she saw something none of us were paying much attention to," he said. "Maybe something really is wrong with that woman." Cain looked out over the ranch as his brother does when deep in thought. He heard the door close behind him as Blair went into the house. He took his cell phone to call Marc.

Chapter 13

Marc hung up his phone with a puzzled look on his face. Geri was in her room dressing. "What's wrong, Dad?" asked Alondra.

"Your uncle says the shoot is off for today," said Marc. "He said something about Deidra disappearing for a while then calling to cancel for not feeling well."

"Is everything all right?" asked Geri, rejoining them.

Marc's eyes settled on her remembering the incident earlier.

"The shoot is off for the day," he said. "Deidra got ill."

"Oh," is all she could say and sat on the couch.

"Funny though," he said.

Geri's eyes went back to him. She heard something in his tone of voice.

"What is it?" she asked.

"Probably nothing; it's just that I thought I saw a glimmer of a car at the end of the drive a little bit ago. But why would they come and then leave without coming all the way in?" he was not really asking, but thinking aloud.

"Maybe someone got lost and was turning around..." Alondra surmised.

Geri's eyes studied Marc. She watched him standing silently for a few moments, and then his expression seemed to change as he looked her way.

Marc wasn't sure it was a good idea for Geri to be alone all the time out there. He felt the two ranches were so far apart that if anything should happen... He didn't want to entertain the thought. "Maybe so, but, Geri, you be careful," said Marc. "I'm gonna be worried about you out here all alone."

Geri readjusted herself on the couch, his eyes had captured hers and she could see that he genuinely cared.

"Marc, I've been here an entire week; I'll be fine," she said, making a failed attempt to relieve his mind.

"I didn't know you a week ago. I do now," said Marc before turning to the door to leave.

Geri left the couch and went to him. "I promise! I'll be careful—no, I'll be extra careful," she said, resting her hand on his arm.

He felt it and something coursed through his body from her touch; something he couldn't ignore. Once again, that familiarity about her came through. He looked down into her eyes allowing them to take him away... and they certainly did.

Alondra watched them, and quietly left the room giving them privacy.

"I'd better go. I'll be back to get Alondra later," said Marc. He released himself from her hold and tried to fight the overwhelming feeling coming over him. It was more than he could bear.

"Let her spend the night," Geri suggested. "You can get her in the morning."

He looked past her, and saw that Alondra was nowhere to be found. He suddenly knew why she had gone. "I don't know..." he began.

"Yes, Dad! Please!" Alondra begged, coming out of hiding.

"I just don't know," said Marc. "I've got the shoot tomorrow, and I'm not sure how early they'll show up. They have a lot of lost time to make up for."

"Dad… take me home and let me get some things. I'll drive the Yukon back here, and bring myself home in the morning," said Alondra.

He simply stared at her. He was still baffled at how she took to Geri in such a short amount of time.

"What?" she asked, noticing his stare.

"Nothing," said Marc. He turned for the door, then, abruptly turned back to her. "Okay—but you behave yourself while you're here. Do you understand? Don't give Geri any grief," He pointed his finger at her.

She smiled happily, and hurried to the car.

Marc turned back to Geri. The mood was right; the atmosphere was heavy. What was between them would not be extinguished. Unaware she was doing it, Geri had moved close to him; and in response, he leaned down to her, their bodies just touching, lips nearly brushing each other's.

"Dad, come on!" yelled Alondra.

The ambiance broken, Marc moved away and caught his breath. Geri turned from him, shaken.

Alondra was in the vehicle anxious to get her stuff, and come back; mostly, because she would get to be away from home for the night, and that was a rare occurrence.

Marc walked to the car but briefly turned back to Geri before leaving. "Just remember what I said. Be careful," he reminded.

Geri clutched her heart as he drove away. This couldn't be happening; she didn't need this now.

"You and Geri seemed to be hitting it off," Alondra pointed out.

"I told you before don't make more of this than it is." His voice was a little gruff.

Alondra wondered what had happened between the time she left, and he came out of the house. She turned to look back at Geri's house as they left. Geri stood on the porch staring after them. Marc caught her in the rearview mirror. He'd have to keep his distance from her, he thought. His emotions were unsettled.

Geri watched them disappear then went into the house and picked up the phone and dialed.

"I need you," she said. "When can you come? No, I'm fine. It's just that I need someone to remind me why I'm here, keep me focused." She moved onto the couch, and pulled her legs into her.

"That's fine. But look, don't just show up. I need you to be inconspicuous. Give me a call when you get into town. Wonderful. See you soon." She finished and sat in a daze. "I can't get distracted," she said aloud to herself. "Got to stay focused." But as hard as she tried, she couldn't get Marc out of her mind. She leaned her head back into the couch and sighed.

Chapter 14

When Marc and Alondra arrived home, she went immediately upstairs to get her things and Marc threw his keys on the table. He was still trying to get himself together after what happened with Geri.

Blair saw them come in and noticed Mark was in a daze. "Did something happen over there?" she asked worriedly. "Alondra ran upstairs, and now you look like you're someplace else."

"Oh, no, nothing happened. Alondra is going to spend the night at Geri's," he said. "That's all."

Blair stepped back, her motherly instincts kicking in. "What? We don't even know this woman, and you're allowing her to spend the night?" she felt a pain in her heart. "I know she's your child and I don't have any right to interfere, but that's our baby up there! I couldn't bear if..."

Marc didn't allow her to finish. She'd been short as of late, but this time she was nearly in tears. He pulled her into a hug to console her. She was usually the one telling him he was too protective of Alondra. He'd never seen her like this.

"Is everything okay?" asked Cain as he entered the room.

Marc looked over to his brother. Cain could see he needed to talk. Marc looked down at Blair and looked straight into her eyes.

"I want you to listen to me," he said calmly. "You're right; she's our baby, all of ours. Ever since Alondra was born, you're the only mother she has ever known. And you have always been free to have your say in what's going on with her. Don't you ever forget that, all right?"

She nodded, her eyes wet.

Marc continued. "And trust me when I tell you that Geri is a decent lady," he said. "She really likes Alondra. She's the one who asked if she could stay. I think she's been pretty lonely over there."

Blair's whole attitude changed as reality struck her. "I hadn't thought about her being out there alone," she said. "I'll go help Alondra pack a bag." Blair went up the stairs.

Marc sighed very deeply.

Cain noticed. "Want to talk?" he asked.

Marc nodded and went to the bar in the living room and grabbed a beer.

Cain watched him, curious. "So what happened?" he asked as he sat down to listen.

Marc took a huge gulp. "Geri," he replied. "I don't know, Little Brother. I keep getting this feeling I know her from somewhere."

Cain shifted in his seat; he knew the feeling. "Yeah, so what else is going on?" he asked. Cain knew that wasn't what had him so shaken.

"We almost kissed!" Marc exclaimed. He then took a gulp of beer.

Cain's eyes grew as large as saucers.

Then Alondra suddenly burst into the room. Blair was behind her. "Dad," said Alondra, interrupting the two men. "Aunt Blair is going to follow me in the car. She wants to visit with Geri and get to know her better."

Marc looked surprised, yet, somehow knew he shouldn't be.

"I know what you're thinking, Marc," said Blair. "But something you said got to me. Geri truly is all alone. We're the only people she knows out here. I just want to visit, let her know she has friends."

Cain went to her. "That's a nice gesture. We're all so lucky to have each other. I wonder if Geri has any family."

"I don't know," said Blair. "When we had dinner together she never mentioned it."

"No, she didn't," said Alondra.

"Well then, that's where we can start," said Blair. "Let's go, Alondra."

Marc followed the ladies out, and Cain went over to get a beer. He thought about what his brother said about thinking he knew Geri from somewhere. He didn't want to say anything to Marc, but he saw it too, the first night they met her. It wasn't that Marc knew Geri from somewhere, rather she reminds him of someone else. He just doesn't realize it.

Chapter 15

Morning arrived, and Deidra was on her way to the Caldwell ranch. But she wasn't feeling any better than she had the day before. "Everything was going just fine until that little twit came along," she blasted.

She hadn't slept much that night. Every time she'd dozed off she would dream about Marc in Geri's house, and Geri in that bath robe. "What did you have under that robe, Geri?" she asked, although no one was around to answer. She struck the steering wheel a few times with her open palm then had to pull over to gain her composure.

"You have to pull yourself together. Rethink this thing through. Anger is not going to get him. Only subtlety will." She talked to herself in the mirror as if she were another person.

Then she began her breathing exercises, slowly inhaling and exhaling, until her body had relaxed. She looked up into the mirror once again. "Good girl! Now keep your cool. You have the upper hand. You've got a plan." She let out a loud laugh as she started up the car, and continued onward.

She pulled up, and saw her crew just leaving the house. She figured they'd just finished breakfast. "So sweet of Cain's wife to offer breakfast to the crew every morning," she said sarcastically. She'd purposely come later to avoid sitting at the table and pretending to be nice and happy and playing glaring games with his nosey daughter. She got out of her Jeep and went to the house to look for Marc.

Having finished breakfast, Marc grabbed a bottle of water and joined his brother for a seat in the living room. Marc read his expression and asked if anything was the matter.

"I didn't want to bring this up in front of Blair. But how are you feeling this morning?" asked Cain.

"Do you mean about Geri?" asked Marc.

"Yep," Cain replied.

Marc thought back to the day before. "There's nothing like a good night's sleep to clear your head," he said.

Cain wasn't satisfied with that answer. "So the almost kiss is not an issue anymore?" he asked.

"I'm not gonna lie. If we were alone again, I don't know what would happen," Marc admitted and turned to gaze out of the window.

Cain nodded knowing this was the truth. "I understand," he said. He wouldn't press him further.

"Hey, looks like Deidra showed up," said Marc. "I wonder if she's any better today."

Secretly, the two men went out to meet her. Deidra had overheard the conversation between the two brothers, and hidden until she wanted to be seen.

So he almost kissed her, Deidra thought to herself. She would have to deal with that; her growing insanity reflected on her face.

"Deidra... are you okay?" Blair asked.

Deidra turned quickly her direction. "Oh! I'll be fine if I may use your restroom," she replied. She pushed her hair back from her face.

Blair pointed the direction Deidra needed to go and watched her slowly stroll down the hall. Blair was lost for words. She didn't know what to think. She didn't like Deidra's deranged look. Maybe that's what Alondra had seen before. Deidra seemed to be going through some emotional breakdown, or was nearly there.

Blair was so deep in thought that she didn't hear Cain enter the house or his footsteps as he came up behind her.

"What time will you be leaving?" Cain asked, wrapping his arms around her waist.

Startled, Blair jumped. Her mind had been on Deidra and a sinking feeling about her lingered. "Cain, you startled me," said Blair.

She hit him playfully with her dishtowel and he put his arms up to shield the blows and laughed. "Okay, okay!" said Cain.

He continued to chuckle, but she stopped and her thoughts once again became serious. She was concerned about the incidents with Deidra. But she didn't have time to think about it any further. She had an appointment to get to. "We should leave as soon as I finish the dishes," said Blair. "Are sure you don't want to stay behind. If you miss the photo session, you'll be another day behind schedule."

Cain slid his hands around her waist and stared lovingly into her eyes. "Your well-being is what's important to me. I'm going with you. I want to hear what the doctor has to say," he said.

Marc appeared in the doorway and was about to speak, but stopped himself. He didn't want to interrupt Cain and Blair.

They saw him and smiled. "Hey, Marc," said Blair, "there's something..." She was just about to mention Deidra's strangeness when the blue-eyed woman reentered the room. Blair decided to hold her peace. She redirected her words to Deidra instead. "Are you feeling any better Deidra?" asked Blair.

Deidra stopped in front of them, and next to Marc.

"You're still not feeling well?" asked Marc. "Maybe we should postpone the session for today."

"No, no, we can't! We're already too far behind!" said Deidra, her voice raised almost hysterically.

The other three stared at her, bewildered at her sudden outburst. Blair felt an alarm go off in her head. Something was definitely mentally wrong with this chick. Alondra was right, she thought. "Calm down, Deidra," said Blair. "You need to take care of yourself."

Marc grabbed Deidra's shoulders to calm her and she looked up into his eyes. Then she did something unexpected. She threw herself into his body, wrapping her arms around him tightly, and began to cry. Marc looked at Cain and Blair awkwardly. Cain shrugged his shoulders and Blair's eyes narrowed with suspicion.

"I can't mess up," cried Deidra. "This is my last chance to redeem myself."

Marc, Cain and Blair looked at each other. Marc pulled her away from him and held her in his sight.

"What do you mean, 'redeem' yourself?" he asked.

Just as curious as Marc, Cain and Blair listened for her response. Deidra tried to stifle the tears, moving from Marc's grasp, and walked further into the living room followed by the Caldwells.

"My father is very rich," said Deidra, trying to explain between sobs. "He is a friend of Ben's. That's how I got this job. If I screw it up, my father will disown me and I'll be out on the streets."

Blair suddenly felt for her, and as Cain looked on, Marc returned to her side. "Don't worry," said Marc kindly. "You're gonna do a great job. Your father may be a friend of Ben's, but Ben doesn't work that way. He thought it was a good idea to use us in the shoot and you just happened to be working for the magazine. It was purely coincidental. He must have seen some of your work and insisted work on the project," Marc explained.

Deidra looked at him through wet eyes and a smiled etched across her face. "Well, he did say he was impressed with my previous work," said Deidra. "He told me I was a natural. You know, until I took up photography, I had no direction. Now I do! That's why my father was happy I got the job. He wants me to fail."

Blair now felt she knew why the younger woman was so dismantled. So much pressure was on her. Her heart went out to her. "Okay, enough of this," said Blair. "Come with me, Deidra. Let's get you cleaned up." Blair beckoned her away from Marc and up the stairs.

"Another idiot with money driving his kid crazy," Marc growled.

Cain nodded in agreement. It's sure sounded like it, as distraught as Deidra seemed to be. "You know, maybe the session should be called off for the day anyway," suggested Cain. "Deidra's not in any shape to do anything, and I'm not gonna be here. Blair's not feeling well and I'm going with her to the doctor."

"Doctor? What's wrong with her? Is it serious?" Marc grew worried. Blair was the closest thing to a sister he ever had.

"No, Bro', it's okay," Cain answered. "I don't think it's anything serious." He tried to ease Marc's mind to little avail.

"But you don't know do you?" Marc added.

Cain's eyes met those of his brother's, and Marc could see he was worried as well.

"I'm going to find out," said Cain.

"I'll go crazy here thinking of what is going on in that doctor's office." Marc began to pace back and forth.

"No you're not," said Blair.

The men turned to see she and Deidra had come back. "I talked Deidra into quitting for the day," she said to Marc. "I think you might want to show her around the ranch, give her a more thorough tour. It'll give you both some down time. Don't you think that's a good idea, Cain?" She looked over to her husband hinting that she didn't need him there. He got the clue.

"I think that's a great idea," Cain agreed.

"That's okay," said Deidra. "The crew and I will go back in to town. I'll just lie down in my room and relax. I don't want to be a bother."

Marc stood there quietly and envisioned her locked up in her room on such a beautiful day as this. "I agree with them, Deidra," said Marc. "And besides, it's too pretty a day to be stuck up in some hotel room. And maybe you can go ahead and take a few pictures—in a more relaxed atmosphere." Marc suggested.

Deidra appeared to think about it for a moment. "All right, you convinced me," she conceded with a smile.

Just then, her crew walked in from outside. She turned to them jubilantly. "Boys! We're going to call it a day. Let's take off and pick up tomorrow," she said.

The crewmen began to mumble. Josh stared at her for a minute, knowing they were already behind a day, and wondering how many days in a row this was going to happen. But she was the boss, so he resisted the urge to complain.

Deidra walked out with them to explain she would still be taking a few pictures and maybe do a small interview with Marc, so they wouldn't get that far behind schedule. She went back to the house happily after watching them drive off. She was finally beginning to feel that things were going her way.

Chapter 16

Alondra just got out of bed from a very restful sleep and left the guest room in search of Geri. She knocked at her door, but there was no answer. She went to the front of the house and saw Geri just coming in from outdoors. She seemed exhausted and was perspiring.

"Geri what's wrong?" Alondra asked, following Geri to the kitchen.

Geri took a bottle of water from the refrigerator and smiled knowingly at Alondra. "I'm fine. I jog every morning. It relaxes me," she explained.

"Oh, okay," said Alondra, relieved. "Well, I guess I'd better get home. I promised Dad I would. He'll have a fit if I'm too long. I'm surprised he hasn't called already."

"You don't want to eat before you go?" asked Geri, not wanting their time to end so soon.

Alondra turned around and smiled. "I have an idea. Why don't you come with me to the ranch and let me give you the tour? We can have breakfast there. I'm sure my Aunt Blair made a feast. She's been cooking enough for the magazine crew."

Geri thought it over. Even though she had tried to fight her feelings for Marc, they still remained, and seeing him would be nice. "Okay, that sounds nice," said Geri. "And I sure would enjoy seeing the lake again." Geri said.

Alondra perked up. "You know about the lake?" she asked.

Geri paused, realizing what she had just blurted out. How could she explain without revealing too much? It would blow everything she had planned right out of the water. She had to think fast. "I told you that I jog. Well, one day I wanted to see how far I could push myself, and I guess I went way too far; found myself well onto your property. I won't do that again," she laughed. "But it sure was beautiful. The lake and the peaceful surroundings were my savior

118

that day, let me tell you." Geri smiled, hoping her ruse had worked and, to her relief, Alondra smiled back.

Good, thought Geri. She knew she would have to be more careful I the future.

Cain and Blair were in the kitchen when Deidra came inside from seeing her crewmen off. When she passed the living room, she saw Marc inside, staring out of the window. She paused at the doorway silently watching, and taking in the view. She hadn't noticed before how red his hair was even though it braided back, the front again covered with a bandana.

"You're worried about her aren't you?" she asked.

He turned his head to her for a moment, then back to the window. She could see his body rise and fall from deep breathing.

"She's like a sister I never had, and I owe her a lot," said Marc. "She's looked after my daughter like she was her own, and I'll always love her for that." Some sadness was evident in his voice.

"What's going on?" asked Alondra, having just entered the room.

Marc turned as she had caught him off guard. He hadn't paid much attention to her arrival as she made her way across the yard toward the house. His mind had been too deep in thought.

"What are you talking about? What's going on?" she repeated.

Marc's eyes held his daughter. What could he say, when he himself had no answers.

"Where's Aunt Blair?" asked Alondra.

"She's all right–" Marc began. He walked toward his daughter, but she backed away and began to call for her Aunt.

Cain and Blair came quickly from the kitchen and Alondra ran into Blair's arms.

"What is the matter child?" Blair rubbed her head.

Alondra held onto her for dear life. "Oh thank goodness," said Alondra. "Dad was talking like something had happened to you." She pulled her head from her, and stared into her eyes.

"Come with me," said Blair warmly. "We need to talk." Blair took her hand, and led her out of the room.

As Marc watched, someone else entered. His heart jumped. As much as he too tried to deny his feelings, his heart told wouldn't let him. Their eyes locked, caressing each other. He felt a sudden warmth building within him.

Geri's eyes glistened, taking in the flow of energy emanating from Marc. She felt as if her knees would buckle. She turned away not able to stand what he was doing to her.

Cain watched it all unfold, as did Deidra through her narrowed eyes. Marc had never looked at her that way, although he had looked at her intently. This was different.

Obstacles—always obstacles, thought Deidra. In her mind, she was fuming. "Marc," she said, intentionally interrupting. "Are you ready to take me on that tour of the ranch?"

The others were oblivious to Cain's presence. He observed everything and wondered if his brother had a clue yet about Geri.

"Oh, yes! Let's go," said Marc. "Uh, Geri! Would you like to join us?"

Deidra tried to hide the fact that her eyes had become large. She desperately hoped this woman would not ruin her plans yet again.

But Geri didn't want to intrude. And she didn't want him to know that Alondra had planned to take her for a tour of the ranch as well. She would have to change plans. "No," said Geri politely. "You go ahead. Alondra offered to take me to check out some cars. I really need to get one. Can't keep depending on other folks, however nice they are." She looked purposefully but nonchalantly away from him, but that didn't stop Marc from rushing past Deidra to her.

"I thought we made it a date for Saturday?" said Marc, a hint of disappointment in his voice.

She glanced at him. Boy, he is huge, she thought. And she was overwhelmed by the intoxicating energy that she felt from him. She moved slightly away to allow some distance between them without him noticing.

"Yes... I know," said Geri. "But you have so many things going on... I don't want to impose any more than I already have."

Marc seemed thunderstruck.

Cain leaned against the wall watching this little scene play out. He hadn't seen his brother so involved with a woman so quickly; not since Clarice. And again he wondered whether his brother had realized the resemblance.

Deidra was puffing hard, but only Cain noticed.

Marc took Geri's arm gently with his hand and escorted her out of the room. Deidra flopped down on the sofa angrily.

Cain could see that she had some strong feelings for his brother. He laughed to himself. "I wouldn't let that bother me if I were you," he said. "Marc always feels like he has to be the protector, especially with women in distress." He sat down across from her.

Deidra grinned slightly. She realized she'd shown her emotions too much today. Now it was time to do whatever was necessary. "I won't let it bother me," she said. "It's just that it would be good to see the ranch, and take pictures too. That way the whole day won't be a bust. You know what I mean? And that thing about Marc and Geri… it's okay," she lied.

Then Cain saw Alondra and Blair returning from upstairs. Everything seemed better. He rose to his feet and went to join them. Deidra followed to see if they had straightened everything out, but the way Alondra glared at her told her to keep her distance, so she walked past them and out to the porch. Marc and Geri were nowhere to be seen.

"I know we just met and all," said Marc to Geri. "But I really want to get to know you better. Hell, I came home and tried to push you out of my head but it isn't happening, Lady; not by a long shot."

She was sitting on a bale of straw and staring up at him adoringly and in disbelief. She tried to absorb everything he'd just said. She'd been feeling strongly for him, and to hear him express that he felt the same for her had touched her deeply. She didn't know what to say.

"Just let me do this thing today and tomorrow," said Marc. "Then, I'll be free. I want to be there when you get your next car. Is that still okay?" He'd given up the idea of pushing her out of his mind. He decided he wasn't going to let her go easily after all. He couldn't.

He seemed so sincere that she surrendered to his plea. "Yes, it's okay," she replied. "I guess I can live two more days being chauffeured around. Not that I really have any place to go."

He smiled. He was pleased he'd gotten through to her. "Good. Then I guess I'd better get back to Deidra," he said, reluctantly.

They left the barn, and didn't notice the pair of eyes watching them.

"I guess I'll have to play dirty," said Deidra. "Real dirty if I'm going to get what I want." She watched them cross the yard and go into the house. She then slipped into the garage and disappeared.

Chapter 17

Marc looked all over the house for Deidra then came back outside and saw her at her Jeep pretending to be looking for something.

"I wondered where you'd gone off to," said Marc.

"I was making sure I had enough film," Deidra lied. "This is a job I want to go smoothly, and so far it seems like it will."

She invited him into her Jeep and he went to the passenger side to get in. As she turned the key she looked over her shoulder to see Alondra and her new friend, Geri, leaving the house and heading into the garage. Her lips curved into a sinister grin.

Alondra saw her father leaving with Deidra and Geri couldn't help but notice the young lady's disdainful look.

"Why don't you like her?" Geri inquired as they made their way into the garage.

Alondra was silent as she went over to her motorcycle and straddled it. She looked at Geri with dark eyes full of anger. "She's no good," she said. "And she's after my father."

Geri let out a small chuckle and came to stand next to Alondra. She paused for a moment and stared at her in a motherly way. "Honey, take that as a compliment to him. I know he's your father so you can't fathom that he's a charming, generous, and really good-looking man. Any woman would be glad to have him in her life."

Alondra looked up and a noticeable glimmer in Geri's eyes. "Does that include you?" Alondra asked.

Geri was caught off guard. She turned away quickly, not wanting to betray the feelings harboring within her, but also not wanting to reveal them to Alondra. "You know," said Geri. "The first time I saw you, I thought that if my baby had lived, my precious little girl, she would have been your age. And I do believe she'd look just like you." Geri changed the subject to an even more revealing one. Her eyes were soft and slowly filling with tears.

Alondra felt her own tears coming to the surface as Geri had opened up and given her a little part of herself. "You lost a baby?" Alondra asked. "We have so much in common."

Geri looked at her unsure of what she meant.

"I lost my mom," Alondra explained. "I never got a chance to see her. She died having me." Alondra turned her eyes to the ground and tried to gather herself.

Geri was stunned with this new revelation. She didn't know that part.

"My daughter died at childbirth," Geri admitted. "It seems we do have that in common." Her eyes went to the far wall, her mind traveling back to that day. Then something else from that day came to the surface. "Except for the father in the story," said Geri. She walked slowly away.

Alondra dismounted the bike, and followed her. "What do you mean, Geri? What happened to your husband?" Alondra pried.

Geri took a seat on the ground with her back against the wall and Alondra joined her. "We were in love," said Geri. "It was like love at first sight, but I did resist him at first. It was a gut feeling I had, but did I listen? No. And it cost me my baby." Geri wiped the tears that were now flowing.

Alondra placed her hand on her shoulder trying to console her. "We don't have to talk about this anymore Geri. Let's do something fun," she said.

Alondra jumped up and assisted Geri to her feet. They went towards the Yukon when Geri paused for a moment, and walked over to the motorcycle. An idea formed in her head.

"Wait," said Geri.

Alondra was halfway in the vehicle but stopped and looked at Geri who had a big smile on her face. She returned to her side.

"Have you ever driven your bike with a passenger before?" Geri asked Alondra.

"Yeah, my dad, when he was teaching me," Alondra replied with a big smile. Could her new friend and neighbor also like motorcycles as much as she does?

"Good," said Geri, happily. "Then you wouldn't have any problems riding with me?" Geri looked at Alondra excitedly and jumped on the back of the bike.

Alondra was speechless. She was very surprised.

Geri sat on the bike grinning. "Come on! I want to fly!" said Geri. She threw her head back with outstretched her arms and mimicked a bird flying.

Alondra grabbed two helmets, gave one to Geri and put the other one on. She jumped onto the bike and started it up.

"Okay, Kiddo! Let's go!" yelled Geri over the roaring motor.

Alondra was excited. She kicked the stand and Geri wrapped her arms around her waist. Alondra revved up the engine and sped out of the garage.

Cain and Blair were locking the door behind them to leave when they heard the motorcycle. They saw it speed out of the garage with the two ladies on it. Blair ran to the edge of the porch and watched helplessly as her niece and new neighbor disappeared from sight. "What in the hell is she thinking?" Blair blasted.

"Well, she's been doing this since she could walk," said Cain. "And she's ridden with Marc on the back; surely she can balance a small lady like Geri!" Cain looked down at his wife who now turned from him and stared away angrily.

"I'm not talking about Alondra," said Blair. "I'm talking about Geri. She's my age. She should know better," she scoffed.

Cain suddenly realized what the matter was and chuckled a little. "Do I sense a touch of jealousy here?" he asked.

Blair turned back to him and glared. "What do I have to be jealous of?" she asked.

He tilted his head and laid a gentle hand on her shoulder. "How close those two have become in such a short time," he answered.

Blair quickly walked away heading toward the garage. "You don't know what are you're talking about," she said over her shoulder.

He caught up with her quickly. "Don't I?" he said, turning her to face him. He bent his knees slightly to come eye to eye with her.

She gazed into his lovingly searching eyes before turning her head. There was no use hiding it. "Okay, you're right," she conceded. "I just don't get it, Cain. The last couple of days, two new women have come into our lives. One, Alondra hates... the other, she embraces. I don't understand."

Cain stood up straighter as his wife paced with folded arms. "It may be the same reason my brother took to her so fast," he said. Cain looked out over the ranch, his mind in a place and time long ago.

Blair was confused by his comment. He then looked at her with a smile. "You don't see it either do you?" he asked.

She stared and then shrugged her shoulders. "No—what? Tell me!" She could see he had the answer.

"Think hard, Baby," said Cain. "Think about Geri. Who does she remind you of?"

Cain watched Blair closely as her mind began churning and deciphering what he had just said. Suddenly, she came to it and her eyes lit up. She looked at her husband in shock. "Oh, my god, I've been so caught up with all the commotion and what was going on with me that I couldn't see what was in front of my face. Do you think Marc sees it?" she asked.

He shook his head. "Not with his outer eyes, but I think he does with his heart," said Cain.

Blair took in a deep breath and let it out slowly.

Cain wrapped his arm around her shoulders and led her into the garage. "Since Alondra's on her bike, let's take the Yukon instead of the car," said Cain.

Blair nodded and got into the vehicle. Cain started it and slowly pulled out of the garage, driving to the doctor's office.

Chapter 18

Marc gave Deidra the grand tour of the enormous ranch. She got out at several spots and took some shots of him. It was apparent he was very proud of his place. It had become his solitude from the grueling road trips he used to take while working.

Deidra truly was in awe of the place. She stood for a while looking as far as she could see, then she joined Marc in her Jeep and followed his directions to the next spot. They came upon a lake in the middle of the property. It was partially surrounded by woods and rich green grass.

Marc pointed out a good place to park and quickly got out and went to the water's edge. Deidra followed, leaving her camera behind, and came up beside him to enjoy the view. It was breathtaking, she thought. Then her mind inevitably began to calculate as it always had. She felt this would be the best place to set her plan in motion. Marc took a seat on the grass under a tree. He watched the ducks, swans, and geese swim peacefully. This was his place of solitude.

"Do you come here often?" Deidra asked as she came to sit next to him.

"Every chance I get," said Marc. "It's a very special place for me."

Phantoms, she thought. Why must there always be phantoms? "I gather this was your 'spot'," she said calmly.

"My spot?" he questioned.

"Clarice's and yours," she said quietly.

He turned to her with an odd expression on his face, and then turned away. "That's none of your business—on the record, that is. But off the record, yeah, it was. We spent many an afternoon here," said Marc.

She was he shared that with her. "On the record I didn't quite get that," she said. "Off the record, I understand."

He smiled a little just then, and returned his eyes to her crystal blue ones. Strange, he thought, her eyes are almost hypnotizing. Suddenly, an urge came over him. And uncontrollably, he caressed her neck with his hand and pulled her closer. Their lips just touched when she held back.

"Wait, Marc," whispered Deidra. "Are you sure you want to do this?" She knew her thoughtfulness would steer him on.

He answered by covering her mouth with his own. She responded with a deeper kiss, encouraging him to do more. He pulled her onto his lap and kissed her passionately, his tongue exploring every inch of her mouth as she moaned in pleasure.

Deidra had never felt such passion from a man before. He released years of pent up need for a loving woman in his life.

"Dad!" Alondra cried. Her voice pierced his ears like a sharp knife. He immediately released Deidra and turned to see two pairs of shocked eyes.

Deidra sat up in his lap seeing one pair glaring at her, and the other was blank. She quickly scurried out of his lap and came to her feet, taking refuge next to the tree. Marc stood up and remained silent for a few moments. He was hesitant to recapture their gaze, but knew he had to face them. His eyes went first to Alondra then to Geri. For some reason he felt like a cheating husband who had just been caught. "Alondra, Geri, what are you doing here?" he said with a forced smile, trying to divert their thoughts from what they'd just seen.

"Don't try to distract me from what you were doing, Dad!" yelled Alondra. "I can't believe you! You brought her here to the place you always took Mom?"

Deidra looked around wondering how they got there.

"It's not what you think, Alondra," said Marc. "We–" he started, but was unsure himself what had just happened and why. He looked to Geri for help, but she raised her hands in protest and went over to the tree eyeing Deidra. She remembered what Alondra had said about her going after her father.

"I don't want to hear it," said Alondra angrily. "Geri is right; whatever will be, will be. I'll be glad when I'm gone from your sight!" she screamed. She turned away not wanting them to see her crying.

"Wait a second, Alondra," said Marc, coming to a revelation. "What are you doing here anyway? You were bringing someone here too," he realized.

"I always come here whenever I need to figure things out," Alondra replied. "I may not know my mother, but for nine months I was a part of her, and that's a connection not even death can break." She returned her gaze to her father. "I wanted to share this spot with Geri because today we bonded in a very special way. And I thought it would be nice for her to be here. So what was your reason for bringing Deidra here?"

He stared at his daughter realizing how much she missed having a mother and he didn't have an answer.

"Okay you two, time out," said Geri, trying to smooth things over.

Marc heard the voice from behind him and thought for a split second that Clarice had come back. He turned quickly around only to stare into Geri's beautiful light brown eyes. They connected to each other for a moment as she walked past to Alondra.

"You're busy, Marc. That we can clearly see," said Geri. "And Alondra is upset, which I can totally understand. So with your permission, Sir, I would like to take her away, have her stay at my place for another night. Maybe some more away-time will do her some good."

Sir? Marc replayed in his mind. That's what Clarice would call him, whenever she was feeling very serious.

"Okay, you're right," said Marc turning to reach for Alondra. "Baby, when this is all over, it's gonna be just us until you leave for college in the fall. How does that sound? We can go anywhere you want to go. It's my gift to you, just for being you."

Alondra looked away and Geri gave her a gentle nudge. She realized she was hurting him and that wasn't something she ever wanted to do. She fell into his arms and held him close. She loved him with all of her being.

Geri smiled seeing them happy and suddenly caught the fierce anger in Deidra's eyes. Geri's eyes narrowed, registering Deidra's expression, and she knew she had to protect Alondra and Marc at any cost. Deidra relaxed her expression, thinking she hadn't yet been observed, and Geri saw that as well.

"So how did you two get up here?" Deidra asked. "We never heard you drive up…"

Alondra realized she hadn't told her father. "Dad, guess what?" she taunted him. He held her away from him looking into her cheerful eyes.

"What Alondra? Am I gonna like this or not?" he hated it when she started with 'guess what'.

"You're going to love it," she insisted. "I rode my bike up here and guess who was on it with me."

He looked at Geri in disbelief.

Alondra began to laugh. Then, unable to resist it any further, allowed her eyes to come to rest on his surprised green orbs.

"Oh really?" he said, regarding her with admiration. "You're full of surprises, dear Geri. I wonder what other surprises you have up your sleeves."

"Come on, Geri," said Alondra. "We'll go back home and get my things. See you tomorrow, Dad." She gave him a quick peck on the cheek and went down the hill.

Geri said an awkward goodbye to Marc and Deidra and left the two alone.

Marc's eyes followed them and saw where they had been sitting at the little picnic area he had created years before. He watched them mount the bike and ride away. Unbeknownst to him, Deidra hit her fist into the tree. He was still watching the two ladies ride away. She was so close until the brat and the busy body showed up. It's okay, she told herself. At least you know he has feelings for you.

Marc came back to where she was standing alone. "I'm sorry about everything," he said.

She hid a bruising hand behind her, not wanting him to see it. "It's quite all right," said Deidra. "Who knows what would have happened if they hadn't have shown up," she said innocently. She tried to make it sound as if it were a good thing they had been interrupted in order to ease his mind. "Do you mind driving back? I'm feeling a bit tired. It's been a long day," she said feigning a yawn, still toying with his emotions.

Chapter 19

Cain sat in a chair while Blair put her clothes back on.
They'd been instructed to meet the doctor in his
office when she was finished dressing. Cain stood up
as she hooked the last button on her blouse. She
stared nervously into his eyes and he caressed her
cheek. "It'll be all right," he said lovingly.

They left the examining room and went down
the hall to get the results. The doctor was sitting
behind his desk reading her file and peered over his
wire-brim glasses when they entered. "Come in; come
in, Mr. and Mrs. Caldwell."

They sat in two chairs in front of his desk while
he finished looking at the chart.

"Well, I'm waiting for the final test. Then I'll be able to tell you for sure what is going on," he said. He sat back in his chair eyes darting back and forth from Cain to Blair.

"Look, Doc, patience is not my strongest virtues, so if you don't mind, please tell us what you think is wrong with my wife," said Cain. His anxiety was getting the better of him.

Before the doctor could speak, a nurse walked in with a sheet of paper and handed it to him.

He leaned forward after taking the paper and scanned it quickly. He then smiled and faced the couple. "Well, you don't have to wait any longer," he said.

Blair was relieved. Cain squeezed her hand.

"All of your tests look normal. You're going to be just fine."

Cain finally breathed and Blair placed her hand over her heart.

"You are definitely pregnant, Mrs. Caldwell," said the doctor.

Cain and Blair then froze in their chairs.

Alondra finished packing her overnight bag and joined Geri in the living room. Geri rose from her chair. It was going to be fun having her spend another night. She was enjoying their time together and finally getting to know her. What's more, she hated being alone, but knew it was the price you pay for your independence.

"Want to go to town and get something to eat first?" Alondra asked as they were heading out the door to the motorcycle.

"No, I'm going to cook. It'll be nice to have someone to cook for," said Geri.

Alondra looked at her surprised. Geri caught this.

"You didn't think I could cook?" said Geri with a laugh.

Alondra smiled; embarrassed that Geri had read her so well. "Well, no. You seem too hippie, you know what I mean?" she explained.

"Hey! Us hippie gals know how to do a lot of things," Geri corrected playfully.

Alondra gave the house a quick glance over, thinking how she would miss the place when she left in the fall. Then she started the bike with Geri on the back and sped away.

Marc and Deidra were coming up the road when the motorcycle tore out of the driveway and turned up the road. Marc sighed heavily. That girl is just too sure of herself, he thought. He hoped she would have the good sense to slow down.

Deidra watched the motorcycle, mad that those two had spoiled her date. But she had a thought. Maybe she could salvage it after all. That is, of course, if his brother and sister-in-law weren't back from the doctor.

Marc pulled the Jeep in the front of the garage. He saw that Cain and Blair had taken the Yukon instead of their car.

Deidra was bewildered. Damn, she thought. Another plan gone awry.

"Do you want to come in, and rest up before you make that trip to town?" asked Mark. "Oh, wait—I've got an even better idea. Let's get something in our stomachs. I know you're hungry." He started to walk to the house.

She hadn't expected this after what had happened at the lake. She was lost for words. But she held onto hope that Cain and Blair would get stranded on the road in the Yukon she had tampered with; and with Alondra gone to Geri's for the night, she and Marc would be all alone. Things couldn't have worked out any better.

"Sure, why not?" she said, catching up and hooking her arm with his.

Chapter 20

"What's wrong with it?" asked Blair. She watched as Cain made another one of numerous attempts to start the Yukon.

"Hell if I know Blair. How often do I drive this thing?" he snapped and gave it one more turn of the key to see if it would turn over. "Shit!" he yelled hitting the steering wheel with both fists. He looked over to Blair who seemed as if she were about to cry. They had just received the most shocking news. They were going to be parents and now this. "It's okay, Baby," said Cain calmly. "I'm gonna get you home, you know that."

She looked in his eyes and found comfort. "I know, Honey," said Blair. "It's just that our lives as we know have changed with one phrase: 'You are going to have a baby'. How everything becomes much clearer," she said.

He nodded in agreement. "Yes it does. I'm gonna check under the hood." He popped the hood and got out to check. Blair could see him fumbling around with something.

"Blair!" he yelled. "Scoot over to the driver's seat and turn it on!"

She slid over and did as asked but nothing happened.

"Damn it!" he said loudly and walked back to the driver's side.

Blair stared at him as he stomped towards her and could see he was getting very upset. "What are we going to do?" she asked timidly.

He glanced at her for a second then looked down the street to the garage. "I'm gonna see if Jack can come and take a look at it. Wait here," he said.

She watched him distance himself from where they were stranded, grabbed the phone out of her purse and called Marc.

"Okay, have him call me when he gets back," said Marc. He hung up the phone, and walked back to the dining area where Deidra sat, and paused at the door with his hands on his hips.

She could see something was wrong from the expression on his face. "Bad news?" she inquired, hoping it was Cain and Blair.

He scratched his head and came to take his seat at the table. "That was Blair," said Marc. "She said the Yukon broke down. Cain has gone to Jack's Garage to see if he can find out what's going on. I hope he can because I just had that thing serviced last weekend. And it's only a couple of years old." He seemed very disturbed.

Deidra stiffened slightly in her seat. She was sure they'd find the loose cable. But it didn't really matter. No one could tie it to her anyway. She relaxed once more. "How unfortunate, Marc," she lied.

Alondra hung up her cell phone, a look of worry covering her face. She looked up and saw Geri just coming from the kitchen where she was making dinner.

"What's wrong Alondra?" said Geri. She was immediately concerned when she saw Alondra's pained look. Alondra's eyes met hers and something tugged at her heart. Those eyes were her father's for sure.

"That was my Aunt Blair," said Alondra. "She and my uncle are stranded in town. The Yukon won't start and they have to get the guy at the garage to come look at it."

"Well cars do breakdown, Honey," said Geri. "Why do you look so upset? The mechanic should get it up and running."

Alondra shook her head and began to pace back and forth. "Yes they do. But Dad just had it serviced this weekend. And it's never done this before."

"Well, that is a little strange," said Geri.

Suddenly, Alondra remembered something. Earlier Deidra had vanished for a little while. Her father had looked seemingly everywhere for her. Then, out of the blue, Deidra appeared and she and her father were leaving together. Where was she during that time? With her mind pondering over that question, Alondra sat in a chair by Geri stared directly into her eyes.

Geri could see something was churning in that pretty little mind. "What is it Alondra? Spill it," she urged.

"Geri," Alondra began. "I know that I just met you, but I feel as if we have known each other forever. I can't explain it, but I feel I could trust you even with my life."

Geri eyes glimmered and tears were forming. "I feel the connection too. It's like you're the daughter I lost," Geri explained.

Alondra was relieved to hear that Geri felt the same. "Okay, now that we got that out the way. I'm about to say something, and I don't want you to judge me harshly for it. This is not something superficial… it is what I've felt from the first time I laid eyes on her."

Geri sat back on the sofa and nodded for her to proceed.

"Our Yukon is practically new. We've never had a minute's trouble with it. How in the world could it go out just like that?" Alondra paused.

Geri sat silently. She wondered where exactly she was going with all of this. Then a realization came to mind, and she exactly where Alondra was headed. "This wouldn't be about Deidra now would it?" Geri asked.

Alondra looked down at the ground fearing she was going to go back on her word, and from the tone of her voice she may have already.

"I promised you I would listen," said Geri. "So tell me, what are you getting at?" she encouraged her to go on. She didn't want to break what was forming between them.

Alondra gazed into her eyes, and saw she was sincere. She took a deep breath and began to wring her hands. "I think Deidra sabotaged the Yukon!" she blurted.

Geri's eyes grew narrow, and she turned her head away to think. Then her eyes came back to Alondra who was observing her reaction. "Okay... What if she did? What would be her reason? What does she have against Cain and Blair?" she asked.

Alondra began to smile wickedly. Geri observed this reaction and figured she had thought this out very thoroughly.

"She wasn't after Uncle Cain or Aunt Blair! She meant to get you and I stranded somewhere," Alondra explained.

Geri allowed this idea to digest. She rose to her feet and began to pace, pondering. Alondra nodded her head seeing Geri was with her on this.

"Remember when we said we were going to be doing something today," said Alondra. "And during the commotion with my aunt she disappeared. My dad went looking for her." She tried to jog Geri's memory.

"Yes, I remember now," said Geri. "We'd come back into the house after he convinced me to let him take me car shopping. I didn't see her outside, and we never saw her inside. But when Marc went outside looking for her..." Geri paused for a moment folding her arms across her chest and rubbing her chin with one hand.

Alondra completed her sentence. "There she was driving away with him," she said.

Geri was in deep thought. "You know what? She has a temper too," said Geri. "I caught that today when you and your father quarreled." She paused again and watched as Alondra neared.

"I know, I caught her doing some breathing exercises geared for anger management," said Alondra. "And the other day she shot me a glare that sent chills up my back. I knew then she was crazy, but what I really think is that she has it out for you. She wants my dad bad, and she sees how he looks at you."

Geri's eyes grew large and her face reddened, which made Alondra laugh.

"Don't tell me you didn't know," said Alondra.

Geri looked away embarrassed.

Yeah, she knows, Alondra said to herself. "Uh-huh, it's just as I thought. You feel the same for him—that's why she's out to get you! You should be very careful. I don't think I'm a threat because she knows I'm leaving in the fall." But suddenly, Alondra was struck with another terrible thought. "Damn!" she shouted.

"What is it?" Geri asked nearly panicked.

"Aunt Blair!" Alondra replied. "She thinks she might be pregnant, she told me this morning. If she is, I don't want her near that psycho!" Alondra became more anxious.

"Alondra do me a favor, and don't say anything to anyone just yet," Geri pleaded. "If she's as crazy as we think, we don't want to alarm her. Who else but a lunatic would want to strand two women out in no man's land just to get closer to a man?"

"I agree," said Alondra. "But my dad and uncle can't always be around. If she gets my dad in her clutches, she'll be there too, and I don't want my aunt left alone with her. I know she will want my aunt and uncle out of the house."

Geri knew she was right, but wanted to give the girl some peace of mind. "Don't worry, you're father loves them too much. He would never send them away."

"She wants us all out of the way," Alondra reminded. "She will do whatever it takes to see it done, I just know it. Watch your back, Geri. You are her biggest threat, and we don't even know yet how crazy she is!" She let out a huge sigh and sat down.

Geri turned away, and walked over to the window looking out. No, she said to herself. None of you know how crazy this bitch is.

Chapter 21

Marc stood on the porch looking out at the land as he usually did after dinner. Deidra had made herself at home cooking and cleaning up in Blair's kitchen. She finished what she was doing and smiled to herself. She was pleased with the way the evening alone with Marc had been developing.

She went to the living room, and peered in discovering Marc wasn't there. She looked through the screen door and saw him relaxing. She was quite knowledgeable of what, or rather, who was on his mind.

She slithered to the bar and poured them some red wine then slinked out to the porch. He'd been deep in thought but looked up when she brushed up against him and handed him a glass. He smiled politely and took it. When their hands touched, he felt a current surge through him.

The atmosphere was just right for something romantic, so she thought. It has to be done just right. Not too subtle, but not too aggressive either, she schemed. She turned to stare out at the land as if she was interested in what he was seeing and took a sip of her wine. She drew in a deep breath.

His eyes went to her rounded chest as it rose and fell with each breath. He quickly took a big gulp of wine, and forced his eyes back out to the evening landscape.

"It's really beautiful out here at night," said Deidra. "It's so quiet and serene." She went to the banister and leaned on it, her hip intentionally pushed outward toward hip.

His eyes moved over her frame, carefully noting how snuggly her curves fit in her jeans. His mind wandered back to their kiss. It had been some time since he'd tasted the kiss of a woman with his tongue. Feeling himself becoming aroused, he excused himself, and quickly retreated into the house.

She straightened up wondering where he was going. But no sooner than he'd left, he came back with a bottle of whiskey and a six pack of beer.

"Wine is okay, but I'd rather have this," he informed her, taking a seat on the porch steps.

She looked down at him agreeing. She could drink with the best of them, but didn't want him to know it. Then an idea popped in her head. "I never had a drink stronger than wine," she lied. "How does it taste?" she asked sitting down next to him.

"You've got to be careful," said Marc. "Whiskey holds a punch," he warned.

"Well, then since I have to drive back later. I'll stop with this glass of wine," she said charily.

"I understand," said Marc. "You're a girl!" he kidded with a wink.

Her mouth flew open and he just nodded.

"Give me some of that," she demanded playfully. "I'll show you who's a girl!"

She tossed the wine to the ground and held her glass in front of him. He smiled and filled her glass. She took it down quickly then jumped to her feet trying to catch her breath. He ran to her and coached her into breathing slowly. She did.

"That stuff burns!" she said between breaths.

"I told you!" he reminded, while laughing.

She looked at him with tears in her eyes. "You ought to be ashamed of yourself," she said. "You knew it would do that!" She hit his arm gently.

"Yeah, that's true," he admitted. Still laughing, he grabbed a beer and gave it to her. "Here, drink this," he said, popping the tab.

She sipped it smiling all the while. He bit the hook, she said to herself. Now to reel him in. She took another sip of beer and walked over to the steps to sit down. He followed, as she knew he would. He opened another can of beer for himself. "Thanks," said Marc. He then took a huge drink of his beer.

Deidra looked at him strangely. "For what?" she asked.

He stared into her clear blue eyes then leaned in and hooked her chin with one finger. She watched his eyes come closer and soon felt his wet lips upon hers. She closed her eyes as his tongue slipped into her waiting mouth. Her can of beer fell to the ground. She wrapped her arms around his neck. He dropped his can as well and pulled her onto his lap kissing her long and hard, not wanting this night to get away. He stood to his feet with her in his arms, and looked deep into her eyes asking something of them. She replied by nodding her head, knowing what he wanted of her. He carried her into the house, and up to his room.

"How could a cable just snap like that?" Cain growled. They would have to stay in a hotel in town until mid-morning at least, until the car was fixed. They didn't want to bother Marc or Alondra to come and get them, bring them home, then come all the way back out in the morning. But Blair didn't seem to mind as she moved around in the hotel room they had taken for the night. It felt good to be away from the house. They left a message for Marc letting them know what was going on, since he didn't answer the phone.

"Cain, baby, look," said Blair. "Let's just treat this like a mini-holiday away from everything. I'm ready to relax. Now I'm going to take a shower, and you can stay out here sulking... or you can come and wash my back," she said lustfully. She eased slowly into the bathroom, looking back at him seductively. He sat dumbfounded for a second, then nearly tripped over his feet trying to run and take his pants off at the same time.

Alondra and Geri ate a fulfilling dinner after their talk, and had turned in for the night. Geri stood at the bedroom door watching Alondra sleeping soundly. She rested her head against the door frame with one hand on the doorknob, and the other over her heart. She let a silent sigh escape and quietly closed the door. She paused in the hallway thinking. Staring into space, she reflected on the past then went to her room and locked the door.

She went to her closet, pulled out a large briefcase, and carried it to the bed. She unsnapped the locks and opened it. She took out a stack of pictures and arranged them on the bed. Though she viewed them all with great diligence there was only one she picked up and stared at for a length of time. Tears began to fill her eyes. She placed the picture next to her heart and fell backward, her head hitting the pillow, she began to cry. "I'm sorry I wasn't here for you," she whispered aloud as she wept. "I was going through so much crap at the time. But I promise you, I'll be here this time." And she drifted off to sleep.

Marc laid Deidra on his bed. She backed up to the headboard and watched as he slowly began to unbutton his shirt. Her breathing was erratic. Her plan was finally coming into fruition. She wanted him badly, now she would have him.

Just then, his eyes fell on the picture on his nightstand. She followed his gaze, noting the distraction, and turned away rolling out of the bed. He looked at her strangely.

"What's wrong?" he asked, watching her head for the door.

"I can't do this," said Deidra. She pulled the door to open it. He laid his hand flatly on the door closing it before she could exit.

"I thought this was what you wanted," said Marc.

She backed away from him, her eyes on the floor. "I did," she admitted. "But suddenly it just doesn't seem right."

He ran his fingers through his hair which now hung loosely. He was ready and now she didn't want it? "You're so strange, Deidra. You've been seducing me all day—no, ever since you got here!" His voice, which started low, was beginning to rise from frustration.

Her head snapped towards him angrily. "Seduce you? You tell me you didn't want this as much as I did? Look me in the eye, Marc Caldwell, and tell me you were reluctant to do this!"

He backed away shutting his eyes trying to decipher through all of this, knowing full well the reason he was angry. It was true. He did want her right now but she was pulling away.

"Marc," said Deidra; her voice bringing him back. "Look over at the night stand. That's where your heart is, not with me." She made it to the door, and rushed out. His eyes went to rest on the picture of Clarice.

Damn, she was so right, he realized. He hurried down the stairs after her, just like she wanted. "Wait!" said Marc. "I can't allow you to leave like this. Please…" He gently caught her by the elbow just as she stepped off of the last step.

"Marc there is nothing to explain," said Deidra. "You love your wife and no other woman will be able to fill her shoes." She never looked at him as she slowly walked into the living room. He followed her, and a smile came on her face, unseen to him. She had him just where she wanted.

The hard liquor, wine, and beer were affecting his better judgment. Normally, he would have allowed her to walk out of the house and back to her hotel room, but not tonight.

"Look, Deidra, that isn't true," he said. "I just haven't found the right woman to help me move on." He walked up behind her draping his arms over her shoulders, and pulling her into him.

Yes! she screamed in her mind. He was hers to do with whatever she pleased, but it had to be played out just right.

"And you never will," said Deidra. "I can guess that you judge every woman by her, and if they don't come up to her standards they're out the door. In the fall, Alondra will be off to school for years; maybe even find someone to love. Then you will be alone," she said, pulling away slowly.

He walked past her, mulling over her words. She watched his blood-shot eyes as he pondered.

"You know, you're right, Deidra," said Marc. "I have been doing that. I can't do it anymore." He sat down on the sofa, defeated.

Deidra looked at him sympathetically, but knew in her heart that this was the time to strike. "You loved her dearly," she said affectionately. "And no one should try to take that from you. She was an important part of your life–the love of your life! You don't have to forget your love for her, you just put her in a special place in your heart, and embrace new love." She came to sit beside him and softly caressed his shoulder.

He looked into her beautiful eyes and felt his heart yearning. "I have an idea," he said, jumping to his feet and buttoning up his shirt.

Deidra watched him with curiosity when he suddenly took her by the hand, and nearly dragged her out of the house. He assisted her to the passenger side of her Jeep, then jumped behind the wheel and drove away into the night. She had no idea where they were headed.

Alondra woke early as always, and went searching for Geri. When she didn't find her up, she thought she was still sleeping and knocked on her bedroom door. It was partly ajar, and slowly swung wider with her touch. "Geri?" she called. There was no response.

Alondra stepped further in and called out again thinking she might be in the shower, but still no answer. Then she remembered she liked to go jogging. She turned to walk out of the room when she spotted the briefcase, and pictures strewn about. She knew it wasn't nice to pry into other people's things, but she's become very close to Geri in the last few days and wanted to know more about her.

She eased over to take a quick look and gasped in horror. They were pictures of Alondra's family. It was her father, her uncle, her aunt. Some of the pictures were old and others were recent. Some were from way back when she was a baby. Then she cast her eyes on a lone picture placed on a pillow. It was a picture of her mother, Clarice. She was young and she was with a girl who looked younger, but very much like her, maybe a sister.

"But Dad never told me my mother had a sister..." Alondra said out loud.

"Because he never met her sister, so he probably has forgotten about her," said Geri.

Alondra turned quickly to face Geri who was standing in the doorway.

Chapter 22

Cain and Blair came around the bend in the Yukon. Even though they'd shared a blissful night, they were glad to be home. They'd got the car much earlier than they thought they would and when they pulled up, the magazine crew was just unpacking. Cain and Blair went over to greet them.

Blair noticed that Deidra's Jeep was there. She was partly surprised because Deidra had been late the last couple of visits. Then she heard the guys laughing amongst themselves and pointing at the Jeep. Cain disregarded it, but Blair could not. She thought she heard something poignant. "Could you repeat that?" she asked walking up to one of the men. The others looked away, sorry she had overheard the sly remark.

"No disrespect intended, Ma'am," said one of the men. "We were just joking around."

She touched his arm. "That's not why I asked," said Blair. "Deidra didn't come in with all of you this morning?" She looked at each and every one of them.

They tried to avoid eye contact, aware that Deidra had been after Marc since the moment she found out about the shoot. "No, Ma'am. She didn't sleep in her hotel room and that's all I want to say." He threw up his hands and backed away as did the others and returned to their work.

Blair looked down at the ground, all sorts of terrible thoughts racing through her mind. Then her eyes went to the house. She started towards it. Soon she picked up her pace, her heart began to pound. A dreadful feeling came over her. Once inside, she spotted Cain and hurried to him. She stopped at the living room doorway and hadn't noticed the look on his face until she walked into the room. He had a horrified look on his face. Her eyes followed his to where Marc and Deidra stood by the unlit fireplace; Deidra was grinning from ear to ear.

"Cain, Honey, what's wrong?" she asked looking from her husband and back to the grinning pair.

His head slowly turned to her then back to his brother and Deidra. "Honey, look," said Cain. "Why don't you let me take you upstairs and lay you down?" He turned completely to her and placed his hands on her shoulders.

She searched his eyes and saw he had a lot going on in there. Shock, anger, and confusion played the biggest parts. "You're scaring me," she said. "Marc, what's going on?" She looked to her brother-in-law with pleading eyes.

Cain bit his lip and turned his head to glare at him then returned his soft stare to Blair. "Promise me you won't get upset," he said. "It's not good for the baby."

"Baby?" asked Marc. "Blair is gonna have a baby?" Marc left Deidra's side and went to Blair. He took her in his arms before Cain could protest. Deidra looked at the threesome and started toward them only to get a stare down from Cain. She stopped in her tracks.

Marc set Blair down gently in a chair.

"Well, Little Brother, looks like we both have good news to share today," said Marc proudly.

Blair could that whatever Marc's news was, Cain didn't like it. "What news, Marc?" she asked.

Cain turned away.

"Show her, Deidra," said Marc.

Deidra was hesitant to near Blair when Cain turned back around and stared at her coldly. She slowly held out her hand.

Blair's eyes became wide. "Is that what I think it is?" she asked. She was in utter disbelief as she stared at what appeared to be a wedding ring.

"Yes," said Marc. "We got married last night. Meet the new Mrs. Caldwell."

Blair felt the blood rushing to her head, and all she remembered was falling into Cain's arms just before blackness overtook her.

Chapter 23

After the initial shock, Alondra made an attempt to flee the room fearing Geri was one of those stalkers her father had warned her about. She began to understand why her father was so protective. This woman had all sorts of pictures of her family. Yet Geri's promise to explain everything kept her there. Somehow, she just knew Geri wouldn't harm her. Nevertheless, she warned Geri against trying anything.

Geri left for the kitchen and Alondra followed.

"Okay, explain!" Alondra ordered. Geri poured herself some coffee and offered some to Alondra who shook her head, no. Geri went to the back door, and stared out picking her words carefully.

"I told you part of my life. It all was true, but what I didn't tell you is why and how I lost my child." She took a sip of coffee. Alondra shifted on her feet listening intently.

"I lived in an upscale neighborhood in Texas. Yeah, I'm from here," said Geri. "In fact, I grew up in this very house. Your ranch and this one were one property. My father sold everything. He wanted to move to the city. That's where we finished growing up." She took another sip staring out of the door.

"We?" Alondra echoed.

Geri turned to her and smiled. "Yes, 'we'," she said. "My sister and I."

Alondra's mouth was slightly ajar. She sat down at the kitchen table. She was getting a mysterious sinking feeling.

Geri stared out the door once again, her eyes fixed on a small hill in the distance. Her mind wandered back to a happier time in her life.

Geri and her sister had been hiking when they heard their mother's voice calling to them. They raced down the hill, as they'd had always done, the eldest of the two winning as usual. They came crashing into the house, and ran through it seeking their mother. When they reached the living room, the older sister came to an abrupt halt, causing the younger sister to crash into her.

"Why'd you stop like that?" Geraldine said with a giggle. Her sister wasn't laughing or smiling. She could see that something was wrong by their parents' expressions.

"What is it Poppa? Mamma?" the oldest girl asked.

Their father took in a huge breath and beckoned the girls to sit down. They obliged. Their mother gazed out the window already knowing what was going to be said.

"I will be selling the ranch…" he began, facing immediately protest from the two girls. He waved his hand to silence them.

"Geri!" Alondra yelled. Her voice invaded Geri's trip down memory lane.

Geri turned and smiled and took a seat across from her at the table. "I'm sorry I was remembering the day our father told us he was selling this land." Geri had tears in her eyes. Alondra was feeling sad for her despite the discovery of her family's pictures in her possession. Then her cell phone rang. "Hello," said Alondra. "Okay, I'll be right there!" Alondra hung up fast and got up from the table.

Geri knew immediately that something was wrong. "Do you want me to go with you?" she asked.

"No," said Alondra. "We need to finish this talk. Until then, I think its best you keep your distance from my family." She was firm and she left the room. She rushed into the guestroom, tossed her things into her back pack, and ran out the door.

"I deserved that," said Geri aloud. "How stupid could you be? Stupid! You knew better than that! How could you leave things out like that? And leave the bedroom door unlocked? And now how can I get her to trust me without having to tell her everything?" Geri sat down on the porch, dejected. Her thoughts roamed back to her childhood once more.

"Look! This isn't easy for me to tell you so please, no more interruptions!" said their father. His voice was louder than they had ever heard it. Their mother glanced backward and his eyes met hers. He nodded and took a deep breath. They were young, and he needed to be patient and understanding. "I love the two of you with all my heart; and you know if it was within my power I wouldn't do anything to hurt you! You do know that don't you?" he asked. His voice was very soft and loving.

"Yes, Poppa, we know," said the eldest sister.

"Good. I have been going to see the doctor for the past two months. I have a rare disease. Soon I won't be able to take care of this land and I don't want your mother or you two to bear that burden. That's why I'm selling everything, and we're moving to the city."

The youngest rose from her seat and walked over to her mother silently. Feeling her youngest daughter next to her, Grace gently wrapped an arm around her shoulders and tried to console her. Then reality hit the oldest daughter. He didn't want them to bear the burden...

"Poppa, are you going to die?" she blurted, causing a stillness to overtake the room.

Her father stretched out his arms for his daughters to come to him. They flew into them willingly. He held them for dear life. "No, my dear child," he said. "That's why we're moving into the city, so that everything I need will be at hand."

Grace stared into her husband's kind and loving eyes and then left him to spend this time with his daughters.

"But a few years later you did die, didn't you, Poppa?" Geri whispered to herself closing her eyes and crying quietly.

Chapter 24

"What?" Alondra asked at the top of her lungs. She then ran from the house with Marc close in pursuit. She wouldn't get away from him easily.

Deidra looked on from the window.

"Honey, look at me," said Marc, grabbing her by the arm and turning her to face him.

Cain stood at his bedroom window observing the scene while Blair lay on the bed with a warm cloth covering her eyes.

"How could you?" asked Alondra, her eyes burning with tears. "You always talk to me about being responsible, and here you go and do the most outrageous thing possible!" She screamed and cried.

Marc placed his hands on her arms trying to get her to calm down. "I know you're upset. Just calm down and let's talk about it," he pleaded.

She saw Deidra staring from the window. She felt instant disgust for this woman. In just a few days she had destroyed her family. "I hate her! She ruined everything!" Alondra shouted. "I will never like her or trust her, and you know this! This is not you! Look what she turned you into!" She looked back into his eyes meaning every word.

"I know, Baby. But that's just it," said Marc. "I've been living this structured lifestyle for so long I forgot how I use to be. She reminded me how much I've missed."

He tried to explain but Alondra couldn't hear what he truly meant. She tilted her head to the side. At that moment he saw his brother in her.

"It's good to know I brought you such a structured lifestyle and took all of your fun," said Alondra. Her voice was low and quiet.

"I didn't say I regretted my lifestyle, or the time I spent raising you," said Marc. "That life was right for me at the time. But soon you'll be off to college away from me. Maybe find some young fella for yourself?

Then where will that leave me? Alone."

"Uncle Cain and Aunt Blair will be here," she said.

He shook his head and turned away, taking a small stroll away from her.

She crossed her arms over her chest glaring into the house at Deidra. Then he turned to look at her. She knew instantly she had angered him. His eyes were darkening.

"Your uncle and aunt will be having a baby in a few months. Hell, they may even decide they want their own place, and God forbid they should entertain that thought," said Marc, glaring angrily.

She felt her heart sink. He had never looked at her in that way. She didn't know what else to do so she ran to her motorcycle, jumped on and started it up.

Marc ran to stop her, but she was too quick. In an instant she was gone. He stood there helpless, and figured she would be going to Geri.

"Babe, don't worry," said Deidra. "She'll come around." She slithered up beside him, and placed a hand on his shoulder.

He shot her a hard glare. "Will she? I need to get out of here, myself," he said. He snarled and headed for the garage.

Deidra started to protest, but thought better. She watched him vanish into the garage, heard his own bike start up, and watched as he sped away. She stood poised for a moment, the anger swelling up in her. Then she walked over to a random bucket, and kicked it as far as it could fly.

"That went well," said Cain, leaving the window to sit next to his wife on the bed.

Blair removed the cloth from her face. She could tell from the sound of the two bikes Marc and Alondra had left the premises. "Alondra and Marc are gone?" she asked.

Cain nodded.

"Where is Deidra?" asked Blair.

"She's down in the yard kicking things," he replied.

She could tell something had just occurred to him. She rested a gentle hand on his arm. "What's wrong, Cain? Something other than this whole fiasco is troubling you. What is it?"

He placed his hand over hers. "Look, you need to get some rest. You already gave me a scare," he said.

She frowned and sat up in the bed. "I'll be okay. But you had a strange look on your face. You're worried about something, I can tell," she continued.

He looked over to her, and rose from the bed rubbing his chin. "Maybe we should think about moving. Marc is just married, and we're having our own child," he said.

"No!" cried Blair. "I will not leave my home or my baby Alondra in that witch's clutches!"

Cain stared at her strangely. He had never seen her so passionate about someone before.

"Honey, calm down," said Cain. "I didn't know you felt so strongly against Deidra." He sat on the bed rubbing her leg gently.

"Oh yes, she is no good, and got just what she wanted!" said Blair angrily.

"What do you mean?" he asked.

"She got Marc," Blair scoffed.

"Marc? She didn't even know Marc until Ben got us to do this shoot," said Cain.

She looked at him and shook her head slowly. "She has known about his celebrity for years. And it just blew her away when both of you agreed to do this project. I wonder whose idea it really was," said Blair.

"What are you talking about? Where did you get this?" Cain rose from the bed and walked over to the window to look out. Deidra was nowhere in sight.

"I got it from her crew members," She nodded her head, and pursed her lips.

Cain shook his head. "Oh, Blair, that's nothing but gossip. You have to ignore that kind of talk," he insisted.

"It's not gossip!" Blair corrected. "They didn't even know I was there when they started talking. When she didn't come back to her hotel room, and they saw that her Jeep was still parked here, they began to talk amongst themselves," she explained.

"Still gossip," he maintained.

Blair thought she heard a noise near their door, and quietly left the bed to go investigate. When she peered into the hall she saw no one, and closed the door.

Deidra leaned quietly against her bedroom door listening as Cain and Blair's door clicked shut. She looked over to the bed where she had spent the most passionate night of her life with Marc. She could still feel him all over her body, taste him on her lips, and smell him in her hair. She moved onto the bed, caressing it with her hands, and laid on her back, longing for more of him. She grabbed a pillow and screamed into it. "More obstacles!" she yelled. She then threw the pillow to the side. "Oh, dear Blair, you will be leaving my house… sooner rather than later," she whispered.

Chapter 25

Alondra sped down the road trying not to cry. She didn't know where to go. Geri had proved to be just as much as a phony as Deidra. And as it turned out, she couldn't trust anyone but her aunt and uncle. They had always been honest and straight forward with her. She came to a familiar entranceway, and paused for only a second before turning onto it. She sped up the winding road, and upon entered the clearing, brought the bike to a standstill.

She sat looking at nothing in particular, void of any thoughts, and overcome with the emotion. She allowed the tears overflowing the wells of her eyes to fall. How long she had sat there she didn't know. And she didn't protest when she felt gentle arms surround her and assist her from the bike. She went freely into the house, and allowed Geri to guide her to the sofa, tears streaming down her face.

"Alondra, what's wrong?" Geri asked affectionately. Receiving no reply, she began to fear the worst and went to the phone to call Marc. But suddenly both Alondra and Geri were startled by a deep male voice.

"I think I can shed some light on this," said Marc. The rumble of his voice coursed through the room.

Alondra immediately came to life, hearing her father's voice. She quickly got up and ran to the guestroom. The door slammed behind her, and they thought they heard a click of the lock.

"Wow! She must really be angry at you if she felt it was safe to come back here," said Geri.

"I don't get it. I thought you two were good," said Marc nearing her.

She looked up and gingerly walked away, not sure how to explain. "We were fine until she found some things in my room while I was out jogging." She didn't look at him, and began to massage the back of her neck trying to relieve the tension building. This was becoming very difficult.

190

"What? It isn't like Alondra to snoop in people's bedrooms!" he boomed. He was shocked and outraged.

"Don't be so harsh," said Geri softly. "They weren't put away, just lying out on my bed. I forgot and went for a jog. I guess she came looking for me, and saw them there."

"Still, she shouldn't have gone into your room. What has gotten into that girl?" his eyes ventured back down the hall contemplating going up to the door and demanding she open it.

"Which reminds me," said Geri. "You were going to tell me what has her so upset."

Marc took in a deep breath and walked closer to her. She studied his demeanor which had changed dramatically. Something was definitely wrong. It was the same look her father had on his face just before telling them he was selling the ranch.

"She's pissed at me," said Marc.

"Wait, have a seat," said Geri. "You look like you need a drink." She went to the kitchen, and emerged a few seconds later with two bottles of beer. She handed him one, and popped the top off the other downing quite bit.

Marc observed this closely as he popped the top on his bottle. "When I'm finish telling you my problem, I intend to find out why my daughter has now turned on the woman she's grown to care for so quickly." He stared long and hard letting her know that was a promise, and that her little explanation didn't cut it.

Geri took another drink and shifted uncomfortably in her seat. This was not going to be good. How would she explain having pictures of Cain, Blair, Clarice and him, or baby pictures of Alondra, and pretending not to know them? Her dilemma, however, was push aside when Marc suddenly explained his story.

"There's no other way to say this than to just say it. Deidra and I were married last night," he said.

His words plowed through her ears thunderously. Geri jumped to her feet dropping her bottle of beer. Her eyes fell on him as the foaming brew poured all over the floor. Her body was paralyzed with shock.

What could she say? What was there she could do? This wasn't supposed to happen. It was her he was supposed to love. At least that's what she felt between them. Was she wrong? It didn't make any sense.

Marc could see all of questions written all over her face and it suddenly made him reflect. A little wine, whiskey, beer, and beautiful woman can lead to stupid decisions. And led to one he was regretting sat this very moment. He was staring into Geri's eyes, seeing the pain in them, the confusion.

All at once, Marc felt he'd betrayed her and something came over him; something greater than the both of them, and it was strong. What was between he and Geri couldn't be denied, and he couldn't resist her any longer. Something urged him to take a leap, so he did.

He rose to his feet, and with a single motion Geri was in his arms, and staring into his eyes. She was bewildered by his news, by this, but in his arms is where she'd always wanted to be. His mouth captured her lips. He kissed her deeply. She felt so familiar, yet so different. It was like holding his Clarice in his arms once again and yet he knew this was Geri. Yes, Geri, his mind called out her name over and over. She was the one who had imprisoned his heart as Clarice had many years ago.

At first, she tried to protest, but soon he could feel her melt into him, surrendering. She allowed him to probe her mouth freely, arousing sensations she had locked up for so long. She moaned into his mouth and wrapped her arms around his neck. She moved more into him, wanting him, but tears fell from her eyes. She knew he wasn't hers to have.

She slid her hands from around his neck and braced them on his chest. And with every ounce of strength in her, she pushed herself away. Their lips unlocked violently. He reached for her, but she walked quickly away.

"Geri, come back," he pleaded.

"You have to go," she said softly trying to catch her breath, and calm her racing heart.

He took a small step toward her but she looked at him with such pain in her eyes, such disappointment, that his heart sunk even lower than before.

"Go, now," she insisted, pointing her finger at the door.

Geri listened as his bike roared away. Its sound faded in the distance until she was engulfed by silence, standing alone in the middle of the room. Her despair was greater than her legs could bear and she collapsed to the floor. She held herself tightly and cried for what should have been.

Marc left the scene, hurt and angry with himself for being so reckless. He knew he feelings for Geri. Why did he go and marry that woman? He has no feelings for her except friendship... and lust. That was the problem. He'd been drinking and wasn't thinking with his brain.

He rode the bike harder than he had in a long time. In fact, not since the night Clarice died. It was like losing her all over again. Those eyes were so much like hers. He passed the rode leading up to his ranch. He couldn't deal with Deidra right now. She would have to wait.

Chapter 26

Blair had gone downstairs in time to see Deidra just coming in the door. She didn't trust this woman, and didn't know how far she should push, but she wanted to at least have a talk with her. "Has Marc come back yet," she asked.

"No," said Deidra, without making eye contact. She'd been sitting on the porch for quite some time, waiting for his arrival. And she'd heard the rumble of a motorcycle nearing, but it faded just as quickly, as if it had gone on by. Many questions were rambling through her mind.

"Maybe it's none of my business," said Blair, "but Marc is my family, and I care for him very much.

So I think you and I should have a very long talk," Blair said sternly.

Deidra scoffed and went into the living room. Blair was close behind.

"I don't think we need a talk, long or short," said Deidra. "In fact, you should understand something. Marc is no longer your business, and this house is no longer yours. Marc is my husband, so I am now the lady of the house. Got it?" She neared Blair forcefully, her glare penetrating deep.

Blair instinctively covered her middle with her arms. Unbeknownst to Blair, Deidra noted this.

Blair's blood began to boil. "If you think you can get rid of us that easily, then think again," Blair spat. Then she rushed up the stairs, pausing momentarily to look down at the wretched woman who had disrupted her home and family. She couldn't hold back the tears any longer and she ran into her room and into Cain's arms.

He tried to console her, knowing it had everything to do with Deidra.

Geri was on her knees on the floor. The pain she felt was devastating. She felt angry with him, yet was equally as disappointed in herself. Secretly, he had touched her deeply, long before she ever had laid eyes on him. And when she did see him for the first time, her feelings for him only grew stronger. "But I didn't act on it in time. Still, how could he have married someone he hardly knew?" she asked aloud as if someone would answer. "So many times you told me how wonderful he was, and he is all you said and more. Yet, look at what he has done?"

Suddenly, she was interrupted by a very curious Alondra. "I think it's time you finished telling me about your past."

Geri was throttled form her thoughts. "Yes… and I think I owe you more than a finished story," she answered, wiping the tears from her face. "I owe you an introduction."

She slowly rose from the floor, her eyes never leaving Alondra's. Then she pulled out a picture, and offered it to Alondra. It was of Alondra's mother and of Geri, arm in arm. The girl was frozen with knowing, yet disbelief. "I'm your aunt, Geraldine," said Geri. "Clarice was my sister."

Alondra felt faint.

Chapter 27

"Cain, that woman is insane, and I know it!" Blair exclaimed as she paced about the room.

Cain sat on the side of the bed. "Blair, come sit down and calm yourself," he pleaded.

But his wife wouldn't hear of it. She continued her ranting. "'Marc is no longer your business' she said, 'I am now the lady of the house'. How dare that woman just waltz in here and think she can take over?" When Blair was finished with her rant, she finally went to Cain. In his eyes, she knew they would have to move out. She began to cry in his arms.

Cain decided he would have to talk to Marc as soon as he got home. In fact, he wondered where he'd gone. And what's more, where was Alondra?

Marc sat on an old branch, staring out at the lake. He threw rocks in and watched them skid across the water, this time not taking notice of the ducks, geese, and swans quacking around the lake. How was he going to remedy this mess? He didn't love Deidra. Why in the hell did he do something so stupid? And Geri... she wouldn't be speaking to him any time soon. The way she looked at him, he should be dead. "Why did it matter so much to her?" he said aloud to himself and skipped another rock. "It isn't like we were in love or anything; even though I do have feelings for her."

He skipped another rock, then another, then took a deep breath and pondered something. It had been a long time since he had genuine feelings for anyone besides Clarice. So it was hard for him to recognize what was going on between him and Geri. As he pondered, everything suddenly began to make sense. The kiss they shared before she kicked him out told it all. He jumped to his feet. "That's it!" he exclaimed. His feelings for Geri were stronger than he'd realized. And he was sure she felt the same way for him. He mounted his bike. He was going to make Geri admit what she was feeling for him.

"You're my mother's sister?" Alondra asked, trying to digest the news.

"Yes," Geri replied.

The two women sat down, Geri's eyes fixed on Alondra, Alondra's eyes to the floor in disbelief.

"Alondra, I know this is overwhelming," said Geri.

"Why are you just now coming into my life?" asked Alondra. "Where were you all of these years? Why didn't you ever meet my dad?" She'd found her voice and her mind was bombarded with questions.

"After my father died, I became very reckless. I did some stupid things. One was marrying a much older man. He was over forty at the time and I was eighteen. It broke my mother's heart."

Alondra immediately interjected, "He was my father's age—and you were my age? Sick! I can't imagine marrying a man my father's age!" Alondra shook her head. Her shock over the initial news was beginning to subside and the mood was becoming lighter.

Geri was feeling some relief and smiled. "Maybe if my father was still alive at the time, I wouldn't have either," she admitted.

Alondra understood and nodded. Geri stood watched Alondra, who was still soaking it all in. "Would you like some ice tea?" Geri asked.

Alondra looked up at her with renewed affection. Her mother's sister was here; someone who would connect her to her mother. "Yes, please," she said softly.

Geri slipped into the kitchen, and moments later returned to tell her story. "He was very wealthy. We left on a long tour around the world," said Geri.

"Clarice and I kept in contact with each other by phone or writing. Mother was still disappointed with me. She became ill a few months after I left. I spoke to her on the phone the night she died. It was sudden; a stroke. We told each other how much we loved the other and then she died." Geri's voice broke, and she began to weep.

Alondra sat her cup down and went to her aunt. Holding her had new meaning. It was almost like finally be able to hold her mother. She suddenly thought she heard thunder in the distance. No… it wasn't thunder, she realized. "Geri, why don't you go lie down for a bit? We have plenty of time to talk," said Alondra. She could see it was taking a toll on her and decided to give it some time.

Geri agreed and went to her room. It had been a very exhausting day. First the confrontation with Alondra, then Marc with his news; she slid into bed not wanting to even think about that disaster. But then the kiss… She lay on her back thinking of him when she heard thunder.

Alondra made sure Geri was in her room before she went out to the porch and watched her father pull up the drive. She glared at him as he turned off the bike and dismounted.

"She's resting," said Alondra. "And even if she wasn't, I don't think she wants to see you."

He'd had just about had enough of her attitude. "Look, Alondra, I know you're upset with me, but nothing you can say or do is gonna keep me from going into that house," he insisted.

"Maybe not, but there's something I can do," said Geri. She was standing in the doorway with phone in hand. "Would you like for me to inform your new bride that you are over here harassing me?" Geri asked.

"Geri, just give me a chance to talk to you," he said, stepping toward her.

She started to dial and he stopped in his tracks. He didn't want Deidra involved, it would only cause more trouble for everyone, and he wasn't going to have that. "Fine, Geri," said Marc. "You win this round. But know something; I will not lose again."

She felt sparks from his piercing eyes and heaving chest. Now she knew why her sister fell so deeply in love with him, his passion. She took a deep cleansing breath.

He jumped on his bike, his eyes lingering on her for some time before he sped away.

"That was gutsy of you," said Alondra.

"Yes, it was," Geri agreed. "But it only puts him at bay for a moment. He'll be back!" Geri knew in her heart he was not going to let go. And part of her didn't want him to. But then a painful thought came to mind. Could it be that he sees Clarice in her, and that it's the only reason he'd interested? Her heart began to sink.

Chapter 28

Blair was sitting on her bed when she heard Marc pull up. Cain was in the bath. She went to the window and watched as Deidra went to greet him. He looked as if he wasn't in the mood to deal with her. Blair chuckled satisfactorily under her breath. We'll see who the true lady of the house is, Blair thought. She had to tell Marc everything right away. This woman couldn't be trusted. She was trying to tear the family apart. She came to the top of the stairs as Deidra and Marc walked in arguing about something.

Blair was halfway down the stairs when a board came loose and sent her spiraling down the staircase. Marc watched in horror as her body rolled down the stairs and came to rest in front of him. He quickly came down to his knees and carefully touched her. "Blair! Blair talk to me!" he yelled upon deaf ears. "Go get Cain, now!" he roared at Deidra who was standing idly by.

She sped up the stairs and called out to Cain, making sure she missed the loose board. She banged on the bedroom door until a drenching-wet Cain swung the door open wrapped in a towel.

"It's Blair!" she cried. "She fell down the stairs!"

He tore down the stairs seeing his wife unconscious in Marc's arms.

"Blair!" he yelled.

"Come on girl, answer me," Marc kept repeating.

Cain took Marc's place and Marc ran to call the paramedics.

"Forget it, Marc!" yelled Cain. "We can't wait for them, she's bleeding! I'm taking her to the hospital!"

Marc stayed with her while Cain through on only a pair of sweatpants and running shoes. Then he picked up his wife and carried her to the car and laid her in the back seat.

Marc watched his desperate brother with no shirt speed out of the driveway. He went back into the house and up the stairs nearly tripping over the loose board. He studied it for a moment. Deidra slowly walked up to him.

"Watch your step," said Marc. "There's a loose board. It's probably what she tripped on. I'm going to take Cain some clothes." He hurried into Cain's room to get what he needed.

"I'm going too!" said Deidra.

As Marc passed her in the doorway, he looked back. "No! You stay here!" he ordered, then rushed down the stairs.

She watched him leave then went over to the loose board. She grinned wickedly. "That's okay, Marc. You go be with them. But if this doesn't get rid of them, I'll think of something a little more drastic."

Chapter 29

Marc called the hospital to let them know that Cain was racing there with Blair. He explained what had happened, and most importantly that she was pregnant. When Cain's car was seen tearing into town, the local police were waiting to escort him safely through. They rushed to the hospital and several nurses came out, wasting no time getting her onto a gurney. She was still unconscious.

Once they got her to a room, a nurse bravely told Cain he would have to leave. His look told the entire staff otherwise. He stood back however, out of their way.

It wasn't long before Marc flew into the hospital himself, searching for Cain. He found his brother despondent, standing helplessly by Blair's side. He briefly saw Blair pale and seemingly lifeless. It reminded him of the day Clarice died. He backed up against a wall. He was beside himself with worry. Then he realized he needed to call Alondra and tell her what happened. He left the emergency room and went outside. "Pick up, girl," he said.

"Geri, I want to know more, if you feel up to it," said Alondra.

Geri had always wanted a passionate man like Marc in her life, but men like that always eluded her—until now. And it seemed her sister had been right; Marc wasn't the type to give up on anything easily.

"Geri!" Alondra's voice carried, penetrated her thoughts.

"Yes?" asked Geri.

Alondra could see Geri had probably had enough for the night, but she needed to know one more thing. "I just have one more question for now," said Alondra.

"What is it?" asked Geri. She braced herself, very much aware this was going to be the hardest part of the family reunion.

"Why didn't you contact my dad when you found out my mother had died? If you loved my mother so much, why didn't you come to check on the baby she left behind?" Alondra had become very emotional at this point. Thoughts of a mother and grandparents she had never met plagued her since Geri mentioned her childhood. Geri held all of the missing pieces for eighteen years.

"It's a long story Alondra," said Geri. "I didn't stay away because I wanted to. I had no choice." She covered her face with her hands and once again fought back tears. "I told you I lost my baby, but I didn't tell you how I lost her. I was so happy when I got pregnant. And Clarice wrote to me and told me she was expecting too. In fact, I think we were due around the same time. During my pregnancy, my husband began to act strangely. Coming home late, sleeping on the couch, and hardly interacting with me. I thought for sure having a baby was something he wanted also. But I was wrong." She grew quiet for several moments and Alondra could see the pain on her face.

"Rumors had started that he was having an affair. I didn't want to believe it at first, but started to realize it was true. He would stumble in drunk at all hours and go straight to bed. He'd lost interest in me. I went out looking for him when he stayed out late, but would never catch him. Then, two weeks before my due date I followed him to her place. He went inside but didn't come out. I waited a long time then knocked on the door. She didn't even have the decency to answer the door in something decent. She wore a sheer robe and nothing else. And she smelled of him. It was unmistakable. Suddenly he came out of the bedroom with no clothes on. We stared at each other, both of us somewhat shocked, then I turned and ran. I couldn't take it. I was so emotional my tears were blinding. That's when it happened."

Geri stopped, her eyes red and wet with tears, her breath shallow. It was clear to Alondra that it was very difficult for Geri to utter these words.

"I ran out in front of an oncoming car," said Geri. "I was knocked several feet into the air and then landed on it. My husband must have run to get dressed because he was suddenly holding me, and his voice was the last thing I remember before falling into a coma. I didn't wake for several months. I guess it was my way of shutting down and not facing what I knew in my heart, that I had lost my baby.

Geri now leaned on the window pane for strength. Alondra went over and wrapped her arms around her as she cried.

It hadn't been an easy road for their family. Geri and Alondra were now the only two remaining.

"When I came to, I called Clarice," said Geri. "And someone told me she had died. He asked who I was and I just went blank. I hung up. It was too traumatic. Everything I had loved was gone. I never thought to ask about the child, and didn't give anyone a chance to tell me. I didn't even know how she died, just that she had." Geri came to grips and left the window to sit down.

"I divorced my husband, despite his protests. Years later, I found out he'd remarried and shortly after had suddenly died in a freak accident. He'd only been married three months to a woman half his age. Radio fell into the tub or something."

Alondra went to sit on the sofa when Geri's phone rang. Alondra gestured for her to remain seated and answered the phone. "Dad?" she said with frustration. "Why are you calling here? Didn't she say she didn't want to be–" She was cut off, and grew silent listening to her father.

Geri unwittingly felt a rush when she heard who was calling. He certainly had passion. And she needed it now. She needed him to ease the pain she was feeling inside. Suddenly, she saw the saddened expression on Alondra's face and ran to her.

"Alondra, what's wrong?" she asked. She took the phone from her hand and listened. There was a dial tone.

"It's Aunt Blair!" Alondra cried. "She fell down the stairs!" She gripped Geri by the arms and stared intently. "Geri, she's pregnant!" Alondra exclaimed.

The two quickly ran out of the house and sped off to the hospital. Geri wouldn't let her make this trip alone.

Marc began to pace back and forth in front of the hospital. He stopped momentarily and looked through the door and down the hall to the emergency room. He should be there with both Cain and Blair. But he needed to gather himself first.

He walked over to a bench and took a seat. He thought back to when he'd met Clarice, how they'd bumped into each other. He thought of her loving light brown eyes. It was a lot like his first meeting with Geri. How could two women be so much a like?

Once again a light shined in his heart because of his thoughts of Geri. But then darkness still looms there as well. How could he marry Deidra? He knew there was nothing real between them. But in a weak moment she'd shown him she knew what was missing in his life and that she could fill that void for him. He sighed wearily. Not many people get a second chance at love, and his moment of weakness may have lost him that chance.

"Dad?" spoke Alondra.

He looked up into green eyes that matched his own. He saw Geri stood next to her. And he saw kindness in her eyes. He stood to greet them.

"Why are you out here all alone?" asked Alondra. Then she realized his reason. "Oh, you don't have to answer. It's Mom, isn't it?"

She wrapped her arms around him and he pulled her close. Geri turned away, not wanting them to witness her tears.

Alondra released her father and turned to Geri when she realized the impact this was having on her. Geri had lost Clarice as well, and had been in the same predicament as Blair was in now. "Geri, I'm sorry, this must be hard on you too," she said.

"What are you talking about?" asked Marc.

"It's nothing, Marc," said Geri quickly. "Don't worry about me. You two should go be with Cain and Blair. I can only imagine what they're going through."

"Yeah, Dad, let's go inside," said Alondra.

Marc started toward the hospital with his daughter then turned back, his eyes fixed on Geri's. She couldn't turn away this time. He had a hold on her. But he continued past her and on to the parking lot where his motorcycle was parked. He removed a bag from it and came back, eyeing her as before, until he went inside.

Geri sighed. That man is something else," she said.

Alondra hurried into Cain's arms. She held him tightly, speaking encouraging words.

Then she raised her head to face him. His eyes were saddened. "What did they say, Uncle Cain? How are Aunt Blair and the baby?"

Just then, Marc approached and handed his brother the bag. "Here's a shirt, and a couple of other things," he said. "How are Blair and the baby?"

"I don't know yet," said a heartbroken Cain. "The waiting is killing me." He took the bag and sat down in a chair. He slipped on the t-shirt while Alondra took a seat and Marc leaned against the wall.

"What I can't figure out is how in the hell did that step get loose?" said Marc. His arms were crossed tight, his brow furrowed hard.

Cain shook his head. He couldn't figure it out either.

"Kind of like the Yukon breaking down all of the sudden," said Alondra.

Marc stood straight up and Cain looked at both of them. Strange things had been occurring. But Cain noticed Marc hadn't truly picked up on that fact. He was looking at Blair's room where the doctor was coming out.

Cain left the chair and rushed up to him, Marc and Alondra at his side.

"What is it? Are they going to be okay?" Cain asked worriedly.

"I checked both Blair and baby out thoroughly," said the doctor. "As of now, they both appear to be just fine. You wife landed in a way that protected the baby. And she didn't break anything. We were able to stop the bleeding, but want to her here under observation for at least a week. She's going to be very bruised and uncomfortable for a while, but everything should be all right. She's a strong woman, Mr. Caldwell," he said with a caring smile. "She's awake. You can go in to see her."

"What a relief," said Marc, holding onto Alondra.

Cain went in to see his wife without delay.

"I'm glad for all of you," said Deidra, who had just walked in.

Marc and Alondra turned around, the astonishment evident on their faces. Alondra's joy soon faded and she went in to be with her aunt and uncle.

Marc's eyes grew dark. Now she was getting to be annoying. "I asked you—No, I told you to stay at the house. You couldn't do that, could you?" he asked, shaking his head.

"Marc, I am your wife! My brother-in-law's pregnant wife just fell down the stairs and you expect me to stay home? Am I not a part of this family?" she asked. She stared at him hard for an answer.

Her words made sense, but nothing else did. He felt like a fool having married her when he was vulnerable, but what was her excuse? Her motives were only one of the things he was asking himself. He couldn't deal with her right now. "Go home," he said. "There isn't much you can do here."

"Fine," she said. "I'll go home and keep it warm." She stared at him long and hard before walking away.

Marc watched her disappear around the corner and then went in to join his family.

Geri had been standing nearby, just out of sight, taking in the scene. Something was definitely plaguing this family. There were too many coincidences. First, the Yukon suddenly broke down, yet had just been checked. Now the step, which had never been loose before, come completely loose causing Blair a near-tragic fall. And after what she'd just witnessed between Marc and Deidra, more 'coincidences' could be yet to come. That was something she wasn't going to allow.

Geri left a note at the nurses' station for Alondra, and then she left the hospital in a taxi. She pulled out her cell phone and made a call.

"Are you ready? Good. Meet me at my place. We need to talk." She hung up quickly. Her plan would have to be accelerated or someone was going to die.

Chapter 30

"Geri, you're good at what you do, pretending to be something or someone you're not to get the job done. But this time you're over your head. You're too emotionally involved. And well, if I may say so, you got a little sloppy!" spoke the voice across the table from Geri.

Confused, she stared blankly at him. "What are you talking about?" she asked, her eyes shrinking.

He turned and looked at her. "The pictures, remember? She saw the pictures which jeopardized everything. So you had to come clean that part in order to divert her attention. Never minding the fact that you almost told her the rest of it anyway," he proclaimed.

"No, no, I never would have told her the rest. I'm not that senseless," she reminded him.

His look softened. "No, you're not, Geri," he said. "But must I remind you what is at stake here? Whatever else is going on, you need to stay focused. A lot is riding on that."

He was right. There was nothing more to be said. She watched in silence as he stood, went to the door and walked out into the night. She knew he would be out there doing just what she'd asked him to: watching.

She walked into her bedroom and pulled out the briefcase containing the pictures and some files. She looked over two photos in particular. The first was of the man she had married at a very early age. "My dear, Stan, you made a lot of mistakes in your life, but you didn't deserve this." She stroked the picture of him gently with her finger then gently placed it back into the briefcase.

"Radio falling in the tub, indeed. One thing you were was a safety freak. You would never have allowed it in the room. How many times did you protest when I suggested we bring it in to listen to while we sat in the tub—countless."

She sat thinking for a moment then looked at the second picture in her hand. A beautiful, tall, slender blonde was poised next to Stan in a wedding picture. She had crystal blue eyes. "Deidra, you thought you got away with it, didn't you? Stan didn't deserve what you did to him. You'll pay; I'll personally see to it. And more importantly, you're gonna forget about my family or you're gonna wish you were never born." She tossed the pictures into her briefcase and locked it for safe keeping. She then decided to get showered and changed. Business was about to pick up.

Fatal Deception: Part II

Chapter 1

It had been a trying time for the Caldwell family. They were embroiled in an emotional windstorm. A sudden new addition to the family was causing tremendous tension between father and daughter, and too many dangerous coincidences surrounding the family remained unexplained. A near-fatal incident involving a mother and her unborn child saw the family restoring their bonds and trying to sort through the recent events together.

Still in the hospital, the maternity staff kept a careful and watchful eye over Blair Caldwell. She had been transferred to a private room and was finally resting peacefully. The news that her child was all right set her mind and body at ease.

Cain, Marc, and Alondra left Blair's room quietly. They were heading outside where they could talk and breathe the fresh air; each was silently deep in thought.

Alondra walked between the two men she loved most in the world, her arms wrapped around their waists. "I'll be back in the morning with some fresh clothing for you Uncle Cain," said Alondra.

"Thank you. You're a good niece," he replied. His voice was still shaky from the stress of Blair's fall down the stairs.

They'd just stepped outside, and Marc stopped and placed a hand on his daughter's shoulder. "Does that mean you'll be spending more time home?" he asked.

Her eyes went from his to the ground; her mind running back through everything that had recently happened. She returned her eyes to his with sincerity. "Yeah, Dad, I'm coming home with you. You shouldn't be alone," she declared. She wanted to check something out; something she'd been feeling inside, but didn't want to alarm either her father or uncle. She thought maybe she could run it by Geri when she went to pick up her things.

"Well now, you know I'm not alone," Marc reminded. "I do have a wife."

Her face crinkled up. "You had to remind me, didn't you? Nevertheless, I'm going to be home from now on, especially, when Aunt Blair gets home," she told them both.

Marc looked at his brother knowing what Alondra meant. But Cain turned and walked a small distance from them running his hands over his head. He felt he needed to say something, and didn't know quite how to say it. Alondra was aware of this.

"What is it Cain?" Marc asked.

Cain turned to face them. His eyes were sorrowful. "I'm not gonna take Blair back there. I'm thinking about maybe getting us a place of our own. I don't want to take any more chances on this happening again," he professed.

The three of them stood silently for a long time not wanting to touch what was said; each realizing how much had changed in such a small amount of time, and would never be the same.

Deidra paced back and forth waiting for Marc to come home. When she heard the roaring bike she was relieved he had finally come back. She ran to the mirror making sure her make-up was in place. She had on a long black sheer lace negligee with matching sheer robe, and wore red heeled slippers. She brushed her hair quickly, and started down stairs to the lounging room. She put out some wine and appetizers. She was going to make this a night to remember.

She stood seductively in the doorway, waiting like a black widow for her prey. She heard the footsteps on the porch, keys jingling; then the lock clicked. The door slowly opened. She watched the door intensely. In walked Alondra.

"Oh!" she cried.

Alondra's head snap around as she closed the door, and locked it. Her eyes were fixed on Deidra.

"I see…" she said. "Planning another night of seducing my dad into doing what you want, huh?" She walked past her, and into the kitchen.

Deidra felt like blowing fire she was so angry. Where was Marc? She came out into the foyer, and gathered herself. She had to play nice if she was going to get anything out of that one. "I didn't know you were coming home or I would have prepared dinner for three," She said, slithering into the kitchen.

"I'm sure you didn't expect me home tonight," said Alondra. "You're dressed to kill!" she said smartly. She then took some bread, deli meat, lettuce, and tomatoes from the refrigerator and put them on the counter.

"Look Alondra," said Deidra. "I know you don't like me, and I understand why." She walked over to the kitchen counter, watching Alondra make a sandwich. She slipped a knife from the dish rack and silently walked up behind Alondra. She brought the knife over the girl's head and down in front of her face.

Alondra, seeing the glittering sharp object just inches from her face, jumped back into Deidra. Deidra placed an arm around the young woman's waist and held her tightly. "Be careful my dear; accidents do happen," Deidra hissed in Alondra's ear.

Deidra's breath on Alondra's skin gave her a chill. The woman then handed Alondra the knife, wooden handle first.

Alondra snatched it out of her hand, and twirled around to face her, pointing the knife. "Yeah, accidents do happen! So take your own advice," Alondra warned.

Suddenly, Deidra's eyes shot past Alondra and conveniently broke into tears.

"What in the hell is going on?" asked Marc. Neither had heard him enter the house, let alone the kitchen. He'd followed the sound of their voices and stumbled upon Alondra pointing a knife at Deidra.

"Ask her," Deidra said, feigning sadness.

"All of the sudden I've lost my appetite. I'm going over to Geri's to get my stuff," Alondra huffed. She left the house and jumped on her bike. She wanted to get her belongings, but also needed to discuss something with Geri.

Deidra was still sobbing when Alondra slammed the front door, and pulled away. She looked up at Marc, and slung herself into him. He kept his arms at his sides. She was crying and mumbling some things he couldn't make out. "Deidra, it's late," said Marc. "And I'm really tired. I'm gonna take a nice hot shower, and go to bed. I'll talk to you in the morning." He pushed her arms away and left the room.

She hardly noticed he had gone.

Chapter 2

Geri opened her door for Alondra and the young lady
flew in quickly, hardly waiting for it to open fully.
Geri knew she was upset. She followed Alondra to
the guest bedroom where she'd slept while she was
visiting. Alondra was tossing her things into her
backpack.

"You're leaving?" Geri asked.

Alondra was simmering "Yes! I can't let Dad stay
in that house with that woman alone. I don't like her,
and definitely don't trust her!" She zipped her bag and
went the living room and threw herself on the sofa.

"What happened? I left you in good spirits," said Geri, taking a seat across from Alondra.

"I wondered when you left," said Alondra. "I couldn't find you anywhere. The nurse gave me your message saying you would talk to me later."

Alondra stared into hers eyes and Geri shifted in the chair. Those were her father's eyes. She looked away. "I didn't feel it was appropriate for me to be there. Besides, the news from the doctor was encouraging. But that still doesn't explain why you're so angry. What happened after I left?" Geri eyes returned to hers as she brought the conversation back to where it started.

"Deidra! Ever since this woman showed up a few days ago everything that could happen has happened. First, the SUV broke down just days after my dad had it serviced. Then a step comes loose on the stairs? My dad and uncle would never miss a thing like that." Alondra sat up, and leaned toward Geri.

Geri's eyes narrowed taking in everything Alondra had just said. Then something in Alondra's face that concerned her. "Alondra, what is it?" she asked.

Alondra looked from side to side as if making sure they were alone. "I'm going to town to find out what happened with the SUV," she began. "And in the morning I'm going to have someone to come over and check out that step." Alondra nodded her head.

Geri's face went grim. "Alondra! What are you getting at?" she asked.

Alondra looked dead into her eyes. "Deidra is a psycho! I have a gut feeling there's more to her than we know. I'm going to find out what it is," she said. She then rose from the sofa and went to the window. She didn't see the displeased expression on Geri's face.

"Alondra! I don't think you should be trying to make something out of nothing. Freak accidents happen every day. It's possible to walk across the same floor every day without incident, then one day slip on that very floor for no reason at all. Or a person could use a plug over and over, then zap get the shock of their lives. It happens." Geri stood to her feet. Alondra turn to stare at her.

"Then imagine this," said Alondra. "A person comes up from behind you, and brings a knife down in front of your face. Then she whispers in your ear, 'Be careful, accidents do happen." She replayed the scenario to Geri, then went over, and picked up her backpack.

"What are you telling me?" Geri asked without emotion.

"Aunt Geri, I have a feeling I may be having an accident… care of, Deidra." She stared at her Aunt for a moment, concern etched across her face. Then turned around and silently left the house.

Geri stood motionless for some time. She had to do something or Alondra was going to spoil things. She was either going to get herself hurt, or even worse… killed. She needed to get her out of the way, but how? Then a plan came to mind. She rushed to the phone and dialed a number.

"Get over here, now!" She yelled into the phone, and slammed it down. She stalked the room like a caged tigress.

Chapter 3

Marc had moved some of his things into one of the
guest rooms, and now sat on the edge of the bed
pondering everything that has plagued his family for
the last few days. It all started with the magazine
shoot. It was all because of Ben. He was always
thinking of ways to make money, no matter what the
cost. And with the entrance of Deidra and the
magazine crew, his family started to fall apart. And
for some reason Alondra took an instant dislike of the
woman. He didn't know why.

At first he thought she might have seen that
Deidra had eyes for him and felt threatened that
someone had come into his life. He guessed seeing

them locking lips at his and Clarisse's special place by the lake didn't help much either. That's when she'd left to go stay with Geri. Alondra was just the opposite with the new neighbor, so happy. Alondra liked her a great deal, and seemed to trust her.

And now Cain and Blair had decided to move away. But he understood the reasons; too many strange things had been occurring. He would take his pregnant wife away too.

Deidra. What was he going to do to solve that problem? No use making a bigger mess. He'd have to do the right thing. He had to make it seem as if he were trying to make things work then ask for a divorce and give her a nice settlement. If she was after his money, that would surely soothe her. But he didn't care, as long as he and his family were rid of her. Marrying her was his mistake and he would have to pay for that. Money didn't mean anything to him; all he cared about was his family.

He decided to take a hot shower. It always seemed to soothe his mind when he allowed the steaming water to run over his face, and down his body. It felt like small fingers massaging his muscles. He undressed and climbed in. He closed his eyes and got lost in the water's caress. Before long, his mind went to Geri. It always led back to her.

He felt a woman's arms encircle his waist, her silky body move into him, her head rest gently on his back. He turned to confront her, thinking it was Deidra once again invading his space. But to his surprise, he stared into the beautiful eyes of Geri... the one who had captured his heart and now held it prisoner.

His eyes roamed over her face memorizing every detail to imprint it in his mind. Her eyes reached out and beckoned for his love. Her face drew closer to his and their lips just brushed against each other's. His body began to go through some noticeable changes, as his mind lingered on the kiss they shared earlier that day, and how tasty she had been. He slid one hand around her and hooked her chin gently with the other. She leaned her head back to give him access to her wanting mouth.

He rested his lips upon hers, gently at first, but the desire was more than he could endure; it took over. His mouth covered hers with such hunger, he didn't know if he could ever release her. She moved her dark, sensuous, body further into him as their souls merged. They made a slow descent to the wet floor of the shower with the water washing over them. Her hands came to the sides of his face holding it, and placing small feather-like kisses on his lips. She raised her head up to him, eyes darkened with passion. She wanted him badly, and needed him to become a part of her more than anything in this world.

Without any warning, and with one smooth gesture she locked their lips in the deepest kiss they had every shared. The vibration of his moan sent currents to every nerve in her body. Their bodies connected, and became one, expressing their love for the other. The sound of the falling water mingled with the sounds of their lovemaking. They floated on the sea of ecstasy as their bodies moved as one, until they came to that point when containment was no longer possible. They released all the emotion they had trapped inside for so many years and gave it until they were drained and spent.

Marc's eyes slowly opened and he looked around seeing that he was alone. It had merely been a fantasy; a very wet one at that. He removed his hand and shook his head realizing what had just happened. He leaned his head back into the wall, his heart beating rapidly, his breathing shallow. This is what it had come to.

Deidra silently backed out of the room shutting the door just as quietly. She turned and rushed back to her room. She had gone to his room to see if they could talk and heard the shower running. She considered joining him, but heard him moan Geri's name. She pressed against the door and tears streamed down her face. She knew Geri would be trouble for her. It was the way he looked at her. He never looked at her in the same way he did Geri. She threw herself on the bed and screamed wildly into a pillow. She sat up, her breath was rapid, and looked around the room for something to destroy. She ran to the dresser, and picked up his favorite cologne preparing to toss it out the window. Her eyes came to rest on the woman in the mirror, she looked crazed and it scared her. She put the bottle back, and looked at herself.

Her reflection began to speak to her. "You've allowed your feelings to get in the way," it said. "You need to take back control, think more clearly." She stared for some time digesting what was just said to her.

"Yes, you're so right," she answered. "The problem with this one is I cared when I shouldn't have. They're all the same. Once they have taken your virtue they seek the affections of another." She walked away from the mirror, and took a seat on his side of the bed running her hands over it.

"Well tomorrow that will all change. I'm going to hit him where it hurts the most. I want to see him suffer when everything he holds dear is taken from him. My dear Geri, I think it's time you and I became friends." She smiled deviously, plotting how she would develop a friendship with a woman she hated, but her husband loved.

Chapter 4

Geri rushed to the pounding door. She was irate. He only does these things to get on her nerves. She swung open the door, and glared angrily at the person on the other side. But she turned abruptly and walked away, leaving him standing on the porch. He laughed and came in closing the door behind him.

"Cage, do you have something you want to tell me?" She asked. Then she turned on him before he could enter the living room.

He stopped and stared seeing she was mad at more than his pounding on the door. But then, if he had a lick of sense, knowing her as he did, he would have figured that out from the tone of her phone call. "No," he replied, trying to retrace things in his mind.

Geri folded her arms across her chest, her eyes narrowed.

Then something brightened in his eyes. She nodded her head in agreement.

"I thought I would tell you in the morning," he said. "I didn't want you to do anything to jeopardize this." He tried to explain, but Geri just paced back and forth keeping her distance from him.

"Deidra could have killed her tonight, and you didn't feel it was important to inform me?" Her voice was slow and quiet. And he knew she was holding back.

"No, she wouldn't do that. She's not that stupid," he said.

Geri uncrossed her arms, and ran her fingers through her hair. Then she went to the window and stared out. "You're right," she said. I'm not thinking straight on this. I shouldn't have taken this assignment. But I thought I could kill two birds with one stone." She shook her head.

"I know! But there's no turning back. You're here now! And Alondra knows who you are. The hardest part is over." He walked further into the room seeing her anger had subsided a bit.

"I'm not so sure of that," said Geri.

Cage was confused, but then she looked up into his eyes and unwittingly gave herself away.

He slapped his forehead. "Oh no, Geri! Don't tell me you've fallen for the dad?" He flopped onto the sofa and waited for an answer.

"Yes," she said softly.

He shook his head. "Of course, which makes this more emotional than before," he said. He rubbed is hand over his face, and gazed at her.

"I know. I'd only considered getting to know my niece, and doing the assignment. I wasn't counting on falling for my sister's husband." She turned back to the window, tears filing her eyes. She couldn't let him know that some of her feelings for Marc had started years before.

"But there is one thing you're forgetting, Geri," said Cage. "There is a murderess in their house. She may be the one who sabotaged the SUV and stairs. A woman and her unborn baby are lucky to be alive." You've got to stay focused on that.

She wiped her face, and took a deep breath allowing it to escape slowly, then turned to him with a new determination.

"You're right," she said. "My feelings for him shouldn't interfere with what needs to be done. It should fuel it all the more, which brings me to why I really called you."

He sat back; satisfied she had come to her senses. "I'm all ears," he said.

"Alondra must get her nosiness from me. She came to me tonight. She's going to get herself knee deep! I don't want that," said Geri.

"Okay. What is it you want me to do?" He asked eagerly, hoping she was planning to use him for more than just a lookout.

"I want you to become a handyman, and become friends with Alondra! You're not that much older than her. And for a girl her age you're probably a hunk—don't ask me why," she teased. He just laughed.

"Sure!" he agreed. How about I check on that step for starters?" He was going to enjoy this.

"That's exactly what I had in mind," said Geri. "I'll give them a call in the morning, and offer to send you over. I'll tell them you're someone I've deemed a good handyman, and who could give the place the once over."

"Thus eliminating any more surprises she may have up her sleeves," he said.

Getting to know Alondra will be nice, Cage thought. From the moment he saw her he thought she was a nice wholesome girl, and also quite beautiful.

Cage was all of twenty-four years old. He was a decent, honorable guy and good a credit to his chosen profession—federal agent.

Chapter 5

The next morning Alondra ran to the door, and opened it up to the most handsome man she had ever seen. He was broad and strong-looking, and stood well-over six feet tall. He had long blonde hair which was tied back, and the deepest ocean blue eyes. Geri had called to tell her he was coming, but she didn't mention he was so good-looking.

"Howdy Miss. My name is Cage. Geri sent me over," he said.

Alondra was staring so hard she didn't hear him at first. "Oh... oh yeah, she called this morning. Come in," she said.

He stepped in assessing everything with one quick glance.

"I guess Geri told you my aunt fell on a loose step," she said, getting straight to business.

"Yea, she did. Where is this step?" he asked looking up the stairs.

She gestured for him to follow her. He could hardly take his eyes off of her, she was very pretty. But he knew he'd better stay focused or Geri would have his hide.

"It's right here," she said. She stepped above it and pointed.

Cage put his tool bag down and began to study the step. There was something there. He reached into the bag and pulled out a magnifying glass. Yes, something was there all right. It was invisible to the untrained eye; a small piece of metal. He picked it out with a pair of tweezers he pulled from his shirt pocket, and then placed it in a plastic bag.

"What are you doing?" Alondra asked

"You may have termites," he fibbed, trying to throw her off. But Alondra stared at him suspiciously.

"You're a cop, aren't you?" she asked inquisitively. "Aunt Geri sent you over because I told her I felt this was no accident. Didn't she? Are you undercover?"

He straightened up and stared at her. She was good, just like her aunt. You couldn't pull anything past her eyes.

"I'm not a cop," he replied. "She sent me over to safe-proof the house, and wanted to make sure all of you were safe. Okay?" He tried to reassure her, but she continued to stare at him taking in what he had said.

"Mm-hm, okay. But know this... I've got my eyes on you," she cautioned. She pointed two fingers at her eyes, then to his and walked down the stairs passing him by.

He took a deep breath. This was going to be like working with Geri, he thought.

"Who are you—and what are you doing?" boomed a deep voice from above him. Cage's head moved upwards, and saw the half-awake eyes staring down at him. He knew himself to be a large man, but this man was an even bigger one.

"Um... hello, Sir," said Cage. "My name is Cage. Geri sent me over. She thought you might need a handyman around. Alondra said it was all right."

Cage remained in the middle of the stairwell and Marc started down them. He came to a stop standing directly above the younger man. He's even larger close up, Cage thought.

"You say Geri sent you?" Marc's voice was little softer with the mention of her name.

Cage thought that was very interesting. The dad has it for Geri as well. "Yes, Sir, I'm a handyman," he reaffirmed.

Marc leaned on the railing scratching his head. "Alondra said it was all right did she? Usually my brother and I do the fixing around the place." Marc paused and looked down at the loose step, and his heart slightly sunk. He would have to go to the hospital, and take Cain some clothes. "But I guess we didn't' do a good job after all. We're wrestlers turned businessmen—not handymen." He looked off still in thought.

"Dad, I see you met Cage, our new handyman. Aunt– I mean Geri sent him over." Alondra caught herself, but Marc didn't miss her blunder.

He looked at her a little confused. "You're referring to her as Aunt now?" he asked.

She shook her head. "No Dad! I was just thinking of Aunt Blair and it slipped out. Aren't you going to see them today?" She quickly diverted the subject.

"Yes, I was just thinking that I need to get Cain some clothes. Are you coming with me?" He asked, going back up the stairs

"No I think I'll just stay here, and show Cage around the place," she said.

With this little tidbit Marc turned and gave Cage a disparaging look that clearly warned him to keep his hands off his daughter. "Okay, Alondra," he said, staring coolly at Cage. "I'll give them your love." He then left the two, however hesitantly.

"Wow, if looks could kill–" Cage came down to stand in front of Alondra.

"You would be dead," she finished, laughing.

Cage shook his head in agreement. "Mind if I'm a little nosy?" Cage asked.

Alondra stared at him curiously and leaned on the railing. "It depends," she taunted. He furrowed his brow.

"On?" he questioned.

"Are you asking as a cop, or as a handyman?" she smiled.

"Neither!" he replied with one brow raised. He noticed she had her father's eyes. She was pretty tall for a woman, taller than Geri. And her creamy skin was a little darker than her father's; it was rich and warm, a sun-kissed blend of brown sugar and cream. He had to stop himself before getting lost in his thoughts. "Uh, what is it your father has against Geri?" he asked.

Alondra was bewildered. "What makes you think my father has anything against Geri?"

"Just the way he asked if you were calling her 'aunt' now, that's all," he replied, walking toward the front door.

"Oh yeah that…" said Alondra. She followed him out the door to his truck. "There is something going on between them, but it's complicated," she admitted. She leaned against the door of the truck, and looked away.

He came to stand beside her. "Like what?" he asked. He felt he was gaining her confidence.

"Dad has a thing for Geri." she said.

"Really?" he queried, urging her to continue.

She bent down, picking up a pebble, and began to walk away from the truck. He was close at her side.

"My dad did something so outrageous. He married this woman he only knew for a couple of days. I can't stand her. She's psycho!" She turned and looked at him.

He could see she was afraid. "She scares you, doesn't she?" He wanted her to know he could see what she was feeling.

She looked up at him, and realized she had someone she could tell everything to and not have to hold back. "Yes she does," she admitted. There's something sinister in her eyes." She was staring out, forming Deidra in her mind.

He listened closely, observing everything about her as she spoke. Yeah, she's a lot like Geri, he thought to himself.

Marc stood at his bedroom window, and watched the two young people talking. He had given Cage the look. What else was he supposed to do? But the ugly truth was that she's wasn't a little girl anymore. Even if he scared this one away there would be others when she left for college in the fall. And he had to admit she was a beautiful girl, thanks to her mother.

Clarice. Hell, she wasn't that much older than Alondra when he met her, and Clarice had told him how her sister wasn't but sixteen or seventeen when she eloped and married some guy old enough to be her father.

He froze in thought for a moment, but then he suddenly realized something. "Well, I'll be damned! I had completely forgotten about Clarice having a sister. What was that girl's name?" He tried to remember it, but it had been nearly eighteen years. He tried to get in touch with her by the addresses and numbers in Clarice's things, but it was like she had dropped off the face of the earth. There was never any response.

"I remember Clarice saying her sister was pregnant," he recalled aloud. "They were due about the same time. Alondra has an Aunt and a cousin somewhere. I think I'll go check in Clarice's stuff in the attic, and get that name. I can hire a private detective to find them. Yeah, I'll do that after I go check on Cain and Blair." He pondered for a while. What a nice surprise it would be for Alondra, he thought. He smiled to himself and started getting ready to go to the hospital.

Chapter 6

"Okay, an hour will be fine," Geri said and hung up the phone. Suddenly, something outside caught her attention.

A familiar vehicle spilled into her yard. She stood at the top of her steps, eyes blazing. "What is it you want Deidra?" Her eyes stared daggers into the woman as she watched her exit the car and come up to the porch to stand below her.

Deidra spoke in a deceivingly friendly tone. "I thought since I'm now your neighbor we could get to know each other on a friendlier level," said Deidra. She then pulled off her sunglasses, and stared at Geri with her clear, blue, lying eyes.

"Really?" asked Geri sarcastically.

Deidra smiled at her suspicion. "Yes, really," she said. "I don't have anything against you, Geri. In fact, you're the only one who's been pretty decent to me." She looked down at the ground pitifully.

"I wouldn't say that," said Geri forcefully. I'd say that Marc has been very decent. He married you didn't he?"

Deidra heard the harshness in Geri's tone and saw this was not going to be as easy as she first thought. For some reason, Geri didn't seem to be the perky little thing she has been so far. She wondered what brought on the change. "That is true," said Deidra. "But Alondra sure hates me. She hasn't liked me from day one." She began to blow her breath on her glasses, and wipe them with a dainty little handkerchief.

"Can you blame her?" asked Geri. "You married her father after knowingly him only a couple of days!" Geri snapped.

Deidra looked over the sunglasses, and satisfied with how they looked, put them back on. Then she turned her attention back to Geri as if bored with their confrontation.

"I denote a touch of anger in your voice," said Deidra. "Could it be that it's not only Alondra who has a little problem with me and Marc?" she taunted.

"Okay let's see here. You're on my property, and I don't want you here. That means you're trespassing. So leave now!" Geri had had enough. Play time was over.

"Well, well, did I ever hit a cord? I'll get off your land, but tonight when you're lying in that big empty bed. Remember... he'll be next to me," she laughed. Then she turned on her heels and made way to the car.

Deidra didn't get far, however, before Geri's anger got the best of her. "Is that so?" she asked. "You know, Deidra, Marc has just the softest lips. And the way he kisses. Mmm.... just makes you melt right in his arms." Geri couldn't help herself.

Deidra nearly tripped over her feet as she fumbled to a stop. If Geri could have seen her eyes she would have shuddered in fear. Without a word, Deidra continued and got into her car, driving away like a mad-person.

Geri dropped down on the porch step, and placed her head between her hands. She shouldn't have done that. This wasn't good. She allowed her emotions to get in the way once again. She knew she had just signed her own death certificate.

"Marc, I'm glad you came. Can I talk to you?" Cain looked up as his brother came into the hospital room, and seeing that Blair was asleep, he escorted him back out.

"Sure, what's up?" Marc was a little bewildered at how his brother was acting.

"I don't know how to say this," said Cain. He paced nervously back and forth in front of his brother until Marc grabbed him by the arm, and brought him to an abrupt halt.

"What's going, Cain? Is it Blair? Is it the baby?" Marc grew anxious, but Cain shook his head to reassure him.

"No, no, they're fine. It's Deidra," Cain admitted.

Marc's eyes narrowed. "What about her?" Marc folded his arms across his chest, eyes fixed on his brother.

"I think she tried to kill Blair," he blurted.

Marc's eyes grew large.

Chapter 7

Geri walked into the house after long thought of what just happened with Deidra. She knew it wasn't a very good idea to anger that woman, but she'd hit a nerve when it came to Marc. And for Deidra to mention them being in bed together... Geri didn't even want to think about that.

Then there was the kiss she'd shared with Marc; the flow of electricity that coursed between them. And in a moment of anger she'd blurted it out to Deidra. She knew she would have to be extra careful. Her life was now at stake.

She made her way over to the files she was now able to leave laying out since Alondra had moved back home. She picked up one file in particular and opened it and began to read. It painted a clear picture of the woman known as the Viper. It was a woman who preyed on very wealthy people. She would marry the men, and become a companion to the women. After some months of marriage or companionship that man or woman would mysteriously die. It wasn't until several months ago that they finally had a lead in the case. And it was Geri who broke it wide open. The key was in a telegram she received stating that her former husband had died.

Geri came back from overseas where she had travelled many times to attend his funeral. She stayed with his sister who loved to talk. She told her how Stan had met a young woman somewhere. She didn't know exactly where. They'd had a whirlwind love affair, and got married very quickly. His sister felt something was odd about the younger woman. 'Her eyes were cynical,' she'd said. The two of them didn't hit it off, and the sister was told she was no longer welcome in their home. The sister felt this woman had sabotaged the relationship between her and her brother. Three months later... he was dead.

The strange part of the situation was how he died. It was said he had come back from a long trip, and was taking a bath when the radio fell in the tub, and electrocuted him. Geri immediately felt something wasn't right when Stan's sister described the events leading up to and causing his death.

Geri had seen the young widow at the funeral. She'd arrived wearing a risqué black dress with a veil over her face. She never removed the veil or socialized with anyone that day. After that, she disappeared.

The house was sold immediately. Everything Stan owned went to this woman, but for a very small portion which went to his sister. That small portion alone was enough to care for her for the rest of her life, so Deidra had truly cleaned up.

At the funeral Geri watched the widow and formed a general description of the woman whose face she could not clearly see. She was tall, slender, had long blonde hair, and crystal blue eyes that pierced the veil before them.

Geri had also been married to Stan. So she knew his quirks, and sitting in the bathtub with any electrical object nearby would never have happened. He happened to be terrified of being shocked to death. So it had been a rule in their home to keep such things out of the bathing area.

That's when Geri pulled the files on the Viper. She did some heavy research on this woman. She became obsessed with catching her, and bringing her to justice. Not only for Stan's sake, but for the other men and women she had killed. Believing that Deidra could be the Viper, Geri tracked her down. She'd been living on a tropical island, and had made her way back to the States. Geri figured if she was back she had picked out her next victim. Surveillance was put on her. She was followed to a big estate in Tennessee. Geri did a background check on who owned the place. She discovered it was an elderly big time businessman, and she felt maybe this was someone whose life may be in danger. He fit the profile of the Viper's victims—old and rich. They had the phones disconnected and sent in undercover agents posing as telephone repairmen to fix them and plant listening devices.

But they discovered that the old man was Deidra's father. Utilizing this new information, they discovered that Deidra had been institutionalized at the age of twenty, and stayed for four years. The timeline meant she was discharged just before the murders had begun.

Deidra hadn't been back to her father's house after being released form the institution. But he hadn't wanted her there either. And her mother died just before she went in. Could that be the reason she'd become so despicable? Had she had a mental break and never recovered?

A conversation between the father and a close friend concerning Deidra's employment peaked Geri's interest. She was working for a magazine and wanted to use two of this friend's clients in a major spread. When Geri discovered the true identities of these two clients, it rocked her to the core.

Deidra had taken up photography and journalism, and got a job with the well-known magazine. They wanted an article on retired athletes. It was her suggestion to use these two particular men. She'd done her research and this was her break for yet another mark. She had it planned well. She went to their agent, Ben McBain, who just happened to be her godfather and close friend of her father.

Geri realized Deidra had been spoiled all her life. She didn't need the money, so why did she murder these people and take theirs? Geri decided to run an investigation on the two brothers; one caught her interest. He was known by many names in his business, and was very popular. She just hadn't put two and two together at the time.

She requested a picture of him, feeling he was going to be Deidra's next casualty. She found out where he lived and that is where everything came to light. She'd discovered something that stalled her abruptly. Everything about him led to another, unrelated, investigation she was conducting; one that was a lot more personal. She was trying to locate her sister's husband, and a child she never got to see. He had changed his name, and gone into a different profession than when he was married to her sister. And she found it difficult to locate him, until now.

Geri had wanted to buy her family's land back for years. Her sister had put the idea into her head. They'd decided to buy the land back together. She would live on one half, and her sister on the other. But they lost touch with each other. And she never knew all that had come to pass. The sisters had drifted far apart. Maybe they both felt they would reconnect at some point, but so much happened in such a little time which changed everything

Finally, some luck came her way. A person who had owned half of her family's land had passed away and his widow wanted to sell. The realtor called Geri, who had left her number with the couple years earlier. Geri bought it without hesitation. She then found out that the other part of the land had been owned by two brothers for nearly eighteen years. She decided she wouldn't bother them about it. The important part of the land was the one she now owned, as their old house was there. That was good enough for now.

But her investigation had taken a startling turn when she found out that the two men she'd been investigating lived right next door. They owned the other half of her family's land. The coincidence seemed so impossible. But then, Geri saw the picture of the older brother and her world stood still. She took out a picture her sister had sent of her and her husband many years ago. With all her heart she knew... this was the same man. Fate had stepped in to reunite her with her family... and even more, to protect them from the venom of the Viper.

Chapter 8

"What in the hell are you saying?" Marc yelled at his brother. Cain tried to get him to lower his voice. He watched as people passed by looking at them strangely.

"Marc, man, calm down! We're in a hospital!" Marc looked around him, and realized he had amplified his voice a little more than needed. He nodded his head.

Cain took a quick peek in Blair's room to see if she was still sleep. She was out like a newborn. Then he pointed down the hallway, and headed down it with Marc close behind. They went out a door entering a patio area.

"Look Marc, hear me out! I'm not just talking out of my head," said Cain..

"Okay, I'm gonna try and be calm here, little brother. What do you mean you think Deidra tried to kill Blair? I don't like what you're telling me." Marc walked over to a table and bench. Cain followed, choosing his words carefully.

Geri closed the file she had just gone over, and anticipated a visit with Deidra's father, and what information she could gather on why she was institutionalized several years ago. She looked up after hearing the taxi cab honking out front. She quickly waved form the door and then grabbed her things. She gave the place sweeping glance then locked the door behind her. He jumped in the cab and made her way to the airport. Her destination: Tennessee.

Deidra was returning to Geri's place. She didn't like their last encounter. Somehow she had to mend the damage done earlier. Her plan still stood, but after being one on one with her, she could see that Geri was more than some plain Jane. Maybe that's what Marc saw in her. This sparked an interest in her, and the need to find out what it was intrigued her. Geri was a mystery she wanted to solve, and that was something she liked.

Deidra had been driving down the road thinking when she saw the taxi pulling into the path to Geri's. She parked a distance away, and decided this was an even better opportunity. She would get in her house while she was away, and find out what were her likes, and dislikes. Then she would lie in wait for her return.

She watched as the taxi went down the road with Geri inside, and headed away from the ranch. When she felt it was safe, she drove onto the path to Geri's home.

"I called Ben last night and told him everything that happened," said Cain. He then paused and waited for his brother's reaction, but he just stared at him.

"I also mentioned your marriage to Deidra," Cain braced himself for the explosion.

Marc took a small walk in a circle with his arms folded across his chest, and then he turned to his brother. "How did he take that little bit of info?" he asked. Cain took a deep breath, and looked at him. "Oh, that well, huh?" Marc slightly chuckled. He loved getting under Ben's skin even if it wasn't intentionally.

Cain sat down on a bench replaying the strange conversation with Ben.

"Actually Marc he's the one who confirmed my suspicions." Cain's eyes crept towards his brother. Marc stared down at him, and saw the worry in his eyes.

"What do you mean?" Marc asked.

"I don't think Blair is the only person who's in danger here," said Cain, revealing his concerns.

Marc slowly came over to his brother, and sat down. He listened very carefully.

Deidra made sure no one else was around, then pried the back door lock, and let herself in. She slowly strolled through the house checking things out. She looked in the refrigerator noting what Geri liked to eat, and in her cabinets seeing her taste in dishes. She went right through the living room admiring her taste in furniture, and headed for the most important place in the house, the bedroom. That's where Deidra's interests truly laid.

She looked over the top of the dresser. "You have very good taste in perfume and cologne, Geri; an

274

expensive and exotic taste at that." Geri was undercover. She was simple on the outside, but definitely something she would like to explore on the inside… in more ways than one, she surmised.

She rumbled through Geri's drawers looking at her most intimate clothing. She could see she was into thongs, and lace. She picked up an undergarment, closed her eyes, and rubbed it over her cheek. She was instantly aroused, her breathing became slow, deep, but her heart was increasing its pace. Her eyes darkened with passion. Geri's taste of under attire proved she was a sexual kitten underneath. Deidra's mind went back to how her voice sounded when she described the kiss she'd shared with Marc. He had brought out her sensual side she'd been trying to hide beneath that rough exterior. And she wasn't that bad looking either. She had tantalizing, silky, chocolate skin and a nice little body.

"If she were a man, I'd have my way with her. Hell, even as a woman." She smiled wickedly, and went over to her neatly-made bed, covered in satin. Yeah, she was something you would want to get under these sheets, and turn every way but loose. She lay out on the bed, and rolled about trying to wrap herself in Geri's scent and to leave hers for Geri to lie in. She began to daydream of making love to Geri. She felt herself become wet with the pleasure of the thought.

"When I told him about the marriage, he said he knew," said Cain. "That photographer, Josh, had just checked in with the magazine, and they called Ben and told him everything. He said he was just getting ready to call me, and see how Blair was." Cain stood and went over to a window staring at people walking by.

"Oh like he even gives a damn about any of us or our families," Marc huffed.

Cain turned to his brother. "Did Deidra ever tell you she got married before—less than a year ago?" Cain had dropped a bombshell, and from the expression covering his brother's face he never knew.

Deidra gathered herself, and left the bed. She was satisfied for the moment, and looking forward to the real deal. She went to the living room to wait for Geri's return, and make the dream a reality.

"Married? Are you sure?" Marc couldn't believe his ears. Cain nodded.

"Ben said when the magazine editor phoned him he called his friend, her father, before the news got back to him another way. The old man wasn't very happy." Cain let Marc know this before he continued.

"I understand that," said Marc. He was more interested about the previous marriage rather than her father's reaction to theirs.

"It seems she met this older guy while overseas or something. I don't know. I wasn't really interested." Cain started.

Marc gestured for him to go on; he wasn't interested in how they met either. Neither man realized how important that information was.

"Anyway, after a three months courtship they married. A month into the marriage he had to go on some business trip for a few days." Cain continued with the information, Marc listened with all ears.

"Okay!" Marc urged him to go on. Cain came to sit across from him leaning toward Marc who leaned in also. He knew it was something Cain didn't want to say out loud.

"Here's the killer, and no pun intended. The very day he came back from his trip he died in the tub." Cain whispered. Marc sat back thinking, and not sure with all of this meant. Cain gave him a look that there was more.

"Dare I ask?" Marc wasn't sure he wanted to know anymore, because this is shedding a whole new light on things that had come about in the last few days.

"The radio supposedly accidentally fell into the tub and fried him." Cain sat back after saying this, and stared at his brother.

Marc sat there for a moment unable to speak, but he finally found his voice. "Accident?" he echoed. "Is she a jinx—or is it worse?"

Deidra sat looking at her watch, and wondering how long Geri would be gone, longing for her to come back. She opened her purse, and took out a small bottle with a handkerchief. She would get her as she came through the door. She smiled at the thought of her plan. It had been a long time since she felt for someone in this way, except for Marc of course. She still wanted him, but his feelings were for Geri. She knew this. So, since Geri has his feelings how ironic it will be for her to have Geri, and him think her feelings for him had changed, and that she will have to do?

"Little Geri will mysteriously disappear. No one will know her whereabouts but me," said Deidra. "Maybe she would leave a nice little note. Yes, that's a better idea; a note to Marc explaining how deeply in love she was with him, and couldn't deal with the thought of him being married to me. Then of course, who will he turn to but his loving wife who will be there with open arms? No one will know I have her locked away. He will belong to me alone. I'll have the best of both worlds: a loving husband, and my little toy." She leaned back into the sofa. Her demented mind was convinced her plan would come to fruition.

"There's more!" Cain told Marc.

"Go on, tell me everything." Marc shook his head not believing what he was hearing.

"The man had money, and everything went to her. She went away for a while, and dropped out of sight. Then one day she shows up on daddy's door step. But she didn't know that Daddy had sent a private detective to find her, and found out about the marriage and everything else that happened."

Deidra was too excited to sit. She left the sofa, and started looking around the room for something to read, or a radio to listen to when her eyes fell on the files Geri had left on the table. She sat in a chair and sat back, crossing her legs comfortably, and looked at the folders. She came upon one named 'The Viper'. It struck her interest more than the others. As she began to read it, she discovered the very first page was about her marriage to Stan.

"So if the father has suspicions about the marriage, and the man's death. Why did he send her to Ben, and to work around so many people?" Marc asked.

"He didn't. She went to Ben with the pitch for us to be part of the magazine article. Ben admitted that to me," said Cain.

"Great! That's just damned great!" Marc's voice boomed.

"There's something else," said Cain.

Mark looked to the sky as hoping for divine intervention. This was beginning to feel like their own personal suspense story.

Cain continued. "Dad said he got a call from some person in the F.B.I. a few days ago. She wanted to come, and talk to him about Deidra, and her past. That's when he revealed everything to Ben fearing there was more to the man's death. And Ben felt there was even more to it than his old friend was saying. Anyway, he has put the magazine shoot on hold. Deidra's out." Cain sat back, and watched his brother digest everything.

"Yeah she's out in more ways than one," said Marc. "I'd better get back home. No telling what accident may have happened since I left."

Marc and Cain stared at each other. Something unspoken went between them. Then Marc left. Cain sighed silently and said a little prayer for his family.

Chapter 9

Geri sat on the airplane thumbing through some notes she had written out, and questions she wanted to ask Deidra's father. She tried to get some information from the institution, but without a court order that was a no-go. And because there wasn't enough concrete evidence against her, she wasn't going to get one either.

Her mind went back to the day she and Alondra discovered Marc and Deidra kissing. She'd seen the rage in Deidra's eyes when Marc tried to console his daughter. Then she'd come over to taunt her about their marriage which had provoked her into confessing she'd kissed him also. She knew then she was marked. It was just a matter of time. For now, she wondered exactly what would be Deidra's next move.

Deidra finished reading the first page and continued on to read about another person who had come into, and left her life. She leaned her head to the side flipping one page after another. This was a file about all of her conquests. And she was named the Viper. But what was Geri doing with this information—and what was she planning on doing with it?

'It doesn't matter what her plans were,' she said to herself. 'As of this moment they are null and void.' She tossed the file onto the table with the others. She now had an even greater determination to see her plan through. And she was confident. After all, she hadn't failed yet.

Geri's plane landed. She walked through the terminal, and out to the curb to hail a taxi. She was anxious to get what information she could about Deidra's stay at the institution. This investigation had become personal, and the safety of Geri's own family was now at stake. She had to find out more about Geri's past and that information might only come from her own family. And the only living relative of Deidra's was her father.

Geri's cab pulled into the driveway of a huge estate. Normally, an access code would be needed to open the gate or someone would open it remotely, but Geri was expected. They pulled up in front of the house. A butler came out to open her door. She thanked him, and paid the driver. The butler informed her that Mr. Elliott was waiting in the study. She followed him as they made their way through the grand home.

"Ms. Paine, sir," announced the butler before leaving the room.

Behind the huge oak desk, was a very old man sitting in an expensive-looking leather brown chair. Geri thought he seemed much too old to be Deidra's father, but he was younger than he looked. His aged appearance was brought on by many years of anguish and illness.

"Hello, Ms. Paine, have a seat," said Mr. Elliott. He gestured toward a leather sofa.

She took a seat when someone entered with refreshments. She sat a platter on a small table next to Mr. Elliott.

"Would you like anything?" Mr. Elliott asked Geri kindly. "I know you have to be famished after that long trip on the airplane." He then whispered something to the other woman who soon after hurried from the room.

"Yes, thank you," answered Geri.

The Butler came back in with some pill bottles and Geri watched as the elderly man took several. He then handed Geri a small plate of fruit and cheese. "I noticed you are staring at the many pills I'm taking. They keep me alive," he explained. The butler sat Mr. Elliott's plate before him, and took the bottles away leaving the two alone to talk.

Geri politely took a few bites from the plate given to her then set it aside and dapped her lips with a napkin. She picked up her notepad and delved straight to business. "Mr. Elliott, I hope you don't mind, but I need to get on with the questioning. Time is of the essence." She noticed he hadn't eaten anything and seemed a bit out of it. She hoped he wasn't too sick to give her what she needed.

"No, Ms. Paine, I don't mind at all. In fact, I welcome the chance to get this load off my chest." He gave her an almost pleading look and she noticed what seemed like relief in his voice.

Geri cut to the chase. "I'd like to know why Deidra was institutionalized."

He pressed his head back into the soft leather chair recalling the night in question. "Ah yes, the night my world fell apart. It was the night she killed my beautiful loving wife... her own mother," said Mr. Elliott, sadly.

Geri was at a loss.

Chapter 10

Alondra followed Cage around the ranch. He wanted to make sure there were no unexpected traps laid about. Alondra watched him carefully. The more she watched, the more she was convinced he was more than a handyman.

"You know, Cage, I'm not as dense as you might think," said Alondra. She walked beside him as they headed for the house.

Cage had finished his inspection. "Alondra, I don't think you're dense, far from it. In fact, I think you're a very intelligent girl," he said with a smile.

Alondra stopped in her tracks and she took a deep breath to contain her changing mood. "Tell me you didn't just call me a girl!" She looked at him sternly.

He stepped back realizing what he had just called her. "Oh, I'm sorry! Let me correct myself, young woman..." He raised both hands in the air, playfully in defense.

She began to laugh. "Thank you." She replied and started toward the house.

Just then, the roar of her father's bike came through loud and clear as he sped up the drive and into the garage. She stopped and listened as it went silent, then watched as he walked out in great haste.

"What's wrong, Dad?" she asked, seeing he was very tense.

"Where's Deidra?" he blasted as he passed her, and into the house with purpose.

Alondra looked at Cage who noticeably watched Marc with interest.

"She's gone. She left this morning," Alondra said after him. "She hasn't been heard from since."

He stopped abruptly at the top of the steps, and turned his head back to the two young people.

"You two have been here alone all this time?" he asked, staring a hole into Cage who nervously shifted from one foot to the other.

Alondra, noticing her father's expression, and what was behind it walked up to her father.

"Dad, Cage is a perfect gentleman. Besides, he is too work-oriented to be distracted from his work… just like you." She said with a noticeable frown.

Cage stared back at her blankly not daring to reveal what he'd been thinking all day.

"Good," said Marc. "I'm glad to hear that. Let's hope he continues to be on his best behavior. I need to find Deidra," he said, with urgency in his voice.

"What's going on?" Alondra asked, following her father into the house.

He stopped again and turned to Cage. "Can I trust you to look out for my daughter? You seem like a decent young man. Don't prove me wrong. I don't want Deidra near her. You get me?" He gave Cage a look, and being the good agent that he was, he could see that Marc had found something out about Deidra.

"You're not wrong, Sir. She's in good hands," Cage assured him.

Marc nodded and ran upstairs to his room. Alondra walked in and saw him tearing the room apart as if searching for something.

"Dad, what is it?" she asked again.

He walked past her, tossing things out of the drawers. "Nothing for you to worry about," said Marc. Then he stopped, and stroked his goatee and went deep into thought. "I'm looking for... oh I know!" He didn't finish as his mind was jolted with recollection. He ran out of the room, heading for a place he hadn't been in nearly eighteen years; a place where so much of his heart had been stored long ago—the attic.

He paused at the door for a moment rubbing his hand over it, as memories shot through him. Alondra walked up behind him, and placed a gentle hand on his arm.

He looked down to her with wet eyes. "What I need is up there," he said and looked back at the door.

"Want me to go with you?" she asked.

"No I'm okay," he said. He patted her hand, opened the door, and stared up the stairs, then slowly ascended them with Alondra watching him go up and disappear.

He looked around at all the stuff of Clarice's, getting distracted from the reason he had come up there in the first place. He found her cedar chest and opened it. He rummaged through until he found an envelope. He sat down pulling the photos from it, and thumbed through them until he saw one he hadn't seen before. Staring long and hard, not sure his eyes were picking up what was being relayed by them to his mind.

He jumped to his feet, and tossed the other pictures back into the chest, then ran back down the stairs. Alondra was with Cage talking when they heard a massive sound coming from above them, then down the steps and toward them.

"Alondra look!" Marc exclaimed. "Tell me I'm not seeing what I'm seeing!"

She looked it over and paused, then looked at her father. He seemed excited, yet curious as to why she wasn't. Then he slightly turned his head to the side, and froze as he recalled something from earlier. Suddenly everything became much clearer as he slapped his forehead, and walked away.

"Dad!" cried Alondra.

Suddenly he swung around and stared at her hard. "How long have you known?" he snapped.

She jumped backward hearing the anger in his voice. "Just yesterday," she confessed. "I was going to tell you, but you hit me with the news of your marriage." She said softly, looking at the picture blurring by the tears swelling in her eyes.

"So calling her 'aunt' wasn't a mistake now was it?" he asked sternly.

Alondra gazed up into her father's eyes, and saw something in them she thought she would never see, disappointment. She'd betrayed him. "No, Daddy, it wasn't," she said. She began to cry. He turned and headed out the door.

She ran to the door and screamed. "Daddy, please!" She knew he was going to Geri's house. "Daddy, stop! Listen to me!" Alondra ran after her father catching his arm, and struggled to stop him from making the second biggest mistake in his life after marrying Deidra.

"Let me go, Alondra!" Marc roared. He pulled his arm from her with such force she nearly fell to the ground.

Cage had witnessed everything and felt this was a good time to intervene. "Um, Sir!" he called, hurrying up to him.

Marc turned around, a glare in his eyes.

Cage felt a knot in his throat causing him to clear it.

"You don't have anything I want to hear," said Marc.

Cage kept some distance between them, but he didn't back down. "I'm sorry, Sir, but I think I do," he said.

Marc's eyes narrowed as he started toward the young stranger. This was one time Cage was glad he had his defensive training. He felt he might need it before this was over.

Chapter 11

"Deidra killed her mother?" said Geri, repeating Mr. Elliott's words. She was shocked at the statement.

The elder man took a sip of water and took in a deep breath as his eyes came over to Geri, never moving his head. "She might as well have," he said. "Her mother loved her so much. She was an only child, and my wife spoiled her rotten. She always wanted whatever she saw, and her mother made sure she had it." He paused as his mind brought back memories.

Inside, Geri breathed a sigh of relief. Somehow she was relieved that at least Deidra hadn't been so deranged she'd kill her own mother.

Mr. Elliott continued. "The day came when she started school and had to be around other children. She would take things she wanted that belonged to the other kids. Her mother spent many nights trying to explain to her that she couldn't do that. That's where we had our problem. The concept never registered in her mind." Mr. Elliott paused once again.

Geri wrote down his words getting the vital information she needed. She saw that Deidra's habit of taking what she wants with no remorse was a pattern that started long ago. It explained her criminal history… and also explained her relationship with Marc. Geri could see that Mr. Elliott was tiring, but wasn't sure if it was illness, age, or just the fact that he was tired of life itself.

"There was an incident at a school outing. A little girl was nearly drowned. She might as well have died that day. She's a living vegetable." He then seemed to drift off.

Geri shifted in her chair. She didn't like this at all. "Deidra?" she asked.

He looked to the ceiling, and then closed his eyes. "Forgive me if this takes some time to tell. It just brings back so many painful memories," he explained.

"I understand," said Geri. "Take as long as you need."

"Most thought it was an accident, but some kids reported that Deidra had argued with the girl before over a beautiful ring she'd been showing off. The girl was seen wearing the ring on the day of the incident, and it was rumored that Deidra could have attempted to take it from her causing the girl to slip off into the water. The authorities said there was no reason to believe that," he said.

"You seem to think otherwise," Geri suggested. She was sensing something in his voice.

"The ring wasn't on the little girl's finger when she was recovered from the water, and they felt it could have fallen off when she fell in." He was still staring at the ceiling as if visualizing that day.

"But you have your doubts…" said Geri. She hoped this wasn't going where she felt, but his eyes fell on her then she knew.

"I have proof," he said despairingly.

Geri stared blankly at him as he opened his desk drawer, pulled out a small envelope and offered it to her. She left her seat, took it, and emptied the contents into her hand. A small ring landed on her palm… and a dreadful feeling pierced her heart.

"What is it you've got to say to me, boy?" Marc was close to his face which caused the younger man to back up. But Cage continued.

"If I may, Mr. Caldwell… Sir… I know you're upset with your daughter for not coming to you about Geri immediately, I understand. But you hit her with some pretty life-changing news yesterday. I don't think she could think about anything else. Won't you just give her a chance to explain?" Cage finished and braced himself for the impact.

Marc stood with his hands on his hips, not saying a word. He eye-balled Cage for what seemed like an eternity then returned his gaze to his daughter. "We have some talking to do, privately," he said before staring Cage down once more. He then went inside with Alondra.

Cage finally allowed the breath he was holding to escape. He was relieved they'd elected to talk amongst themselves, for he had other business to attend to. He had to contact Geri. He had two major concerns: Deidra, and her whereabouts.

Geri was stunned. There it was right in her face; the ring of a little girl whose life was taken away by a selfish little child who didn't understand she couldn't have everything she wanted.

"Where did you get this?" asked Geri, her voice shaking as she fought back her emotions.

"My wife found it years later; the night Deidra was sent to the institution," he said, continuing to stare out the window.

"A child's life was destroyed... your wife finds the ring that could give the girl's family some closure... and all you do is put Deidra in a sanitarium?" Geri felt her blood begin to boil.

"Not exactly," said Mr. Elliott. "My wife confronted her. I was just getting in from a business trip when I heard them arguing. Of course I went to see what the commotion was about, and that's when I was informed by my wife what she had discovered." He turned back to Geri, who said nothing.

Geri was angry, but she controlled herself. She knew an outburst would serve no purpose. And she'd learned something very important about Deidra's past. She was definitely home-raised sociopath.

"Deidra begged her not to tell me," Mr. Elliott continued. "She was furious with her mother and called her every name in the book. I became so enraged at her disrespect for the only person who loved her more than life itself that I raised my hand and brought it down across her face. She fell back over her bed, and the look she gave me as I admonished her would have turned your blood cold." He paused again.

Geri thought she heard him sniffle, but couldn't tell as he'd turned away yet again. "That's when I knew what we had spawned," he said. "She sat quietly for a few moments. We thought she was digesting the whole situation. Then she looked at her mother, rose to her feet, and walked to her. She wrapped her arms around her. My wife began to cry, and held Deidra tenderly. I saw it before my wife could feel it. She had a letter opener in her hand we hadn't seen as she had concealed it in her other hand blind to us. She lifted it up and came down. I was quicker in those days. It hit me in the arm as I shoved my wife from harm's way. Deidra lifted the knife and tried to stab me again, but she was shoved into the wall with great force. Funny thing about a mother's love... it's very unpredictable." He turned to stare at Geri.

"So you institutionalized her? And you never told the police?" Geri was feeling only contempt for him at the moment. She gripped the little ring in her hand.

Mr. Elliott stared at her for some time, not saying a word, just deep in a thought. "Ms. Paine, you are not as knowledgeable as you might think. So I suggest you sit there, and listen to what I have to say without the shrewd remarks." He was calm when he'd reproved her, but a hint of firmness was present in his voice.

She sat back in her chair and considered a comeback, but thought better of it. She was there in a professional capacity, and as far as he knew... it wasn't a personal one. She knew better than to show her own emotions when questioning a witness. "I apologize, Mr. Elliott. You're right. It's more important that I hear what you have to say. So much is counting on it," she conceded.

"Not only pretty, but smart too, as I knew when you first contacted me," he said. "Now where was I?" He leaned back in his chair staring into the ceiling.

"A shove into the wall by your wife..." said Geri.

His eyes shot towards her for a moment, and then back to the ceiling. "Oh yes, we locked her in her room sending the staff away for the night, and then I called in a doctor friend of mine. He happened to own a quaint sanitarium out of town. It's a very upscale and secluded place. No one but the very elite knows of it. Most of them go there for rehabilitation from drugs and the like."

The way Mr. Elliott spoke of the sanitarium sounded to Geri as if he were describing some sort of resort for the very privileged. She held her tongue with great difficulty. She tried to maintain a professional level of decorum, but the truth was that unlike any other case, this one was personal. And she had trouble containing her distaste for the haughtiness she heard in Mr. Elliott's story. She wanted to tell him she didn't give a damn about where the 'elite' went or why. What she cared about was protecting her family and others from his venomous daughter.

She took notes on every detail. It was clear that a child's life had been diminished due to Deidra's uncontrollable desires, and that Deidra didn't seem to care or feel a shred of remorse. She'd also tried to kill her mother, which brought Geri to her next question. "You said Deidra was responsible for her mother's death—how so?" she asked. She looked up from the notepad.

Mr. Elliott sat very still at first, and then slowly leaned on the desk and stared into Geri's eyes. "After that night her mother became ill. She wouldn't eat or drink. Finally, I had to have a home nurse come in. She was hooked to IVs for hydration and nutrients, but that didn't help. She lingered seven months and then died. Her will to live was gone. She never got over all that Deidra had done, and that the child she had brought into this world had tried to take her out of it."

He turned away, and left his chair for the first time. He walked to the double doors, opened them, and went out into the fresh air and a beautiful garden.

Geri left her seat, following him, when he fell suddenly to the ground like a fallen leaf. Geri ran to him and lifted his upper body into her arms carefully. "Mr. Elliott! Are you all right, Sir?" She was frantic as she shook him gently. He gazed into her eyes.

"You are a beautiful and charming young woman," he said, trying to catch his breath between words. "If I had a wish, I would have wished for as decent a daughter as you. But you have to play with the hand dealt you. I don't have much time, so listen to me well. In my desk is a large yellow envelope. I put it there for you alone. Get it and then call my butler. Go! Save that young man who my daughter has married. His life isn't worth two cents to her. Especially, when she finds something or someone else she wants."

Geri gently laid him down, and ran to the door calling for help. The butler appeared almost instantly. He was running and was bewildered when he saw Geri. She pointed to the double doors and he saw Mr. Elliott lying on the ground. He ran quickly to lift him and carried him to the sofa as Geri called for emergency assistance. The butler then covered Mr. Elliott with a blanket which was nearby. Geri felt sorry she had brought this on by bringing up too many painful memories.

The butler kneeled down, his ear close to Mr. Elliott as he tried to speak. He then rose to his feet, went over to the desk, and pulled out a large yellow envelope. He gave it to Geri. "Mr. Elliott wants you to go now, and to take this. It will help you greatly," he said.

She took it and then looked at Mr. Elliott one last time. "Will he be all right?" she asked.

"Yes, Ms. Paine. He has made his peace. Now maybe you can finish what needs to be done." She understood that he knew about the story, and that

Mr. Elliott was now ready to die. She walked over to the elderly man. His eyes were closed and he was barely breathing. She could hear the sirens in the distance. She gathered her things, turned away, and left him to his serenity.

Chapter 12

Marc had listened quietly while his daughter relayed how she found out that Geri was her mother's sister. "No wonder I couldn't contact her," he said. "She was in the hospital recovering from an accident... and she'd lost her own child. Looking back, I do remember a woman calling once about Clarice. It was about a year after she died." His eyes seemed full of new awareness.

"Aunt Geri?" Alondra asked.

"I suppose it could have been," said Marc. And after all this time it seems she wasn't sure how to tell us."

Suddenly, Cain walked into the room.

Marc immediately jumped to his feet. "What are you doing here? Is everything all right?" he asked.

"Everything is fine," said Cain. "Blair just wanted me to come home and check on you two."

"Good, I don't need any more shocks today," said Marc. He let out a long hard sigh.

Alondra ran up to her Uncle and hugged him. "Should I go stay with Aunt Blair?" she asked.

Cain held tightly to his niece. Little did they know, he wanted to be with Blair, but was just as concerned as she was about Marc and Alondra's safety. "I think that would be a very good idea, and it would ease her mind to see you," he said. He looked down at her smiling face.

Alondra gave him a peck on the cheek and gave her father the same before running upstairs to get ready. As soon as she was out of sight, Cain's eyes shot straight to his brother's. "Okay... what did you mean by 'another shock'? And where on earth is Deidra?"

Marc took a deep breath before telling his brother about Geri.

"Damn, Geri—where are you?" said Cage. "And why aren't you answering your cell phone?" He'd made numerous calls to her without any response. She'd told him she'd found a lead on the case and had to briefly leave town, but insisted she would check in with him. In fact, she had not checked in, and he couldn't reach her with the news that Marc knew who she was, and more importantly, that Deidra had vanished.

Cain sat across from his brother on the living-room sofa. "I noticed the resemblance right away, but I didn't know Clarice had a sister," said Cain.

Marc was stunned. "You saw it?" he asked and shook his head wondering why he hadn't.

"Yes," said Cain. "So did Alondra… and so did you. Why do you two think you were so swept away by her? You saw Clarice but didn't realize it." Cain wanted to make him see the connection between his feelings and why she had seemed so familiar to him.

Marc thought for a few moments, and then nodded his head. She was a lot like her sister. "You're right, Cain. I saw it but didn't see it," he said. He then began to get anxious. He looked at his watch. "I wonder where Deidra went off to." Marc looked at his brother, who shrugged.

"I don't know, but we can be sure she's up to no good," said Cain.

Suddenly, something in Marc's gut made him jump to his feet. His mind traveled back to a few days earlier, when a car pulled into Geri's drive and then left. Deidra had mysteriously left the ranch around that time, without anyone knowing her whereabouts. Then she'd phoned Josh, telling him she wasn't feeling up to the shoot that day. Coincidence? He didn't think so.

"Geri!" He yelled realizing the absence and the incidents that has surrounded this woman's presence in their lives. Everyone was accounted for except Geri and Deidra, which could only mean one thing. Cain sprung up looking at Marc their eyes telling the other what was in their hearts. Without further hesitation they ran towards the door nearly knocking over Cage as he came into the house, and still trying to contact Geri.

"Hey you can leave anytime you want. Alondra is going to the hospital to be with her aunt." Marc stopped long enough to address Cage who was wondering where the fire is!

"Okay, is everything all right?" he asked. Marc paused wondering if he should tell Cage.

"We're going over to Geri's. She may need help," Marc told him.

Cage stiffened. Did they know something he didn't?

"What do you mean?" He was wondering if something had indeed happened since he couldn't get in touch with her.

"I haven't seen my wife all day, and we feel she may have gone over to Geri's. They don't care for each other." Marc decided to tell him as he was acquainted with Geri.

"Oh okay! You had me worried for a moment. Geri did tell me yesterday she would be going out of town this morning, and said she probably won't be back till the morning sometime. So I doubt if your wife would be there." He didn't need a bunch of amateurs interfering with the case.

"Really? Kind of sudden don't you think?" Marc was wondering where she had taken off to so abruptly, and why.

"I have no idea of what her mind frame is Sir! I only do the handy work for her." Cage wanted to throw off the fact that they were closer than just being a handyman working for her. They were partners. Marc's eyes narrowed.

"I don't either. I guess she's just a secretive person. Well, anyway, Alondra won't be here so you're free to go on your way." Marc headed back towards the house with Cain staring Cage down as he passed him by. Cage turned away from him looking up into the sky.

If another oversized wrestler gives him a look today. He was going to give them a good old butt whooping FBI style, he thought to himself.

"Who's the young guy?" Cain backed in the house eyes fixed on Cage's back.

"Some guy Geri sent over to look the house over. She didn't' want any more accidents." At that moment Alondra came bounding down the stairs.

"So you met Cage, huh Uncle Cain?" She smiled brightly. Marc was thinking when he heard her tone, and turned to look at her. Cain tilted his head, and then the two men looked at each other, back at her simultaneously, and then let out a deep sigh.

"Sir, if you don't mind I think I'll tag along with Alondra. Never can be too safe!" He suggested. Marc and Cain's heads turn towards Cage as he came into the house. Marc pondered for a moment. If they hadn't done anything all day he was sure they wouldn't be doing much now.

"Sure, I'll feel better if someone rode into town with her." Marc nodded. Cain continued to stare at him, then remembering his manners introduced himself.

"I'm Cain her Uncle!" He walked over to him with an extended hand. Cage took it, and felt the strong grip with a slight pressure on it as a warning.

"Cage!" He replied taking what Cain was giving.

"Come on Cage, I'm anxious to see my Aunt. You two can play the macho game later." She told him as she pushed her way between her Uncle and Cage.

"Alondra did Geri mention anything about going out of town to you?" Marc asked.

"No, not a word! Why?" She turned to her father.

"We were heading over there, but Cage informed us she had gone out of town. That was a little sudden, don't you think?" He looked over to her feeling she knew her better than anyone since she had spent the most time with her.

"Why were you going over there? Is there something I should know?" She looked at her Father, then to her Uncle. Cain headed towards the door and stood there.

"Nah! Nothing to worry about. Just wanted to thank her personally for being so considerate by sending her handyman over to check the place out." Marc didn't want her to know about his concerns for Geri's safety.

"Oh okay. Maybe it was a spur of the moment thing. You know with everything that was going on." She reassured him, and then grabbed Cage's hand leading him out the house. Cain walked to the door, and stared out watching them get into the SUV.

"Our little girl is growing up!" Cain said sadly as the SUV disappeared from his sight. Marc smiled, and shook his head at his brother.

"Growing? More like grown!" He informed his brother. He saw Cain's chest inhale and exhale. Then he turned away, and sat down near the phone. Where could Geri have gone without telling anyone? Oh yeah, except her handyman! Maybe Alondra was right.

He picked up the phone, and called Ben. He owed him after sending that demon to his house. He asked him some pertinent questions; got the information he needed, and sat back in the chair. Cain had come in on his conversation, and sat down listening.

"What is it? You have that far away confused look." Cain asked. Marc was in deep thorough, trying to cypher through what was told to him by Ben. Then he looked over to his brother remembering their earlier conversation.

"Didn't' you tell me Deidra's father got a called from some FBI agent who wanted to ask him some questioned about her?" Marc asked. Cain nodded his head wondering what this had to do with Geri.

"The FBI agent. You said she!" Marc reminded him.

"Yeah that's what Ben said." Cain still not getting where this was all leading.

"Wait, I'm going to call Deidra's father, and pretend to be looking for my agent." Cain sat down confused with his brother's actions. Marc dialed the number Ben had given him.

"Hello! One of my agents was coming out to interview a Mr. Elliott concerning an ongoing investigation." He started. Cain shook his head almost laughing. His brother has looked at too many spy movies.

"I haven't been able to contact her all day. Is she still there?" He continued the farce. Then grew quiet as the person answered.

"Okay, thank you. I'll just wait for her arrival." Marc told them then hung up the phone. He was silent for a moment as Cain watched, and waited for him to say something

"He said Ms. Paine had left some time ago!" Marc relayed to Cain.

"Ms. Paine?" Cain was confused.

"That's Geri's last name." Marc informed him. Cain thought for a moment allowing this to register, then his mouth flew open!

"Wait a minute! Are you thinking what I'm thinking?" Cain asked him. Marc nodded his head bewildered by this revelation.

"Either Geri's going to get herself in a lot of trouble posing as a Fed or else…"

"Or else?" Marc couldn't let it come out.

"She really is F.B.I." Cain concluded.

Chapter 11

Alondra drove down the road rambling on, but Cage was half listening. He was worried about Geri, and they were nearing the path that lead to her house. He debated whether or not to get Alondra to take him by and see if she had returned or if indeed Deidra had caused her some harm. As they neared the road he got an idea.

"Oh shucks!" he yelled.

Alondra eyes darted over to him.

"What?" She continued to drive.

"I just remembered I left my other tool box over Geri's. You think you could swing by there for a minute?" Alondra pulled to the side.

"Cage! Don't play with my intelligence. You just told my Dad and Uncle, she was out of town." Alondra reminded him. He looked at her then out the window.

Damn. Forgot about that, he said to himself.

"Well, yeah! But I left it out in the garage so I can run in, and out without disturbing anything. Alondra looked at him with some suspicion, and knew he was lying.

Okay, she thought to herself. I'll play along with him.

"Sure!" she said, driving further up, and turned into the path. They went a distance before coming into the opening.

Deidra was sitting and waiting for Geri's return. She was getting very impatient wondering what was taking her so long to get back. Then she heard the car coming into the yard, and ran to the curtain peering out.

Damn! She said to herself, turning away from the window. Alondra! Then an idea flowed through her head. Some insurance Geri will be cooperative, so she waited for her to get out the car, and come up to the door.

Double damn, she yelled in her mind. She wasn't alone. Who was that with her? That plan was a bust. But that's okay. Plan A was still in effect. She continued to stare out through the curtains concealed, and watching their every move.

Alondra turned off the vehicle as Cage jumped out, and ran up the porch. Alondra exited the SUV, and stood staring at him. He began to knock on the door pacing up, and down the porch knocking nervously on the door, and pacing some more. She took this in. He jumped off the steps, and ran to the back. She could hear him pounding, and calling from there. She leaned on the car, and observed his behavior. Why did she get the feeling there was more going on between her Aunt and Cage then met the eye? He finally came back around the front and stared.

"I thought the tool box was in the garage?" She looked towards the garage, then back to him. He turned his head to look at her, and she saw something there that made the hairs on her neck stand up.

"I just remembered I left them in the house." He answered with a shaken voice.

"Well, it doesn't matter. Geri isn't home remember?" She reminded him of what he had told them. He turned and walked silently back to the SUV. Alondra got back in, started up the car, and then drove away. Cage continued to stare at the house, and hoped everything was well with Geri.

Deidra took a peek out the curtain, and watched the two leave unknowing she was in the house. She moved away from the window, and went back to the sofa.

Soon, very soon she will have her biggest possession.

Geri went through the contents of the envelope given to her by Mr. Elliott. She couldn't believe the overwhelming evidence this man had. He had his daughter followed since the time she left the institution, and until now. She shook her head. All the people whose lives had been destroyed by this woman over the past three years. She was above deranged.

She was snapped out of her thoughts by the overhead intercom announcing their approached to the airport, and for them to fasten their seat belts. She looked out the window to the jigsaw puzzle representing her home. She was anxious for the plane to land, and could only hope nothing had happen while she was away.

Cage would have called her if it had, then a thought touched her mind. She reached into her purse to give Cage a quick update, and see if everything was going well. She continued searching her purse realizing her cell phone wasn't there. She didn't have it. In her haste to leave she had forgotten it. Anything could have happened. She pressed her head back into the headrest. This was depressing. She had to get home to catch the Viper, and save her family. She just prayed she wasn't too late.

Chapter 12

Marc paced back and forth thinking. Cain sat back on the sofa watching him. The two had derived that Geri had left town in search of information on Deidra. Either posing as a FBI agent or she actually was one.

"Here's what we have. Geri was posing as an agent to get something on Deidra!" Marc stopped in the middle of his pacing.

Cain leaned in towards his brother. "Yeah! But wouldn't' the old man be smart enough to check out her credentials?" Cain injected. Marc stood for a moment, thinking about what Cain had just said. Then his eyes went over to him.

"Right! I'm sure he did!" Marc stared at Cain who nodded his head.

"Then that means only one thing. She is a Fed!"
Cain stood and began to mimic his brother's pacing.
Marc crossed his arms over his chest stroking his
goatee.

"Maybe she's just vacationing since she just
retrieved her family home. Well, at least part of it.
We're living on the other part." Marc informed Cain
who stopped, and looked confused. Marc smiled.

"The Anderson land and this one once belonged
to Clarice and Geri's family. It's a long story." Marc
told him. Cain reclaimed his seat on the sofa as a cue
he wanted to hear it. Marc shook his head, and began
to explain to his brother.

"Their Father became ill. He had to sell the land,
and they moved to the city. A few years later the
father died, and Geri ran off with some man old
enough to be her father. You know that' part. I later
met Clarice. The two kept in touch by letters and
phone calls." Marc took a seat in a chair. Cain shook
his head.

"Did you ever talk to her?" Cain asked. Marc
shook his head.

"No! It wasn't' that much calling. Only when
Clarice felt lonely. Like whenever I went out of town
on business. They both discovered they were

pregnant at the same time right after their mother's death. You know the rest." Marc told him. Cain left his seat and stood silently.

"This is so confusing. What if she is on a case that involves Deidra, and the husband who died?" Cain thinking out loud, trying to make sense of all that had come about the last few days.

"But didn't' you say Ben told you that her father got a call from the FBI person in regards to the death of the husband?" Marc reminded Cain whose eyes brighten.

"Yeah!" He answered snapping his fingers. Marc ran over to the phone, and called the airport to inquire about a flight, then quickly scribbled down the information slamming the phone down, and rushing for the front door with Cain following him.

"Where are we going?" Cain closed the door and locking it. Marc was already getting in the driver's seat of the Car.

"To the airport to catch Geri!" He informed Cain as he got in the passenger side of the vehicle. Marc had turned the car on and was heading out.

"Then what?" He asked.

"I don't know Cain! I just don't know!" Marc admitted. Cain turned his head from his brother to leave him to his thoughts, and stared straight ahead.

The plane had to circle a few more times. It moved away from the airport, and cleared the air space until they could land. Geri was losing her mind, and wanted to get home to her family if she still had one. Who knows what that woman was planning? After a half hour of extra flying the plane was cleared for landing. It made the turn back towards the airport, and lined itself up with the runway, then slowly began to descend. Each minute that went by felt like years to Geri, then she felt the plane coming down and the bump as the plane's wheels hit the runway. This gave her some relief causing her to finally exhale.

Once on solid ground she stared out the window as the plane slowed down, and she could make out what had once been a blur. It taxied towards the terminal, and came to a complete stop! She sighed loudly. The overhead intercom announced that they could unfasten their seat belts which Geri did with haste, and as soon as the doors were opened she was the first to jump to her feet, and spill into the aisle pushing her way through the passengers, and down the ramp plowing through the crowd. She was a desperate woman. She hailed down a cab on the outside of the busy airport, told the driver where to go, and how much she would pay him if he got there as fast as he could. He sped away.

Just then, Cain and Marc drove up to the curb. Marc jumped out and Cain slid over to the driver's side.

"I'll go in and see if I can find her." Marc yelled back to him. Cain nodded his head, and watched the towering figure of his brother scanning the crowd, then go up to an information desk and ask a question, then turn around parting the crowd as he made his way back to the car.

"She already left. Her plane landed minutes ago. She may have just left." Marc informed Cain as he opened the door and jumped in. At that moment they heard a loud crash before their car plunged forward, and caused them to fall into the dashboard.

"What the Hell!" Marc yelled looking back. Cain jumped out of the car, and rushed to the back of it. Marc soon followed. Someone not watching what they were doing had crashed into the back of the Car.

"Look what you did to my car!" Cain roared inspecting the damage. The man had slowly exited his car as his eyes grew larger than life when he saw the two giants emerge from the car he had just collided into. He had been on the phone, and not paying attention to what he was doing.

"Damn! I don't need this shit!" Marc yelled putting his hands on his hips. He looked in the direction of his home, and Geri! Then away and down to the ground dejected. But high hopes ruled the day as he saw something heading his way that could help him in his quest.

"Hey stop!" He yelled with outstretched hands to the oncoming yellow cab. The cab came to a screeching halt just inches from the huge man standing in the middle of the street, and directly in his path. Marc rested his hands on the hood of the cab staring down the man inside who was already holding the full bladder that threaten to flow at this moment in time. Marc stood straight up coming to his full height, and walked around to the passenger side of the taxi. The driver's eyes followed Marc's every movement as he opened the door, stepped in causing the cab to rock. The driver looked out the corner of his eyes hearing the door slam.

"Take me to Mockingbird Lane!" The sound of his voice was just as intimidating as his size. It shook

the cabbie's foundation. He didn't have to say it twice
before the cabbie lifted his feet off the brakes without
any hesitation.

"Marc! I'll be there as soon as I take care of this
here! Good luck, brother!" Cain hollered at his
brother as the cab started off.

"Wait!" He said touching the shoulder of the
cabbie whose foot hit the brakes, and caused the cab
to jerk forward.

"Okay! Let the police know what we suspect!"
He yelled out of the window. Cain gave a quick wave,
then turned back to the person who had rammed the
back of his car.

Chapter 13

Cage made his way through the back way of Geri's ranch heading for her house a road he had often taken, since Geri called him. He had thought he spotted someone peeking out of the window as they drove away, and a jeep parked inconspicuously behind a tree in the far back when he had went around to knock on the door. He informed Alondra of his suspicion, and told her to go to town to notify the locals. After a few minutes of arguing he had to tell her who he really was, and why he was there. He left out the part about Geri also being a Federal Agent. He felt she should be the one to tell her family. But he put emphasis on how dangerous Deidra was. Reluctantly, she went on to town. She had argued she could call with her cell phone, and come with him. But he wouldn't have it. He explained to her it would distract him worrying about her, and that's something he didn't need.

He made his way up to the field and over the hill to the backside of the house, and sat observing things for some time trying to detect any movement in the house. He could see someone moving from the kitchen towards the living area. And with his keen eyes he could make out it wasn't Geri they were too tall which left only one person, Deidra! He took this time to move towards the other side of the house using the setting sun as his shield, and came around the side furthest from the living room knowing no one could detect him from there.

He eased himself upon the porch, and went to the room where he saw the silhouette entering. Just as he thought, it was Deidra walking around, and from this view he couldn't spot Geri anywhere so he crawled underneath the window, and peered in the other direction. No Geri in sight. He sighed with relief, and from what he could get from Deidra's body language she was alone, and waiting. Was she lying in wait for Geri?

He quietly moved around to the part of the house never used. Geri had told him she didn't quite know what to do with this part of the house. It had been her family's rooms. He quietly jimmied the window open and slowly lifted it, then silently made his way inside, and turned to let it down when he felt something was off. He froze hearing movement from outside. He pulled his gun, and braced himself to confront them. A shadow came pass the window, and paused for a few moments. He wondered how Deidra saw him. He was the best when it came to these things.

He watched as the figure came back to the window, and began to lift it up, then the body poured into the room clumsily. He took cover in the shadow of a corner observing their movements as they crawled in, landed on the floor of the room, and came to their feet searching the dark room.

He relaxed letting a small sigh escape, and holstered his gun. His record remained unblemished. Deidra hadn't discovered him coming to the house. It was someone he had sent for back up, and decided to follow him.

"Alondra!" He whispered grabbing her from behind, and covering her mouth with his hand. She struggled for a moment before finally planting an elbow in a certain spot of his side. He released her instantly bending over, and cringing in pain. Her father had taught her that move.

"Let that be a lesson to you to never grab a girl from behind. Especially one who is scared." She scolded him. He looked up to her, and started to say something when the lights in the room came on. They paused for a moment, and then turned their heads to see in the middle of the doorway stood Deidra with a gun in her hand, and pointed at Cage's head.

"Well, well! Now what do we have here? What a pair! My dear step-daughter and who are you?" She looked Cage over. But before he could answer she cut him off.

"It doesn't matter! I thought I heard some noise coming from back here when I came closer I heard you two going on in here. Toss that gun this way." She ordered him. He did as asked.

"You two will be my insurance policy." She told them, and picked up the gun waving hers directing them out of the room.

"I told you, you would distract me!" He whispered in her ear as he walked up to her.

"Do something!" She whispered back. He let out a huge sigh. She's been watching too many movies.

"No talking!" She said, backing out of the doorway, and into the hall. She didn't want either to get too close to her. Then she made a gesture towards the front of the house. He gave Alondra a gentle nudge as an 'I told you so'. She elbowed him with less pressure than before as a warning.

Chapter 14

Geri stared out the window of the cab as it made its way towards her house. She was thinking about everything she had been told by Mr. Elliott. Deidra was a psycho case from a child. Sort of a bad seed as to say. The sun was making its way behind the horizon. She wanted to get home, and take a nice hot bath to relax her nerves. But she needed to call Cage first to let him know what she found out about Deidra, and get an update of his day. Suddenly a flash of light caught her from the side. She straightened up, and looked around.

"Wait!" She yelled to the cabbie. He immediately put on brakes.

"I thought I saw something off the road. Back up would you?" She said turning around in her seat. He did as asked. She looked off the road in the direction of the light.

"Stop!" She told him, and jumped from the car before he could come to a full stop. She grabbed something out of her purse, and proceeded to investigate the object of the light. It was the SUV sitting off the road. She slowly approached it with gun in hand, and heart pounding. What was Alondra's vehicle doing here? She walked over to it, and peered inside for any foul play, but it was empty. Then she moved around it cautiously searching the surrounding area. Nothing seemed to warrant any struggle. The SUV was locked. Then she saw the footprints of two people heading out on foot towards her ranch.

"Why are they going to my ranch on foot? Did the car go out on them again?" she asked. Then a voice interrupted her thoughts.

"Is everything all right?" The driver had gotten out of the car, and was standing off the road watching her. She was heading back towards him.

"I need you to go back to town, and inform the police they are needed at Mockingbird Lane!" She

340

instructed as she walked by him to the taxi removing her purse, and briefcase from it.

"You gonna be okay?" He asked staring at her tucking the gun in her belt.

"Very!" She said, and headed towards the SUV. He stared after her for a moment, then jumped in the car making a U-Turn in the middle of the road, and headed back towards town. Geri threw her things under the SUV for safe keeping, then started out towards her ranch. She had a gut feeling something wasn't right. The taxi was nearing town when he saw his brother in the taxi heading out of town. He waved him down. The other came to a stop in the middle of the road. Marc could feel his temper rising.

"Hi," he said looking inside the others taxi, and saw the man nearly taking up the whole back seat.

"I'm kind of in a hurry here! I'll talk to you later!" The man said nervously.

"Yeah me too! I just wanted to warn you that there's a woman back there that I let off the road. She was carrying a gun. There was this SUV she spotted, and told me to go straight for the police to tell them what happened." He told his brother. Marc heard what he had said, and got of the car rushing over to the other taxi.

"Take me where you dropped her off, and you go get the police." Marc threw around the orders, and then jumped into the other's taxi. Both taxis made U-turns in the road and headed for their destinations.

Geri came up back of her ranch, and paused looking down at the house. She could see a flicker of light now that the sun had set. She didn't remember leaving a light on. Then she spotted movement, and could barely make anything out, but three silhouettes passing a window. She ran swiftly across the open field, and came up the other side of the house quietly moving in the direction the three were heading, and stopped to make out who exactly were in there. She heard them talking, and could make out one was Deidra.

"Alondra," she whispered. They seem to be arguing about something.

"That girl is going to get a good talking to, she shouldn't be in there." She said softly to herself, and the other shadow she saw had to be Cage's.

Boy am I going to kick his ass for putting my niece's life in danger, she said to herself. Though she probably already figured out that this was more of Alondra's idea than his. The women voices grew louder as Cage's voice joined them. He was trying to get Alondra to calm down. Suddenly, there was silence. She got an eerie feeling this was the quiet before the storm. She peered into the window trying to get a definite location of where everyone was situated. She could see Deidra had a gun, and was slowly stalking up to Alondra. Geri moved back from it, and braced herself against the wall. She took in a few long breaths then relaxed. She knew it was now or never, and slowly moved pass the window. Cage had seen the dark flash by while they were talking, and knew it had to be only one person. Geri! He tried to buy her some time by stepping between Deidra and Alondra. Geri eased up on the porch, and gave a quick glance into the window to see how close Deidra had gotten to Alondra. She saw Cage had come between the two women, and had nonchalantly looked over her way.

"Good boy!" She murmured. He knows she's there.

In the distance, sirens could be heard. Deidra turned her head alerted by the sounds, and that's when Geri made her move kicking in the door with gun pointed at Deidra. But at the same time Alondra had plans of her own, and leaped towards Deidra in her distraction by the sirens. But just as quick Cage grabbed her, and flung them backwards into the table causing the lamp to come crashing to the floor. The room went black, except for the flashes from the gunshots!

The cabbie had dropped Marc off where he had left Geri. He paid him and searched the area spotting the top of the SUV, and headed towards it. While he was looking it over noted the doors were locked, and Geri's things were underneath it. He took them from under the car, reached in his pocket for his keys, opened the door tossing Geri's briefcase on the passenger side and was just starting the car up when he heard the sirens, and saw the flashing red lights racing down the road in the direction of Geri's place. He took off over the field knowing he would get there before them. It wasn't long before he pulled up to the open field outback, and saw the lights on in the house, then go pitch black. And what he heard next made his blood curdle.

Gunshots!

He put the SUV in full speed driving like a madman up to the house facing the headlights towards it to see what was going on inside. He jumped out, and ran upon the porch peering inside.

"Geri!" he yelled. At this moment, the police cars poured into the huge open space in front of the house. They came out with guns in hand. Marc was already in the house looking around. Deidra lay in a pool of blood, Alondra was being held by Cage, and Geri was on the floor holding her shoulder with little trickles of blood flowing between her fingers.

"Geri!" He ran to her, and picked her up in his arms. She looked at him half conscious.

"Marc? What are you doing here?" She said before passing out. The police were creeping into the house with guns in front of them. Cage left Alondra, and began talking to them flashing his badge, and then moved over to Deidra, and placed two fingers to the side of her neck. She was still alive, but barely.

"We're going to need an ambulance. This one is still alive, but not for long." He told them. Marc took a seat on the sofa holding Geri in his lap. Alondra ran to get a towel, and came back to him.

"Press this against the area. It will stop the blood, and clot it." She instructed him. He took it, and placed it as she had said, then his eyes went back up to her. She knew what was coming.

"You're grounded, young lady. What are you doing here?" He asked, eyes glistening. Cage came over to them. Marc's eyes narrowed.

"Wait Daddy! Cage tried to get me to go to the police. I followed him." She explained before her father blew up. He looked at him hard, and then his eyes went back to Geri in his arms.

"I gather the two of you are partners or something like that? And this was a case you were on." Marc deducted eyes still regarding Geri. Cage shifted from one foot to the other. He didn't want to reveal much while Geri wasn't able to defend herself.

"Yes Sir, I am a Federal Agent. But I feel it's Geri's place to explain everything to all of you." He said this and walked away hoping that would end it. The Paramedics entered the room. Two went to Deidra and began tending to her. Marc rose to his feet with Geri, and walked outside to another ambulance coming up. He stood there while they brought out the gurney, then gently placed her on it, and backed away watching as they loaded her up.

He turned to his SUV when he saw them bringing another gurney out of the house. It was carrying Deidra with the sheet covering her. Her long psychotic struggle had ended. His heart felt a little for her. He turned away and made his way to the SUV.

At that moment, Cain drove up jumping from his Car, and walked up to his brother, then looked around at all of the commotion. His eyes caught them loading the covered body in the ambulance, and looked to his brother who seemed very distraught, and placed a gentle hand on his shoulder.

"Geri?" He asked, but not sure if he wanted to hear the answer. They had just found the one person who could connect them to someone they had lost, and who was so dear to them only to lose them too.

"No! Deidra. Geri just left. She had been shot, and could have been killed Cain! I don't know!" He said and drove away from the crazy scene.

"Uncle Cain!" Alondra called to him as she came out of the house with Cage at her side whose badge was hanging from his shirt pocket to identify his presence.

"You're a Fed too?" Cain shouted. Cage stopped a short distance away.

"Uncle Cain, please don't embarrass me." She walked up to him, and gave him a big hug.

"Young lady you're grounded for life." Cain shot Cage a look.

"You're too late, Daddy already grounded me, and I also explained that Cage tried to get me to go to the police, but I followed him." Alondra explained once again. Cain just stared ahead.

"How bad was Geri hurt?" Marc hadn't divulged that information being too shaken up.

"She was shot in the shoulder." Alondra informed him. Cain shook his head. What a crazy last few days. It felt like a hurricane hit them.

Hurricane Deidra!

Blair was in her bed when she overheard talking outside her door. It was about some shootout at the Anderson's ranch. They said one person was dead, and another shot. They were on their way to the emergency room.

"Geri!" She whispered to herself. Deidra must have gone after her.

Oh No! Alondra was there too. What if she killed one, and injured the other. She unhooked herself from the monitors, and took the IV solution off the pole, then slowly walked over to the wheelchair, and sat down. She couldn't wait for Cain or Marc to tell her anything. She headed down to wait in the ER area. She had to know. At that moment, the siren announced the arrival of the ambulance. She braced herself for the worst, and watched as the Doctors and Nurses assisted the Attendants in unloading the gurney. They race through the door. Blair saw the face. It was Geri!

"Wait!" she called out.

"Ma'am! We have to get her to surgery immediately." One of the nurses stopped and told her.

"That's my sister-in-law. I need to talk to her." Blair grew anxious. If Geri was alive, then that meant only one thing. Alondra wasn't.

"No! Stop!" The weak voice said. They did as asked. Blair wheeled herself up to the gurney, and stood to her feet to look Geri in the face.

"Alondra?" Her voice cracked, and tears started to stream down her face. Geri weakly looked into her eyes. She had lost a lot of blood.

"She's fine!" She consoled her as she passed out once again.

"Move IT!" The Doctor yelled, and the gurney sped away leaving a relieved Blair standing there. Her baby was fine, she thought to herself.

So who was dead?

Just then, another ambulance came up. Blair sat and watched as they unloaded the gurney, and pulled it slowly into the ER.

"Is this the expired one?" The Nurse asked. The Attendants nodded.

"Take them down to the morgue. We'll wait for the next of kin to come, and make arrangements.

"I'm her kin. May I look at her for one last time?" Blair asked, standing up once again. She lifted the sheet, and stared at the crazy woman who had tried to destroy her family. She felt no love lost for her. She threw the sheet back over her face, and sat down in her wheelchair, then headed off to see how Geri was coming along.

Chapter 15

Marc drove into the garage, and started out of the SUV when his eyes fell on Geri's briefcase. He reached over and picked them up, then left the car, and headed towards the house. He made his way across the open space, stepped onto the porch and looked out at the landscape he always had. Except everything had changed. After a few moments his curiosity got the best of him. He opened the briefcase, and out fell a badge. Geri's!

So she was an agent. So now the thing is, were they just part of a case, and being duped to think she was the long lost sister of Clarice? Or was she truly Clarice's sister?' He thought as he held the badge in his hand.

'My ever cynical Marc! How many times have I told you not to follow your head, but your heart?' The voice flowed ever so gently through his heart. Clarice's voice.

"I don't know Babe! My head is a better judge. My family almost got torn apart by these two women. What am I gonna do?" He was stumped.

'Follow your heart.' The voice repeated as it faded away. Then something happened. He felt something leave him. He didn't know what exactly, but it left a void in his heart. He sat down, and a picture fell out of the briefcase. It was one of Clarice and Geri! It must have been one of them before their father died, before they split up. He hadn't seen this one before, and saw it was one of them younger. They stood side by side with arms draped over each other's shoulder smiling. They seemed so happy, and something tugged at his heart. So much to think about. A car pulled into the yard, and Alondra exited it while it continued on into the garage. She slowly walked over to her father, and took a seat on the rail staring down at him, and could see he was in deep thought. That's when she saw the picture.

"Is that Mom and Aunt Geri?" She jumped down and squat next to her father to get a good look. He looked up to her.

"That' was a very dangerous thing you did tonight." He said softly to her. Cain made his way towards them, and stopped midway hearing his cell phone going off. He opened it and began to talk.

"I know! But I don't know Dad! I think I might be better off going into law enforcement. I think I'll be good at it." She said and waited for him to answer.

"I'm against it, but you have to do what makes you happy. You're grown up, and I can't tell you what to do with your life anymore." Marc rose to his feet studying Cain on the phone.

"All right! I'll let them know." Cain closed the phone, and started towards his brother, and niece.

"That was Blair! She got wind of what happened. Boy, did she chew my butt off. Is it still there?" Cain twisted around to see his butt. Marc just stared. Alondra gave a light chuckle.

"Something else she thought we might want to know. Geri is in surgery. But word is she's gonna be all right." Cain told them.

"What is Blair doing? She's supposed to be in bed resting. I hope you chewed her butt out!" Marc snapped. Cain looked at him strangely.

"No, Bro'! I didn't chew her out for caring about her family." Cain came back at him.

"Family? We're just fine. Did you tell her that?" Marc told him. Cain shook his head.

"Geri was almost killed tonight by a woman YOU married. Wait! Why am I standing here? I'm gonna go to the hospital to be with my wife, and the sister of a very special woman who came into our lives, and now that specialty has graced us once again. I don't want Geri to wake up, and no one is there for her." Cain turned and walked away. Alondra looked at her father for a long time, then she ran pass him after her Uncle Cain.

Marc stood alone on the porch watching as the Car sounded up, and pulled out of the garage disappearing out of his sight. He fell back in his seat on the porch, and bent over cradling his head in his hands. What to do?

Chapter 16

A week later, Geri sat on the bed in her hospital room waiting for Alondra to get her discharge papers, and take her home. She rubbed her shoulder where the stitches were, and adjusted the sling on her arm. Up until the day she had been released, Blair had been her constant visitor along with Cain, Alondra, and Cage. They had been great supporters through this ordeal, except for one. Marc never once came to see about her for whatever his reasons. She sighed as her thoughts were interrupted by the beautiful niece she had come to love dearly. Alondra bounded into the room with a huge smile etched across her face followed by Cage with a wheelchair.

"Ready to go Auntie Geri?" She said proudly and glad she didn't have to pretend anymore. Geri answered by quickly jumping off the bed.

"I won't be needed that." She told him and proceeded to walk out the door, but only to be stopped by Alondra.

"I've already gone a round with him. It's hospital policy. You have to be wheeled out, and once you're out of the building you can do whatever you want. We felt you would feel better if one of us did it so Cage volunteered." Alondra explained. Geri looked from Alondra to Cage, and then nodded in confirmation to what she had just been told.

"Sorry, Geri! This is the only way you can get out of here." He half laughed. Geri didn't find it at all amusing.

"Oh all right! Let's get the hell out of here." She snapped and flopped down in the chair. Alondra couldn't help but chuckle under her breath. Cage gave her a quick smile pushing the chair through the door. On the way home Geri thought of what she would be doing next. Her boss already told her she would be off duty for a few months. Maybe she could take a long vacation. But not until after Alondra goes away for school. She wanted to spend as much time as she could before that.

"So Alondra why don't you tell your Auntie here about your change of plans." Cage broke the silence, bringing her out of her thoughts. Alondra could be heard shifting in the backseat.

"I don't think she wants to hear about my plans right now. I have plenty of time to talk to her about that Cage!" She had a bit of anger in her voice. Geri looked at Cage who was smiling, and got the hint the two have become very close.

"No Alondra I would love to hear it." She turned in her seat, and looked at her niece who was looking strangely at her.

"What's the matter? Is there something I missed?" She looked back at Cage who shrugged his shoulder.

"I feel your niece should be the one to tell you." He looked over to Geri. She turned her head back to Alondra, and got this sinking feeling in her stomach. Alondra looked down at the floor, then out the window.

"I wanted to wait a while before I told you, but big mouth here decided to open the can of worms so

here goes. I've decided not to go to college after all!"
She started. Geri's eyebrows rose.

"And how does your father feel about this?" She
inquired. Alondra looked at her.

"He's okay with it and accepting it, but really
doesn't like it." She informed her. Geri stared in space
for some time, and then turned around in her seat.

'What is Marc thinking?' She shook her head very
confused with his reaction to this decision.

"Tell her the rest Alondra!" Cage interjected.
This time Alondra slapped him gently in the back of
the head causing Geri to stared at the two, and
observe their interaction. Yes, these two have really
gotten close, and she noted Cage was smiling from
ear to ear.

'Kids!' She thought. But was curious to what it
was that Alondra didn't want her to know.

"There's more?" She finally asked. Alondra
turned towards the window not wanting to see her
Aunt's face.

"I'm not going to school because I'm going to be
an FBI agent," she said quickly, then braced herself
for the fallout. First there was this foreboding quiet
that flowed through the car.

Then!

"STOP THIS DAMN CAR!" Geri's voice exploded like an atomic bomb. Cage's foot slammed on the brakes causing the car to come to a screeching halt, and no sooner than that Geri had spilled out of it slamming the door behind her. She stomped back and forth yelling profanities.

"Wow! I didn't know she could get that angry!" Alondra stared out the window.

"Oh this is nothing! Wait until she gets finish. That's when the fun starts." Cage warned her.

"Oh!" She said, watching her aunt flinging one arm around, and mouth moving faster than a locomotive. After a few moments of releasing days of anger, Geri composed herself and started back towards the car.

"Oh boy not good!" Cage gave Alondra a heads up on her Aunts demure as she approached the car. Alondra took this in mind, and sat back in her seat still as a statue watching as the door open, and her Aunt entered the car calm as a cucumber. Cage started it up again, and came to the road leading up to Geri's ranch, but as he started up into it.

"No take me to Marc. We have something to discuss." She commanded. Cage didn't argue as he could tell by her quiet voice she was really angry, and he felt better Marc to be at the other end of the anger than him. Alondra sunk down in her seat covering her face.

Chapter 17

Marc sat up in his room at his desk pondering over two pictures. One of Clarice and him on their wedding day. The other with Clarice, and Geri standing side by side smiling at some event. The house was dead silent and empty. Cain and Blair were over Geri's planning a welcome home party. He had elected to stay out of it. In his mind he wasn't sure of his feelings for Geri, and didn't know if his love for her was due to her similarity to Clarice or because of herself.

That's was one of the reasons he didn't call or go to see her while she was in the hospital. He felt it was best he kept his distance. Yeah, he knew for Clarice and Alondra's sakes he should try to make her feel comfortable with being a part of the family. But how was he to do this knowing she would only take it to mean something else? Something he knew he couldn't give to her now knowing that she wasn't some stranger who dropped into their lives, but the sister of the one woman he has loved for all this time. He wasn't ready to give that up or fill that void.

That's why marrying Deidra was so easy. He had no real feelings for her. He had to admit he used her as much as she used him. So he couldn't be angry at her after all the information on her came out. She was just someone to keep him from coming home to an empty bed at night, and to keep the single women at bay. It was safe to be with her knowing that she would never threaten his love for Clarice or help him to move on.

Geri on the other hand was another story. She could and probably would be the one to accomplish what he feared. His thoughts were interrupted by his door being swung open, and crashing into the wall.

"What in the hell is wrong with you?" Geri barged into the room making Marc jumped to his feet, and stared down at the little fury yelling at him.

"What in the–" he started. He was confused and peered past her seeking Alondra's whereabouts. He knew Cage and her were picking Geri up from the hospital.

"You're really going to let this go without saying anything?" She continued pacing back and forth in front of him.

"What?" He was still confused. Then, an idea suddenly came to him as to what this was all about.

So he thought.

"Oh I see!" He stared down at her figuring she was talking about him not contacting her while she was in the hospital.

"Do you now?" She turned to him, and caught the expression on his face.

"I'm sorry I didn't' come to see you at the hospital," he said. He put one hand on his hip, and gestured with the other. Her eyes watched his hand moving in front of her face, then moved up to meet his and what he saw in them made him move the hand out of her face without any hesitation.

"You arrogant, pompous, oaf!" she yelled. "Do you really think I would be this angry because you didn't come to see me in the hospital?" She walked away from him, and then turned around staring at him for a long time reading his face. She shook her head at him with a great disappointment. Marc stared at her blankly.

"Well, what' else could there be?" he had to ask.

"You know," she half-smiled, then looked to the far wall forming the right words to say that would have an impact on his ego, and make him realized the severity of it all.

"I thought you were someone special due to all that my sister had told me. Then I met you, and those feelings didn't change. They only grew. But after the last couple of weeks, and the things I've seen you do made me realize that, that was someone completely different she spoke to me about." Geri turned back around eyes fixed on him with a lot of regret in her heart, as something slowly flowed from her. He wasn't the one she loved. That man was just a fantasy she had created. He stood silently allowing all she had said to him sink in.

"Then why did you come?" He gazed on her with a new respect. She was moving toward the door, and slightly turned to the side to address him.

"Your daughter, and my niece, plans not on going to a traditional college, but to pursue a career in the FBI. She said you didn't say much about her decision. Maybe you should." She informed him. He tilted his head to the side.

"She has a mine of her own. She's a lot like her mother and aunt. You were the reason she decided. You're one, so what's the problem?" He challenged her. She paused for just an instant, then turned fully around to face him, and made a couple of steps towards him. She wanted him to get what she had to say.

"You see this here?" She pointed to the wound on her shoulder.

"Could just have easily been there!" Then she rested her hand over her chest where her heart was still beating.

"Then we wouldn't be having this conversation. That's how it is." Her eyes never released his as he tensed a little with this revelation, and a peek into the life she had lived for some time.

"So you may want to show a little more interest in her, and not so much in yourself. After all, you lost a wife. You don't want to lose a daughter too." She slowly backed away staring him down one last time, then turned to walk out of his room disappearing through the door.

He stood for a few moments, before Alondra rushed in having heard everything that had been said. His eyes regarded his daughter with so much love as they captured her for a moment, then he gathered her in his arms as they held each other for some time. They will discuss her decision later. Right now all he wanted was just to hold her close, and knew no matter what it was her decision to make.

Chapter 18

Geri had walked out of Marc's room, and ran into
Alondra. They stared at each other for a length of
time, and then Geri walked over to her niece, and
stroked her arm gently. Alondra placed her hand over
her aunt's hand. She was happy for her
protectiveness, and having her around has made her
feel close to the mother she never knew.

Geri left her niece, and started down the stairs
where Cage stood at the bottom waiting for whatever
may occur. She paused in the middle of the steps
hearing Alondra's footsteps going into her father's
room, and then continued onward passing Cage as he
watched her go out the door. He turned his head up

the stairs thinking, and then he ran to catch up with Geri who was already in the car waiting.

"You all right?" He asked, starting up the car, and steering it away from the house.

"Yeah, I'm just dandy." She said, looking out the window. Cage took a quick glance over to her, then back to the road.

"Cain and Blair are at your place. We were going to give you a welcome home party. I thought I should tell you so you can decide if you feel up to it." Cage told her. She shifted in her seat bringing her hand up to her mouth.

"It's okay! I don't want to be alone. A party with people who care may be what the doctor ordered," she said with a touch of sarcasm in her voice. He could tell by her tone that there was something more bothering her than Alondra's choosing to become an agent.

"You know, Geri, I spent some time with your niece, and she's a hell of a girl or young woman. You don't have to worry about her. She has a good head on her shoulder, and Marc did a damn good job raising her." Cage broke the silence, and wanted to reassure Geri that Alondra was wise beyond her years.

She seemed to allow this to register before she turned her head to him.

"I know he has along with Cain and Blair. She is wonderful, and I know my sister would be very proud of her. But it's just that..." Geri couldn't find the words.

"Too much like you?" Cage finished for her. Geri straighten up in her seat.

"What do you mean?" She asked a little annoyed. Cage pulled the car over to the side of the road, and shut it off turning to face her.

"You can get as angry with me as you want, but you are going to hear me out." He started. Geri just stared, stunned.

"Alondra isn't you or her mother. She is a combination of you both along with her father. She's not going to run away from pain, and do something stupid. Not that I'm saying what are you did was, but that she's not going to. Look how she handled her father marrying Deidra?" He reminded her. If she was going to do anything stupid, wouldn't that had warranted it? Geri thought for a moment.

"Yeah, I guess. I thought with everything she was doing was the same as what I did." Geri looked at him.

"But then you know she wouldn't. There is something else bothering you. Spill!" He stared at her knowingly. Geri turned away from him eyes fixed on the road ahead.

"Nothing! Take me home please!" She spoke barely above a whisper.

"No Jerry! Not until we get this settle. It's not about Alondra as much as it's about Marc not coming to see you in the hospital." He laid it out on the line. The statement hit home and caused her to snap her head around to stare out the side window. She didn't want him to see the tear forming in her eyes.

"It's okay Geri! We've been partners too long not to know what's eating away at the other." She turned to smile at him. He was right. They had grown a bond to know each other. He continued onward to her house.

Chapter 19

Cain and Blair had prepared Geri's house for her homecoming. Cain had filled her in on everything from Geri being Clarice's younger sister, how this land had belonged to the sisters' family, about the dad getting sick, and selling the farm, then moving to the city.

"Wow!" Blair shook her head sipping some punch she had prepared. Cain took the bottle of beer to his lips and took a swig.

"So she's been trying to find us all this time, and it took that psycho to lead her to us." Blair rose from the sofa, and walked over to the window staring out.

"Yeah. I guess in a way we owe Deidra." Cain injected. Blair slowly turned her head towards her husband, and nodded her head after thinking about what he had said.

"I guess in a way we do." She concurred. Then her head turned back to the window hearing a car approaching.

"It's them!" She ran over to Cain, and waited for the sister of her closet friend to enter. The door opened, and in walked Geri with Cage. Cain and Blair looked at the two with smiles, then past them.

"Where's Alondra?" Blair asked going to the door, and peering out.

"Oh she's coming. She wanted to stop by her house, and pick up the SUV." Geri wanted to advert any further questioned. She wasn't up to going through the emotional replay of the events. She walked over and took a seat. Blair came to join her.

"Cain filled me in on everything. Wow! Clarice's little sister. Who would have thought?" Blair beamed. Geri smiled.

"Me! I searched for all of you for so long. But the names had changed, and that was then, this is now." Geri nodded her head. Satisfied everything turned out okay. Well, almost everything.

"Everything looked nice. Thank you so much for all of this. You don't know how much I needed this today being surrounded by people who care." The tears began to form in her eyes. Blair looked at her, then to Cage who went to get her something to drink.

"Here Geri, drink this." He handed her the glass.

"You know what, why don't we get something to eat? I'm sure we're all hungry." Blair suggested.

"Starting the party without me?" Alondra walked through the door. Cain strolled over to the door, and peered out hoping his brother had come to join them. He has been a pure asshole towards Geri who's the sister of the woman he claims to love so much. And further more is very aware Marc loves Geri. Stubborn comes to mind.

"Looking for Dad, huh?" Alondra came up behind her Uncle. He turned his head to stare in her eyes.

"Yeah! For once I wished he didn't' allow his emotions to rule his decisions, but I guess wishes don't always come true." He placed an arm around her shoulders.

"Come on you two, let's get this thing going." Blair hollered over to them. Cain turned to see her moving around doing things.

"I thought I told her....." He started towards as Alondra laughed watching her Uncle scolding her Aunt, and placing her next to Geri on the sofa.

"Just remember you're still mending too. So both you Ladies will be taking it easy. Alondra, Cage and I will serve you Madams." He told them. Geri began to point a finger at Blair giggling like a school girl taunting the other. Blair folded her arms across her chest and pouted. Cage had made his way over to Alondra under the watchful eyes of Cain.

"How was your Dad when you left?" He asked knowing she was concerned about him.

"Quiet. I don't know Cage. Dad loves Geri; I know this. Why is he acting like this towards her?" Alondra began to sniffle. Cage looked around, and saw Cain glaring at him, then turned back to Alondra.

"Come on Alondra. Let's join the party, and for a while forget all the bad stuff. We have plenty of time to solve them. Okay?" He looked in her eyes, and she smiled in agreement. Cain took all of this in. First Geri diverts questioned, and now those two huddle up. He can see Alondra is upset about something. Yeah, something is up, and he plans on getting to the bottle of it.

As the day wore on, Geri seemed a little exhausted from the day's events began to yawn, and lean back into the sofa relaxing. Blair observed this.

"You know maybe we should call it a day." Blair started. Geri sat up and looked at her.

"Oh No! I'm fine. I'm really having fun." Geri didn't want them to leave. She didn't want to be alone to think. This was distracting her from Marc.

"Okay! Only if you go get you a nap and we'll be here when you get up." Blair told her. Geri looked at her, then everyone else in the room who all nodded their heads.

"That sounds like a deal." She rose to her feet, and headed for the hallway stopping at the entrance, and looking back at the room full of people who were there for her. Then her thoughts went to Marc. She broke and turned away leaving them. Blair looked over to Alondra wondering what was going on, and then started to get up to go after her. But Alondra rested her hand on her Aunt's shoulder signaling she would go see about her. Blair looked over to Cain, then Cage searching for an answer.

"What's going on Cage?" He looked over at her, then to the floor.

"Something happened on the way here that was upsetting to her, and having all of you here welcoming her home, and showing her so much love was just too overwhelming." He informed them hoping this would suffice the inquiry, but Cain felt it was more to it than that.

"What happened?" Cain came straight to the point eyes revealing he was not up to any bullshit! Cage looked at him, and took in a deep breath.

"Dad is what happened." Alondra's voice flowed into the room causing Cage's head to swirl in her direction, and relieved at the same time. She took a seat next to her to Blair. Cain nodded his head with this grimace across his face.

"What happened?" Cain asked her with an equally stare as he had given Cage, as he inhaled and exhaled deeply.

"Um!" Alondra started trying to format in her mind how to explain what went on between her father and Geri, and most of why without revealing all.

"What did he do?" Blair stood to her feet angry knowing how he has treated her. He didn't even have the decency to come to the hospital, and see her or call. Nor come over to help them welcome her home after the shooting. She began to feel a little light-headed. Cain noticing this came to her side placing a gentle hand on her shoulder, and helped her back down in her seat.

"Now sit and don't move from that spot until it's time to go home." He ordered. She looked up to him starting to protest, but saw the look in his eyes, and knew it was better to concede.

"Now you two stop with the games, and tell me what did Marc do to upset Geri?'" Cain looked at the two young people with the same eyes he had just given his wife. Cage looked away.

Cage was right. The anger didn't stem as much from the career choice of Alondra as the fact Marc never came to see her while she was mending from the injury. Not even a phone call. Yes it hurts. Maybe this was fate telling her it was wrong to be in love with her dead sister's husband. She hadn't planned on it, but reading the letters her sister had sent her, and seeing how happy he had made her. Caused her to fall in love with him too.

"Why didn't you come to see me in the hospital? Not even a damn phone call. I thought you and I had a friendship at least!" She began to cry until she succumbed to the exhaustion, and drifted off to sleep.

Marc sat alone staring at his wife's picture, and then inadvertently would look over to the picture he that sat next to him. The one of Clarice and Geri. His eyes went upwards. How much he had loved Clarice. But then they fell on Geri, and as much as he didn't want to admit it she had truly filled that void left by the loss of his wife.

"Well Cage told Aunt Geri about......" Alondra paused remembering neither her uncle nor aunt knew about the choice she had made. Cage looked on with interest.

"Aunt Geri?" Blair injected. Alondra looked over to her Aunt, and realized there was another person who was now holding that title. She turned to the one who had been there for her from the time she was a baby, and saw her though everything a child could endure, and much, much more.

"I'm sorry Aunt Blair. I wasn't thinking. I never ever want to hurt you, and if calling her Aunt makes you feel bad, then I won't." She said sadly feeling the tear forming in her eyes. Blair allowed a smile etched across her face, and took her hand brushing the reddish hair back from Alondra's, and gazed into her eyes with all her love. Alondra basked in them feeling the love.

"Baby, you saw it before any of us. From the very first day Geri approached us at the restaurant until now, you felt the connection. She is your Mother, and my dearest friend's sister. I would have it no other way." She assured her, and then Alondra's face lit up like a candle.

"Thank you Auntie." She hugged her Aunt dearly relieved she had taken this stance.

"You do know soon I will be having a baby to tend to, so it looked like we both have new additions to our lives." She reminded her. Alondra smiled nodding her head with the thought of having a cousin to help raise.

"Not to mention you gonna go to college." Cain added. Cage took this time to inject himself into the flow.

"Oh!" He started, as if remembering something.

"Alondra you forgot to tell them!" He added smiling mischievously. Alondra threw him a glare that would match both her Father and Uncle's.

"Yes finish telling us." Cain looked from Cage, then to Alondra who turned her attention from Cage to her Uncle and Aunt. She would deal with him later.

"We were on our way here when she got some news that didn't sit well with her." Alondra drifted off trying to talk around what caused the situation in the first place.

"What bad news? Oh, maybe you can't tell us." Blair asked. But then as an afterthought, repeated the question looking towards Cage.

"Oh no it can be told. Can't it Alondra?" Cage informed them looking at Alondra with this silly grin paste on his face. He was enjoying himself. Alondra knew this and shot him a glare. This time Cain and Blair caught it, and looked to each other sensing something was up with these two.

"I told you two to quit playing games. Get to the point!" Cain's voice boomed causing Blair to sit back on the sofa not wanting this to come her way.

"Okay! But promise me you'll let me finish before you go off." Alondra sped through this sentence. Cain took a deep breath and held it, then allowed it to escape through his mouth knowing if Alondra was rattling on like this; it wasn't going to be good.

"All right I promise." He said through clenched teeth.

"I made a choice a couple of days ago, and Dad knew about it so Cage told Aunt Geri." She paused. Blair shifted on the sofa getting this foreboding feeling, but Cain stood silent trying to keep his promise.

"Go on," is all he would say.

"I decided to forget about college, and pursue the law enforcement. I want to be a FBI agent!" She said this just under her breath. Cain's eyes narrowed as he tried to contain himself.

"What?" Blair screamed jumping to her feet. Cain caught her, and gave her a look encouraging her to reclaim her spot he had put her before.

"Let her finish," he said calmly. But Blair knew better, and so did Alondra.

Maybe it would have been better not to make him promise. At least by now most of his anger would have been exhausted. She thought to herself peering into her Uncle's eyes, and could see he was seething.

"That's about the reaction Aunt Geri had. Boy, can she blow a fuse." Alondra began laughing looking around to everyone, but no one was laughing. Cain and Blair just because they didn't find it amusing at all and Cage because he knew better. Alondra cleared her throat.

Not good. She thought.

"So when she found out Dad knew, and didn't press me on it. She told us to take her over there." Alondra continued.

"Oh!" Blair said knowingly. She would have done the same.

"She jumped out of the car before Cage could stop it, ran into the house and up the stairs, came to Dad's room and swung opened his bedroom door, causing it to slam into the wall, and went off on Dad. At first he thought she was angry because he didn't come to see her at the hospital, but she set him straight, and asked him why he hadn't been mad at her." Alondra reenacted the encounter.

"I'm sure." Blair snorted. Cain folded his arms over his chest still simmering from the revelation of her choice. Alondra avoided eye contact with him.

"And then?" Blair coaching her to continue. Alondra gave her Aunt a quick glance just to see where she stood with her, but she hid what she was feeling.

"After that she left the room. We passed each other in the hall, then she left with Cage, and I went to Dad." She finished. Cain allowed another breath he had been holding out!

Chapter 20

Two weeks passed since Geri's release from the
hospital. Her healing process was coming along as
expected. The wound had become a scar, and she was
now doing therapy, and able to move her arm without
pain, but she has to remember to be careful. She
entered the house after her morning jog, walked over
to the refrigerator, and pulled out a bottle of water,
then took a seat at her kitchen table to get herself a
rest before she took her shower.

Her thoughts automatically went to Marc.
Something else that has been a routine. Even after she
changed her jogging route. She didn't go towards his
ranch any longer. She ran in the opposite direction. It
was too unbearable, though Alondra, Blair, and even

Cain had been her constant. They were always around to make sure she was doing all right. Alondra spent most of her nights with her, and Cage was also there until he was reassigned to another case, and had to go back to D.C. And since she is officially on medical leave there's nothing for her to do but jog, sit, and think.

She put a lot of thought in her next plan of action. She was going to lease her ranch out, and moved back to D.C to be near her job. There was nothing there to keep her, and she could always come back to visit Alondra, Blair, and Cain or better yet have them come visit her. But staying there was not an option. It was too painful. So not to be persuaded by them to stay, she decided to leave them a letter informing them she had gone, and where to contact her. It was the only way to do this.

Marc had been hard to deal with for the last couple of weeks. He'd been grumpy, grouchy, and crabby toward everyone. Cain has promised to drop him on his head if he didn't get his act together. Blair just stayed clear of him since she was pregnant, and one thing you don't do is get an expecting woman upset. Her hormones ruled over her emotions, and who knows what may be the outcome. But one thing is known the perpetrator will get the worst end of it.

Alondra seemed to be the only one he didn't snap at, and had become his confidante. He could let his guard down with her, and allow her into his deepest thoughts save for one. The love he harbored for Geri. It had become increasingly clear what he felt.

He had come to the conclusion of his feelings. It wasn't because she was Clarice's sister, but because she was Geri, and just felt he was betraying his love for Clarice by loving Geri as much as he did. And as much as he tried to hide his feelings the more prominent they became. Alondra knew he cared for her Aunt, but was just too stubborn to do anything about it.

"Cage, how are you?' Geri had phoned him.

"I'm doing okay. Just wrapped up another case, and waiting to be assigned another one. How are you, Geri?" Cage was concerned. He knew her to well. If she was calling him something was up, and that didn't mean a good thing either.

"I'm mending. I'm back to jogging, and can finally move my arm without pain. I finished up therapy yesterday." She walked around holding the phone. Cage sighed.

'This is definitely not good.' Ran through his mind.

"Okay, Geri, whatever it is you're planning, don't do it." He begged her. Geri went over to the door and stared out.

"I need a favor. Can you take a couple of days off? I'll fill you in when you get here." She told him. He jumped to his feet, and ran his hand over his face. She's going to do it. She's going to do what she does best. Run! Before it was different. It was only her she was hurting, but this time she has a family that loves the hell out of her. His thoughts went immediately to Alondra. This will devastate her.

One week later Cage dropped by Alondra's to see how she was doing. He had left Geri to finish her packing. She had leased her place out, and the real estate agent was going to oversee everything for her. His problem wasn't so much as she had to leave, that part he understood that part, but her not telling her family wasn't setting well with him.

"Cage!" she screamed, running through the door and into his arms. Cain was in the garage working on something when Cage drove up, and he saw Alondra's reaction.

He shook his head with a grin, and went back to his business.

"Wow! Where did that come from?" He joked. She'd punched him in the arm.

"Stop playing! What brings you here?" She stared him in the eyes. At that moment, he felt a tingle flow through his body. Then something touched his mind. They had been so caught up with what was going on with the older folks in their lives; they had never explored what they meant to each other. This is something he'll have to deal with later. Right now they have more pressing matters. He gently took her by the arm looking around to assure they were alone, and then led her from the porch, and to the side of the house.

"I'm not supposed to say anything, but I couldn't live with myself if I didn't." He started. The smile slowly left Alondra's face. Something was wrong. Her gut was warning her.

"Go on!" She said softly not sure if she wanted to hear it or not.

"I thought all of you should know Geri is leaving today." He revealed. Alondra's eyes enlarged and her lips parted, as her legs felt as if they would collapse from beneath her as she tried to decipher what was just told to her.

"Leaving? Leaving like what? Going on a vacation? What?" She turned away from him walking, and searching the ground for something or nothing at all.

"Leaving Alondra! Like she leased out her ranch, and moving back to D.C. That's the reason I'm here to take her back with me." Alondra stood silently still trying to comprehend all of this. Tears filled her eyes as it struck her. She was going to lose again. The closest thing to her mom was leaving her. She turned back to him eyes overflowing. She placed the back of her hand over her mouth to prevent the scream pleading for release from escaping, and held her stomach to still the pain that was growing within.

He walked towards her wanting to take her in his arms, but knew better. She wasn't the type to allow a man to comfort her; not one who wasn't her dad or her uncle. Cain had come back out of the garage, and saw they were not on the porch but at the side of the house, and could tell from that distant something was wrong.

This can't be happening, she thought as she peered up into his eyes begging them to comfort her, and tell her that this wasn't so, and that it's a dream she will wake up from, and see everything is as it should be. But they couldn't as she saw they confirmed everything he had said was true. His heart began to sink seeing her so sad and helpless. For the first time since they had met, he'd witness a part of her he hadn't before. Her vulnerability.

"No, Cage. This can't be happening. I just found her, and now she's leaving me?" Then without any more reservation Cage took her in his arms, and held her tightly. Now he knew she meant more to him than he had thought, and may even love her.

He heard the footsteps approaching from behind them with great haste. He knew from the impact to the ground it had to be one or the other of the brothers. If it was the Dad he would give him a piece of his mind, for the pain he was causing the two women in his life who he loved dearly. And if it was the Uncle. Hey, he will have to deal with the fact there will be another man in Alondra's life.

"What's going on? What did you say to her?" Cain's voice enshrouded them. Cage continued to hold Alondra as she sobbed, and found comfort in his arms. He turned to stare in the eyes of the oncoming Cain, and for the first time he knew why Cage was a Federal Agent. He stopped in his tracks, and in his eyes he saw that this day he wasn't backing down.

"Sir! I came to tell all of you something you should know, because I care for Geri, and don't want her to make a big mistake." Cage started. Alondra slowly moved away from him leaving the security of his arms, and turned away to stifle her tears. Cain nodded urging him to continue.

"Geri called me a week ago stating she needed me to take a couple of days off, and that she would fill me in when I got here. I knew she was going to do something crazy. I know her! You don't work together for the years we have, and not know the other." Cage walked pass Cain eyes to the sky. Cain could see the concern on his face.

"I understand." Cain acknowledged.

"I told Alondra she's leaving today, and had leased the ranch out." Cage looked back at Alondra. Cain noted this, and could see this young man cared deeply for his niece.

"My damn brother!" Cain shook his head knowing why all of this had come about. He looked over to Alondra who was still attempting to pull it together.

"Baby I'm sorry! I know how important it was for you to have your mother's sister near." Cain walked up behind her, and put his arms about her.

"It's because of him! I will never forgive him for hurting her so much that she had to leave me." Alondra finally found her voice, and broke away from her Uncle's embrace yelling to the top of her voice. Anger, pain, and sadness could be heard in it. Cain was allowing her to vent when she ran pass him and Cage towards the house.

"Alondra!" Cain called after her to keep her from making a big mistake. He knew where she was going. To confront her father.

Marc was where he spent most of his days lately. Up in his room sitting on the edge of the bed, staring at the pictures of Clarice and Geri when he heard the commotion coming from downstairs, and getting louder as it flowed up stairs towards his room. He jumped to his feet when the door came crashing in. Déjà vu! He's been here before, but this time it wasn't Geri. But his daughter.

"What the....?" He never got a chance to finish as Alondra was up in his face.

"I hate you!" She screamed at him. He stepped back wondering where this was coming from.

"I'll never forgive you! Never!" Marc had never seen her so angry with him. He had never seen her angry at anyone like this except for Deidra. And even that may not have been as severe.

"You ruined everything!" She continued the assault. Marc stood there bewildered. What had he done or ruined to make her so irate with him?

"Baby....." He walked towards her, but she shrunk back.

"Don't call me baby! Never ever, call me baby again! All you do is care about nobody but yourself. No one else matters."

Blair had come into the room after hearing the pandemonium.

"Did you care about any of us when you married that psycho? Or that she almost killed Aunt Blair and her unborn baby? Huh? Did you even give it a thought of how I felt about her? That I hated her. No! You didn't. It's what are you do best. Shut down or run. Yeah, I know why you became a wrestler. You didn't really want the responsibility of raising a child. It would tie you down, so you left me to be raised by Aunt Blair." Her nose was flaring as she fought to suck in the air she had expended in her angry rant. Marc eyes grew horrified. Who was this person in his daughter's body spewing such venom towards him?

"Okay Alondra, that's enough!" Blair came over to her, and put her arms around her shoulder. Too much had been said to take back now, and she wondered if the wounds cut so deep would ever heal. She turned into Blair, and allowed her soothing touch.

She broke down and began to wail. Blair looked over to Marc concerned for his frame of mind, but he was dazed, and couldn't be reached as he stood as a grand statue in the midst of the room. She took Alondra from her father's room, and pass Cain heading for the stairs. Cage was standing there watching and hearing all. He turned to followed Blair and Alondra down the stairs.

Cain stepped further into the room closing the door, and shielding his brother from the outside. He needed him after the way Alondra had torn into him. Some may have been true, but not all. His love for her was always his priority. The profession he had chosen was one long before she was a thought, and leaving her in the good hands of Blair was the trust he had she would be well taken care of. He will deal with her later. No matter what the things she said wasn't warrant. And now he will help his brother to not make the biggest mistake in his life.

"Alondra got some bad news about Geri" He started. Marc's eyes went from bewildered to shock. Something happened to Geri? He came out of his trance, and stared at his brother. He became as stiff as a board feeling all the color rush from his face as his heart dropped to his feet. He grabbed hold of the bed post to brace himself, for the answer to the question he was about to submit.

"What?" he asked.

"She's leaving. Gonna move to D.C. She's put her ranch on lease. Cage is taking her back today. He's going straight there to take her. She wasn't' gonna tell us 'til she left. But Cage didn't' feel that' was the right way to do things. Smart boy." Cain added the last as for his benefit. He was getting to like this young man. Alondra could do worst.

Cain watched as his brother went through his changes. That's all Cain needed to know. Marc loved that woman, but was too stubborn to admit it. He did all he could as he headed for the door, opened it, and paused to observe his brother. Now let's see what he does with the information. He left him to his thoughts.

Cain came down the stairs, and saw that Cage had already gone. He had filled Blair in on everything and left. Alondra wanted to go to Geri and confront her, but Cage explained to her to do that would be disastrous. He let her know that Geri was in a fragile state at the moment, and she didn't need that. Reluctantly Alondra yielded. Cain sat down and stared at Alondra as she returned his gaze. She knew what was getting ready to happen and braced herself.

"I understand you're angry, hurt and confused. But what' you said up there was uncalled for and untrue. Your father loves you more than anything in the world, and would give his life for you." He was very stern, but gentle. Blair sat back quietly. If he hadn't straightened her out, she would have.

"I know Uncle Cain—" she started, but was cut off.

"Do you? That man up there lost the love of his life, your mother. He has done nothing but devote his life to seeing that you are loved and protected. Yes, in a momentary of lapse judgment he made a mistake. But now someone he truly loves has come into his life. He's fighting within himself fearing this one will replace your mom, and that's something he can't deal with."

Cain rose and walked over to the bar to get a bottle of water. Alondra straighten up on the sofa, and looked over to her aunt who nodded in agreement.

"You think all of this has been easy on him?" Cain asked. "No, it hasn't. It's easier on you because you never got to know the beautiful woman your mother was as we did, and how painful it was for us to lose her. It was even worse for him."

Tears began to form in Alondra's eyes. She'd said some awful things to her father; things she couldn't take back.

"I don't ever want to hear you speak to my brother like that again!" His voice was hard and cold. He turned away from her, and walked out of the room leaving her to her thoughts. Blair brushed her arm, and left the sofa to go to Cain. He too was in pain.

Chapter 21

Geri was looking at her watch, and wondering where Cage gone off to when she heard his car pulling up. He got out of it but wouldn't look her in the face, and then she knew what he had done.

"You went to them didn't you?" She started on him. He turned to face her, and saw she was angry he hadn't gone along with her plans.

"If my arm wasn't injured I would kick your butt!" She yelled. He stared at her in a way she hadn't ever seen before, which made her grow grew quiet as he came to tower over her with all of his six feet five inches.

"What are you are doing is wrong Geri, and I refuse to allow you to screw this up!" He was very firm in what he was feeling. She took a step backwards stunned never had ever experienced this side of him.

"Before it was just you free to come, and go as you pleased. But not anymore Ger. You have a family now. Yes, that's what are you got over there a family who care so much for you, and for you to even contemplate walking out on them without even a 'have a good life' is wrong!" He stared her down, then turned away from her, and began loading up her luggage. She was astonished with how much he had come to care for them. Or was it Alondra? She took a few steps around in a circle setting a course for this plight. What he had said was true. This can't be done.

"Let's go, but take me to them!" She got in the car. He looked over at her grinning from cheek to cheek. She looked over at him.

"You think you're all that don't you? She shook her head, and then looked straight ahead.

"No Geri! I know you are!" He turned the key starting up the car, and drove away.

"Just don't make it a habit to confront me. I'll give you this one, but next time you won't fare so well." She warned never looking at him. Her mind drifted off to how to explain, and make things right with the people she had come to love, and call family.

Alondra had settled down, and was sitting on the sofa thinking about what her Uncle had told her. Cain and Blair were in the dining area talking. And Marc was still secluded in his room, when a reflection passed over the window. Alondra lifted her head, and stared out the window. It was Cage! She moved up on the sofa, and parted the curtain. He wasn't alone. Geri was with him!

"Cage is here! And Aunt Geri is with him!" Alondra jumped from the sofa, and ran from the living room making a bee-line out the front door. Cain and Blair heard her, looked at each other, then bolted after her fearing her mental state, and what she may say to Geri. But they came to a halt seeing the scenery before them. Alondra was in Geri's arms balling like a baby, and Geri wasn't much for the wear either as the tears streamed down her face. Cage was turned the other way shielding his face, and they felt maybe he was shedding a few himself.

Geri looked up to Blair her eyes saying something to her which caused her to start in too. Cain pulled her into his arms, and cast his eyes away not wanting to get caught up in this emotion whirlwind.

Marc was trying to piece himself together after the being attacked by his daughter. Her words struck hard and true, slicing his heart. He never thought she would turn on him, speak in him in that way.

He saw a reflective light shine in his room like a beacon signaling to him. He heard Alondra's proclamation, then the sound of her running. He went to the window and saw her. It was Geri. She was with Cage. They stood by the car and Alondra ran into her arms. Both women seemed to be crying. He wondered if Geri had changed her mind.

"I don't have much time to say what I have to say. My plane leaves pretty soon," said Geri to Alondra. She pulled away and looked affectionately into her eyes. Then she noticed Cain and Blair had appeared. They stood on the porch and watched in silence.

"I had to say good bye the right way," said Geri. "I've been so use to being alone, and up to now every decision I've made was for me. But not anymore. Cage helped me to realize... you helped me to realize, I have a family to consider now. And whatever decisions I make affect us all. I'll call and let you know where I am. We'll keep in touch, and I'll come to visit. And hey, you can come to visit me." She was promising this to them all. She wanted them to know how sorry she was for being so careless in the way she handled everything.

Blair stepped off the porch, and stared into Geri's eyes. What was said between them didn't need words as they embraced each other. She looked up at Cain who was making his decent.

"Thank you for coming and making this right," said Cain. "Too many wrong decisions have hurt this family enough, and now it's time for us to move towards healing, and binding together. We'll be awaiting your call, and your return."

Geri hadn't realized how important she was to all of them. She only knew how important they were to her. They all said their good-byes.

Cage and Geri drove away. As they disappeared around the bend, Marc remained at the window from the window as she vanished from his sight, and out of his life.

"I'm glad she came. This feels so much better even though she's still leaving, but we know now we'll be in touch." Blair walked into the house accompanied by Cain and Alondra. He looked to his niece, and saw she was smiling.

"Feel better?" He asked as he wrapped his arm about her shoulder. She looked into his eyes.

"Yes, a lot better," she replied. She then went into the living room where Blair had taken a seat.

Suddenly, they heard a loud crash upstairs, and they all jumped. Cain rushed to see what had happened, but was met with the sound horses rumbling across the ceiling and down the stairs. The ladies froze as Cain's eyes enlarged to what he was witnessing. The source of the calamity blew right past him, and out the door, sending it crashing into the wall.

"What was it Cain?" Blair asked anxiously.

"Marc!" he exclaimed.

Chapter 22

Geri and Cage were well on their way to the airport, and Geri had been crying the entire time. She was wishing she hadn't made the choice of leaving without consulting with them, and now it was too late. She couldn't go back on the lease.

"It's okay Geri! I know how hard that was, but this wasn't about him or you. It was about the ones who have given you so much love." He pulled the car over to the side.

"It just hurts that he didn't say goodbye. He couldn't even do that." She began to sob some more.

Cage rested his hand on her shoulder. He had never seen her like this before. She had always been a strong, independent, woman, and usually a force to be dealt with.

"Where in the hell is he going?" Blair peered out the window after seeing the SUV peel out of the garage like the hounds of hell in pursuit.

Cain and Alondra eyes met, and hoped he would be in time.

"I'm going to get out, and let you pull yourself together." Cage touched her shoulder lightly, and left the car.

Geri felt him leave the car as the absence of his weight lifted it, and heard him close the door. The tears began to stream down her face, and once she had finally had enough of the crying over spilled milk, wiped the tears from her eyes regaining her composure with a greater determination to move on with her life.

She was getting ready to leave the car, and call for Cage to come back when she heard his footsteps coming back to the car. She stared down at her watch. They just had enough time to check in her luggage, before their departure. She quickly checked her face in her compact, and then continued to look out the window not wanting him to see what was in her eyes. It was pain.

The door opened, the car sinking from his weight, then the door closed again as the car started up, and they were on their way. She didn't move. She was lost in her thoughts. Out of Marc's life forever, she thought to herself.

They were silent for some time. Geri was deep in her thoughts as they headed towards the airport, and the end of this era.

Alondra stared out the window and saw her father's SUV pulling up the drive. She wondered why her father had changed his mind and come home. She darted outside to meet him. Cain and Blair followed.

As they moved down the highway, they passed the road that Alondra had turned on when they came upon Marc and Deidra. Geri's eyes fixed on it as another wound reopened. Without warning they turned up onto that road. Geri sat up straight, bewildered. "Where are you going?" she blurted, confused. She turned quickly to Cage and surprised, she let out a loud gasp and frozen in her seat.

Alondra stood steadfast as he opened the door, and got out. Alondra, Cain, and Blair were speechless.

"Cage!" Alondra exclaimed.

"I'm taking you to a special place, Geri. We need to talk!" Marc looked at her, then back to the road with a satisfied grin, contented he had pulled it off.

Geri looked at him for a long time. She was dumbfounded, but sat back in her seat without a word of protest.

Silence ruled the moment as the vehicle made its way down the road. The tension was so thick even a knife couldn't slice through it. Geri's eyes were fixed on the side window. She had no idea what to say about the events leading up to now. She had no idea what had come over Marc, or what was going on. She watched as the scenery became familiar to her when he turned off the main road onto a smaller one she knew exactly where he was taking her.

"Special huh?" she scoffed, but he never looked her way as he continued his course. To Geri, special meant something or someplace held above all others. "I'm not in the mood for 'special'," she cautioned.

She turned to him for an explanation. He never looked at her. He just smiled and knew she was stewing.

Oh no, Geri, he thought. You're not going to spoil it this time. He shook his head.

She saw that she wasn't getting a rise out of him. Then the place he had been with Deidra came into view. Her eyes lowered as they approached the area. So many terrible things happened since that day. He wound up marrying that evil woman, a woman who eventually tried to kill her. This had led to the confrontation between Marc and Geri. Cage was right. Her anger didn't stem as much from the Alondra's career choice as it did from the fact that Marc never came to see her while she was in the hospital he hadn't even called.

She turned to him as they came up to the place. She wanted to get it straight. There would be nothing but answers when they came to a stop. But stop they didn't.

Her eyes were hard upon him; his eyes were on the road. She suddenly realized they were passing by that area; he wasn't stopping there at all. She watched as it was lost further and further behind them, then disappeared behind a small hill.

"Hey, you passed the, 'special place'," she said aloud. Her sarcasm was evident.

"I said I was taking you to a special place," said Marc. "You just assumed that was it, and you were wrong." He returned his attention to the road.

Geri stared at him for several moments. Her mind was going a million miles a minute. She felt like a fool. She elected to remain quiet for the rest of the trip. She'd said and done enough wrong for the day.

They drove along a winding road through dense the woods. There wasn't much to see but the road ahead. The road went up and up until there was a clearing in the trees. They were driving by the lake. It stretched much further than she realized when she'd seen it before; all the way to the horizon. The trees in the background were like a painted picture. It took her breath away and she gasped.

Marc secretly looked at her. He was happy he'd begun his quest to make this a day she would remember; a day to make things right.

"This is beautiful," she breathed. She was forced to turn in her seat as she watched it too vanish from sight. The road turned into another heavily-covered area with trees. It was dark and secluded. She settled in her seat once again not sure if this was where she wanted to be… then they moved into a clearing.

Before her was a cabin with three steps leading up to the porch. There were two rocking chairs with a table between them. The car came to a stop under a carport on the side of the cabin. Marc exited first and Geri watched as he came to her side and opened the door. She gazed into his eyes for the first time in a long while, and he peered deep into hers. Electricity swirled around them. Suddenly, they were apart from the rest of the world, in their own special place.

She placed her hand in his and he gently closed his hand around hers assisting her out of the car. Her eyes scanned the area taking in the enchanted place. She could still see portions of the lake. There was a small boat docked on a pier. She felt Marc's hand at the small of her back his touch sent waves of current through her body. She wanted him badly, and in this place who knew what could happen? Something good, she hoped.

He led her up the porch steps. She wanted to stop at that moment, and kiss him deeply, throwing away her inhibitions, but she resisted. She allowed him to follow through with his plans uninterrupted.

"Have a seat," said Marc. "I know it's been a long day, I want you to relax." She stopped in front of a rocking chair as he went to the cabin door.

"Did you bring Clarice here often?" she asked. Her mouth was never one to know when to open, and when not to.

Marc's head shot towards her as he fumbled to find the right key for the door. "I only wished." He said solemnly.

Geri waited patiently as he found the right key for the door.

"When I said it was a special place," said Marc, "I meant that. No one but the builders and I knew about this place. Not even Alondra." With that he turned the key, and opened the door. Geri watched him disappear into the cabin.

He moved around inside the cabin with ease. He had come here a thousand times over the years, but never went inside until now. It was to be a home away from home. Initially, it was a big surprise he'd planned for Clarice when she had the baby. He was going to bring them here when she was strong enough to enjoy it. But fate stepped in, and that dream died along with her. He'd closed the place up, and left it for many years hiring a caretaker to tend to it. That was until the last few days when he had a change of heart.

He had made a decision, but didn't know it until Geri came by to say her goodbyes. He knew it was now or never. It was going to be now. He ran from his room and down the stairs out to his SUV, flying down the highway to stop her from disappearing from his life. He wasn't about to lose her. She was the one to carry him through the rest of his life.

He looked the place over making sure everything was in place. He was satisfied she would like it. He made his way into the kitchen, and poured some juices. He was going to make sure she took good care of herself. She may think she healed enough to go running around like crazy. But not him. He took a deep breath, and headed back out onto the porch.

Geri was rocking back and forth in one of the rockers staring at the lake, and watching the swans, ducks, and geese gliding on the water. She heard Marc before she saw him, as his footsteps announced his arrival. He handed her a glass of juice which she took, and quickly began to drink it. She didn't know how thirsty she had been until the moisture touched her lips. Marc turned and walked over to the steps taking a seat, and stared out as he would do at his ranch.

"Marc I'm so sorry for being such a hard- ass. I just assumed—" she began.

Marc took a sip of juice. "Yeah, you were pretty difficult, but I brought it on myself. I should have called or better yet come to see you." He said taking another sip.

'Boy, could he do with some good ole Jack Daniels, and a beer, but he needed to stay sober. They had some things to get straighten out. He was remembering the last time Jack Daniels, beer, and a pretty woman cause some very bad chain of events.

"I deserved that. But yeah I wished you had." She said softly staring into her drink.

Marc's head slightly turned in her direction, and regarded her with such feelings that not even he knew the depths. She was Clarice's sister, his beautiful dead wife. She was so much like her, and yet so much different. Now he knew why he could see it, but couldn't. They're similar, but opposites.

"What was it like with you two growing up?" He asked out of the clear blue. Her eyes rose to meet his own. Marc stared deep into them. Her initial reaction was to pounce on him. She would not be living in her sister's shadow. But then her mind changed. There was something in the way he looked in her eyes that tugged at her heart. It wasn't about her being Clarice's sister anymore. It was about Clarice being hers.

"We were happy. That's the best description I can give. We ran and played together. We were inseparable. We loved each other so much, and as much as we played hard, we fought just as hard." She added and began to laugh. This got Marc's attention. He turned towards her and leaned against the rail post.

"You two fought?" Marc seemed surprised.

"You mean Clarice never told you that part. My dear sister always the one to keep things in." Geri grew silent staring her in her glass, then out into the lake. She sat the glass of juice on the table next to her, and covered her mouth with her hands as the tears began to stream. Marc sat his glass down, rose to his feet, and came to stand in front of her.

"I think you need to get some rest," said Marc. "Come with me." He extended his hand out to her. She looked into his eyes and placed her hand in his. She rose to her feet and he led her into the cabin, stopping in the doorway not sure if she should or not. But a gentle squeeze from his hand helped her decision.

"There are four rooms." He taking her down the hallway, and then coming to stop at a door.

"Here, take this one. While you're napping I'll fix some dinner." He opened the door to one of the rooms.

She looked at him, and then placed the palm of her hand on his chest. He covered it with his own, then she slowly turned away and slipped into the room closing the door behind her. He stood at the door for a few moments contemplating should he forget everything, and take her now. But instead he pulled himself away. On the other side of the door Geri leaned against it, and hoped no wished for him to come in, and make mad love to her. But that was soon doused when she heard his footsteps grow dimmer at each step he took away from her. She sighed hard and went to the bed to lie down. It was much needed as no sooner than her head had hit the pillow, she was out like a light.

Chapter 23

Cage had relayed to them how he'd been trying to console Geri and pulled to the side of the road to talk, when he saw the SUV pull up behind them. At first he thought it was Alondra coming after them, so he told Geri he was going to give her some alone time before they went on to the airport. As he left the car, he saw it was Marc. They didn't say a word to each other; Marc just tossed him his keys and continued towards the car. Cage hadn't protested in the slightest.

"So here I am, and there they go," Cage finished, shrugging his shoulders.

With Cage at her side, Alondra went over to her father's favorite spot, and sighed nervously.

"Worried?" asked Cage, leaning against a post, observing her closely.

"Yeah. Dad has been acting strange ever since Deidra and Aunt Geri came around. He's been different." She shook her head; her voice was full of concern.

"Emotions can be tricky," said Cage. "You can only keep them at bay for so long. Then one day something, or someone, comes along and you find you can no longer control those emotions." He took a deep breath. He didn't want to show that he too was worried. Marc and Geri were like two firecrackers waiting to be ignited. One false move from either one of them could really set the other one off.

"I think dad was okay with Deidra being around, but when he saw Aunt Geri I think she kind of shook his foundation." She kind of chuckled at the thought.

"And yours," Cage added.

"Yeah, she did," Alondra agreed. "It was so strange how it happened. When I first saw her there was a connection right off. I can't explain it." She rose to her feet, and began to walk a few steps before coming to a stop; a comforting thought passed through her mind. "It's like my mother sent her here when we needed her the most," she said.

Alondra figured that was a good way to summarize everything that had happened to them over the last several weeks. Even in death, she was still looking out for them.

'They're all together now,' Cage thought to himself. "If only Geri will see it through.

The pleasing aroma of cooking food circled through the air, crept under the door, and made its way to the bed, tantalizing Geri's nostrils. She slowly stirred from her nap, and flipped over on her side still partly in her dream world. The scent became stronger and she realized she wasn't asleep anymore, but in that place where unconsciousness slowly fades away, and the senses take over. She sat up, rubbing her eyes and searching the unfamiliar room. Then she remembered. She was in a cabin; and not just any cabin, but a special place where Marc had brought her. Now her stomach was fussing from hunger, and the smell from the food in the other room was sending a very tempting invitation. She wasn't about to resist.

Geri slid to the edge of the bed and sat for a few moments, gathering herself. She slipped on her shoes, and opened the door in anticipation of what was on the other side; food for her stomach, and a little something for her heart, she hoped.

Marc had made some hearty hamburgers, and fries. This was one thing he did know how to make, and he was hoping Geri would enjoy it.

He'd peeked in on her while she slept. She seemed to sleep peacefully, so he'd decided to relax himself with a shot of dark whiskey and a glass of beer. However, one turned into a few, and before long he was feeling pretty good. But he didn't realize just how much he'd had, and it was a bit more than he'd intended.

He was sitting on the steps of the porch thinking and drinking when he was startled by the soft touch of a hand on his shoulder. It was Geri coming to sit next to him.

When she sat, he looked down into her gentle eyes, and she could see he had been drinking. She looked out at the lake, and felt so calm, at peace.

"Sleep well?" he asked.

She nodded, and continued to look away.

"Good," he said, rising from the steps.

She looked up at him curious to where he was going.

"Are you hungry?" he asked, staggering slightly as he entered the cabin, and bumping from one side of the doorway to the other. She jumped to her feet, and followed him into the kitchen where he had thrown one of the hamburger patties between two buns, and was eating it before she entered the kitchen.

"Marc, sit down. I'll make your plate. You shouldn't have been drinking on an empty stomach. What got into you?" She took the food from his hand, and gave him a gentle push towards the kitchen table where he took a seat in one of the chairs.

"You got into me," he answered. She stopped what she was doing to stare in his eyes, and saw such longing in them, matching what she was feeling. She cast her eyes to the floor closing them tight. She had faced so many dangerous situations in her career as an agent, and never backed down from anything as she went full force in each assignment given to her. But when it came to a relationship. She just wasn't very good at them. That's why she had been alone all of these years. Yeah, there have been men, but none who stuck around. Why would this one be any different? She opened her eyes with a thought.

"Maybe we should leave. I can hold up in town at a hotel. I'll get you home safely." She turned away from him, and stared out the kitchen window watching a deer make its way up to the back of the cabin hesitant, and afraid that something would pounce on it without notice. She was feeling a lot like this timid creature.

"Naw! You don't have to be afraid of me. I brought you here for a reason. To talk, and that' we will. It's been a long day. Get you something to eat. I'm gonna call it a night, and see you in the morning." He slurred his words.

Geri turned around to him after hearing him getting up from the table, and stumbled towards his bedroom door, stumbling into it, then backing up a few steps swaying, and   leaning backwards almost falling to the floor.

Boy, he must have really tide one on, she thought to herself. She then made an attempt towards him, but he turned his head and waved her off. He moved back to the door, grabbed the knob and pushing the door open, pouring into his room, and closed the door behind him.

Geri could hear the bed give under his great weight as he fell into it. She shook her head rethinking if this really was a good idea. She sighed, and went to the kitchen to prepare her a plate. One thing was true she was starving. She went out on the porch, and sat the plate on the table next to her taking a seat in one of the rockers, and sat admiring the beautiful landscape relaxing while she ate. She could really get into this, it was so soothing.

"My thing is where did Marc take Geri?" Blair wondered. Alondra didn't know." She looked over to her husband as he came to sit beside her, then pulled her legs into his lap, and began massaging them. He could see she was tired no hiding that fact from him.

"With my brother who knows. He has been on a roller coaster of feelings for the last few weeks. It can't be easy for him to let Clarice go." Cain gently rubbed one toe after the other. Blair was feeling the effects, and began to relax her head into the pillows.

"No it couldn't. With Deidra he could do two things. Have her to quench that lust, and still hold onto his love for Clarice. But Geri was a whole different story. It's going to be very hard to do that with her. She is going to fill the void he has held onto for so long. How he will deal with it remains to be seen." Blair yawned. Cain noticed, and saw her eyelids getting heavy. He placed her feet on the ground, and rose to his feet taking her hands into his, and led her up the stairs to their bedroom.

Geri finished eating, and went into the kitchen to clean up, and put the food away. She headed towards the bedroom door where Marc was sleeping and stood for what seemed like ages before quietly opening it. The sun was just beginning to set, and the room was dim. Marc lay sprawled out over the bed. She smiled and went in to cover him with a blanket, then moved around to where his head rested, and bent down to give him a gentle peck on his cheek.

"Sleep tight my love." She whispered in his ear. She could say this without reservation knowing he was asleep, and wouldn't be able to hear her. She quietly left and closed the door behind her.

"Yeah, you too Geri." He mumbled turning over onto his other side, and drifting back to sleep.

Geri was in a deep slumber, but dreaming of a fog horn sounding out as she walked through the haze seeking from wench it came, and as she moved further away from the mist it grew louder until finally she emerged into a bright light, and the sound became very distinctive. She shot straight up in bed. The groaning was emanating from outside her door, and in the other room. She quickly grabbed her robe leaping from the bed, and opened the door stopping short in it taking in the sight before her.

Marc was sitting at the table bent over, and holding his head. It was him making the sound she had heard in her dream. She tried not to laugh at him, but he deserved the punishment for drinking on an empty stomach. She walked passed him, and into the kitchen to make up a concoction. He hadn't looked up, but heard her come in. She slid the drink over to him.

"Drink it will help." She informed him. He reached over, took it in his hand, then took a sip frowning, and set it back on the table.

"Drink I said!" She ordered. He lifted his head slightly hearing the voice from some place long ago, and determined eyes; He reached for the glass once again, and downed it in one gulp, then replaced the empty glass on the table. She stood waiting and knowing, then without any warning he jumped to his feet, ran into his room straight for the bathroom, and hurling could be heard. Satisfied with her deed for the day smiled as she nodded her head.

"That should teach him." She said to herself, and went into the kitchen to prepare breakfast. She was just sitting the food on the table when Marc slowly made his way out of his room. She glanced his way and continued with what she was doing.

"Feeling better? She asked, watching him take a seat at the table.

"That wasn't very nice. You knew exactly what that stuff was gonna do," he snapped. She paused focusing her eyes on him for a few moments.

"No one told you to load up on Sir Jack Daniels, and his buddy Mr. Beer on an empty stomach. You know better than that!" She shook her head, and began preparing him a plate. It just seemed like the natural thing to do.

"No, no one told me to do it, but considering the circumstances I had no choice. What would you have me to do?" He rambled on without really making any sense to her so she was very confused.

"What are you talking about? What circumstances?" She stood waiting for him to explain. His eyes narrowed almost into slits.

"I told you why I got drunk, so don't play dumb with me." He turned away from her, and down at the food shoving it away from him.

"Play dumb? Did you just say, 'play dumb' to me?" She glared at him.

He stood to his feet towering over her as if trying to be intimidating. "Yes, I did Geri. I told you that you made me drink. You're confusing, and I don't know what to do with you." He had one hand on a hip, and the other was moving about as he spoke.

She stepped back still trying to make some sense of what he was saying. And a little annoyed with his stance. She never sent him anything but what was there. What was so confusing about it?

"You don't know what to do with me, Marc? I tell you what, nothing! Not a damn thing! I forgot what an ass you can be." She turned away from him. His head shot towards her.

"Yeah! Well I forgot what a little tease you can be. Always playing these Damn games! One minute you're standoffish, and the next your touching me in a come on way. Even kissing me on the cheek, and calling me your love." Oh he was really feeling his oats this morning, as his mouth was writing a check his jackass wasn't going to be able to cash.

She was stunned he had heard what she said to him last night while he was sleeping, but more hurt with his accusation of her playing games with his heart. Games were the last things she was playing. What she was feeling for him was for real, and he just trampled on them.

Her eyes narrowed, and turned dark as an abyss. Then he got first hand why you should choose your words wisely when addressing the 'Lady' known as Geri! She turned on her heels, walked away distancing herself from him, and began to use every profanity in her arsenal. His eyes turned into large green pools. He didn't know she could curse like that. She even puts a Sailor to shame. Then suddenly everything went silent. She stopped in her tracks, turned, and glared at him for what seemed like forever. Then her mouth opened, but this time noting obscene exited it.

"Take me into town, and I'll get a hotel room, then reschedule my departure, and after this day I never want to set eyes on you again." She stormed passed him into her room slamming the door behind her. He wasn't going to allow her to get the best of him so he went to his room, and slammed the door even harder causing the whole cabin to shake. She jumped from the intensity of the impact.

"No Geri! Not this time!" He shook his head standing just beyond his door, then turned towards it, and swung it open as it crashed against the wall. She heard the great impact as the walls to the cabin vibrated, and heard him leave his room as his footsteps pounded the floor, coming her way. She waited to see to where he was going. It wasn't long before she found out.

His footsteps stomped towards her room, and this time it was her door that flew open with a determined Marc standing in the door way. She stood to her feet eyes fixed on him. Her destiny.

She knew no amount of ranting or raving she might have tried to warn him off would stop what she saw in his eyes. The longing, desire, and a thirst that needed to be quenched, and only she would be able to do that. As much as she saw in his eyes, he saw it in hers. She wanted him too, and there was no denying it any longer. Her whole body came alive with this moment they had tried to fight off.

This was it!

With just one look she told him what was in her heart, and without any more delay his long strides reached her in a second. She sucked in a deep breath knowing there was no turning back as his passion will rule this night.

Instantly she was caught up in his arms, and being carried out of her room into his. He gently lay her down onto the bed gazing into her eyes, and there were no words to express this moment in time. One that had eluded them in days pass, and even years.

Now here they were. It was like fate had gestated time for them to come to this place. He smiled at her eyes full of so much want and need. She replied with a half-smile of her own eyes desiring something of him. He knew what she wanted, and moved closer to her pulling her into him at the same time. The heat from their bodies went up a degree. He lifted her head upwards as his mouth covered her lips parting them, as his tongue slid inwards. She let out a heavy moan as their physical, and mental emotions finally collided. The repercussion from all the years of shutting themselves down.

Inhibitions freed, and cast into the wind they allowed themselves to let go, and loved each other in a way no one else would have known or even been able to do. Their two souls were made for each other, and their ivory and mocha bodies intertwined expressing that in every way possible. They melted into each other, and gave to the other just what was needed, and on this day they would leave nothing wanting. And when they thought they have given all that there was to give, they realized it wasn't enough, and gave more not wanting to deprive the other of anything desired.

Finally, drained of all their emotions both physically and mentally. They laid wrapped in each other's arms exhausted, and drifted off to sleep pleased they hadn't held back satisfied there would be no doubts in each of their minds how much they were loved by the other.

A few hours had passed when the sun made its descent in the west, and Marc began to stir from his sleep automatically reaching over to the other side seeking his love. Another round of what they had experience was definitely a must. But he found the other side of the bed vacant, sat up in bed searching the room. He jumped out of the bed putting on his jeans, and made his way out of the room towards the living quarters figuring she was there in the kitchen preparing something for them to eat. But she wasn't there either so he went through the cabin and outside seeking and calling for her without any response. His heart dropped when reality set in. He was alone.

He headed back into the bedroom, and sat on the bed staring into the mirror on the dresser, wondering what was going on. That's when he saw the answer to the question. A note placed on the mirror. Addressed to him:

I opened up to you, thinking maybe you wanted me, as much as I wanted you. Today I realized that you did, so I let myself go. I wish it didn't have to end this way. Our lovemaking was more beautiful than anything I have ever experienced. And I know you have feelings for me, but I think there are things you need to resolve. You called Clarice's name while you slept. That's when I knew. She will always be a ghost in our bed. When you look at me, she will be there. I can't live with that, so I'll go... taking with me the most wonderful day in my life. I love you, Marc Caldwell.

Always, Geri

Marc allowed the note to fall to the floor, his heart nearly stopped. He'd spoken aloud during his dream, and Geri misunderstood. How was he to go on, after finally letting Clarice go? That's what the dream had been about. He was saying goodbye, and Clarice was wishing him well.

"No damn it! You can't leave me; not after what happened in this room today. It can't be this way."

He sat on the edge of the bed, his head in his hands. He was heartbroken. He'd lost the greatest love of his life for the second time.

He laid back, his eyes fixed on the empty space next to him. Loneliness pained his heart. He closed his eyes and began to drift away, when he felt the bed sink slightly behind him. Someone gently touched his shoulder. He turned over to see a loving pair of light brown eyes. He was in disbelief. He rubbed his eyes to clear them, but the image before him was real. Those welcome eyes gazed at him lovingly.

"What–" He began, but was met with a finger to hush his lips.

"I was about to make the biggest mistake in my life," she said sorrowfully, "Until a voice flowed softly through my ear. It said, 'turn back, he loves you more than he can say'. So here I am." She sat down and went deep into thought.

Marc rose up and sat next to her. "The voice was right, Geri."

Geri suddenly had a strange expression on her face.

"What's wrong?" he asked, curious. She looked as if she had seen a ghost.

"I think the voice was Clarice," she admitted. "Does that sound crazy?"

Marc stared for a moment taking in what she said and began to smile. "No, it doesn't," he replied. "I dreamed I was saying goodbye to Clarice. She was wishing me well. I think this is what she wanted, and knew it's what we both needed." He took her hand into his, and brought it to his lips.

"I love you so much," said Geri. "I can't see life without you in it. You've been on my mind for so long, and now you're really here."

Marc didn't say a word; he could only show her again, and again how much she meant to him. And he did, until the morning sun ascended over the eastern horizon, and for the rest of their lives.